# Witch Fulfillment
## WISHING FOR A MAGICAL MIDLIFE
### BOOK THREE

TEE HARLOWE

M&F BOOKS

Copyright © 2023 by Tee Harlowe

All rights reserved.

No part of this book may be reproduced in any form or by any electronic or mechanical means, including information storage and retrieval systems, without written permission from the author, except for the use of brief quotations in a book review.

Cover design by Karen Dimmick/ArcaneCovers.com

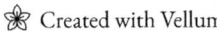 Created with Vellum

# Prologue

**BEFORE**

Isabella Westfold stormed from the little cabin in the woods. Rain pounded around her, soaking her hair, her clothes, but she didn't care.

She thought she heard a voice call out her name, though the rain and thunder rolling overhead masked it. That voice, though, it made her stop, hesitate, turn. When she did, no one stood behind her, the green door to the cabin firmly closed. She curled her hands into fists and whipped back around, stomping toward her car.

She couldn't believe he'd said all those things to her, unforgivable things. She'd given that man, whose name she didn't even want to think right now, her heart, and he'd turned around and crushed it.

The things he said echoed in her mind, even though she tried to block them out.

*You're too stubborn for your own good.*

*You hold onto grudges that keep you from growing, from moving on.*

And the worst accusation he hurled her way.

*You don't know how to love.*

That was the one thing she'd always been afraid of—that he was right and she didn't know how to open her heart, to be vulnerable, to feel that deep unending passion for someone. The kind of passion that would make her put someone else before herself. She fumbled with her keys, and before she got into the car, looked back at the cabin one more time, hoping that maybe he'd come out, tell her he was sorry, that he loved her. Maybe he'd gather her in his arms and press a kiss to her lips.

If he did that, she'd cave. She knew it. For all her bravado, she'd forgive him if he'd only give her the chance to. But the door didn't open. The curtains over the windows didn't sway, not a bit. He wasn't coming after her.

She swallowed and got into her car, and that's when the tears came. Isabella didn't cry often. In fact, she hadn't cried in years. Another reason many thought her cold and distant: her inability to show emotion. But just because she didn't show it, didn't mean she felt nothing. She started the car, and her shoulders shook with the sobs that wracked her body.

It was over. It was truly over.

She could forgive a lot of things, but she couldn't forgive what he'd done, what had caused their fight in the first place, especially not when he wasn't even willing to bend, to fight for her or their relationship. Well, she wasn't going to fight for it either. It wasn't a relationship worth having.

Not anymore.

The tears slowly came to a stop. She straightened in her seat, pushing on the gas pedal, and drove away from the cabin for what would be the last time.

Isabella made a vow to herself in that car: she would never love again.

A vow she would eventually break. But she didn't know that. Not yet.

# Chapter One

My daughter stood in front of the full-length mirror, twirling in a circle as the bottom of her shimmering blue dress fanned out around her. The dressmaker bustled about, dipping her wand in a vial that sat on a small table nearby, then touching the wand to specific places on Remy's dress. She tapped the waist and it cinched tighter, then she tapped the thick shoulders, which fitted around Remy's muscle and bone. Each tap of her wand made the dress fit to Remy like a glove. I couldn't believe my eighteen-year-old daughter was going to her first-ever Samhain Ball.

After I'd left my life of magic behind at the young age of nineteen, I never dreamed I'd witness something like this. Sure, I knew I'd see my daughter go to prom, homecoming, and every other high school event under the sun, but I never thought I'd see her attend a witch ball. It brought up memories of my own Samhain Ball, a night I'd never forget.

I held back my tears, not wanting to make this moment about me and my feelings. Remy turned, examining her figure in the full-length mirror. I knew this was a momentous occasion for her as well. She'd just discovered magic was real four months ago, and now here she was, learning magic, attending a witch academy, dating a . . . vampire. Well, I thought she was dating a vampire. She hadn't exactly updated me on that situation.

I settled into the pink couch sitting near the back of the room. Silk brushed my ear and I looked behind me at a rack lining the wall, stuffed with dresses of all colors.

"So is this the one?" I asked, my attention straying back to Remy.

The dressmaker stepped away, pressing her wand to her chest, nodding in answer to my question, even though the question hadn't been directed at her.

Remy stared at herself in the mirror, a smile on her lips. "I think so."

I squealed. "Oh Remy, you look absolutely stunning."

She tugged at the spaghetti straps and pulled the A-line up. "Do you think he'll like it?"

She didn't say his name—she still hadn't told me that little tidbit. But I knew who she was talking about. Her mysterious vampire crush.

"He'd be crazy not to, Remy," I said, standing and walking toward her. She turned to me and gave me a tight hug.

"Okay good. I kind of still have to tell him I want to go with him, but you know . . ."

"Remy!" I pushed her to arm's length. "You still haven't said yes? He asked you a month ago!"

She bit her lip. "Well, Mom, it's complicated."

I clearly didn't understand teenagers and their weird dating habits. "How? He asks you to the Samhain Ball. You say yes."

"Except I said no!" Remy said, twisting her hands together.

She'd told him no when he first asked, afraid she couldn't live up to one of the most popular boys in school asking her to a dance.

"Yeah, but I thought we talked through that whole situation? You said you were going to tell him how you changed your mind."

Remy looked down at her feet. "I know, I know. I just . . . he's been so moody toward me, so distant. And that kind of made me mad. I mean, I know I turned him down, but he's acting so immature about it. Makes me question everything."

I laughed. She might've been eighteen, but sometimes I felt like my daughter was at least a decade older. Other teenage girls might pine after their crushes, do anything and everything to get their attention, forgive easily, overlook red flags, but not Remy. She was wise beyond her years.

"Listen, kiddo, you just have to talk to him," I said. "You hurt his feelings, his pride."

She opened her mouth to argue, but I continued, my words gaining speed.

"That doesn't excuse his behavior." I tucked one of her wild brown curls behind her ear. "All I'm saying is that people aren't perfect. Don't start making excuses to shut him out before you've even given him a chance."

Remy blew a big breath out. "I guess maybe you're right."

"I'm sorry." I put a hand to my chest. "Can you say that again?"

The door to the little dress shop burst open, Martin standing in the doorway, phone out, no doubt recording this moment. "I knew it," he declared, his green skin flushed red as he huffed and stomped into the room. "I knew you were here."

"Are you recording this, Martin?" Remy asked. "I thought we talked about this."

"You told me you'd already found your Samhain Ball dress, but I was walking down the street, and whom did I see through the window? A certain Remy and her mother." He sent me a pointed stare. "A Clara Westfold."

I rolled my eyes at the imp. He could be incredibly dramatic. "Martin, I'm sorry we lied to you."

He crossed his arms.

"We just wanted a nice mother-daughter outing, is all. I know you wanted to be there for Remy's special moment."

He circled Remy with his phone, tears pooling in his eyes. "Oh, you're so beautiful."

Remy's expression softened.

Ever since we'd arrived in Whispering Willows five months earlier, the town had seemed to adopt Remy, looking out for her, loving her, wanting to be a part of her life. I appreciated that everyone loved Remy so much, but sometimes, they took it too far, invading parts of our life that we wanted to keep for ourselves. We'd agreed that it would just be Remy and me going dress shopping. She might have teased me about how she wanted someone with more fashion sense to accompany her, but at the end of the day, she said she didn't want anyone else by her side. We knew it might hurt some people's feelings, so we told a little white lie to everyone. Clearly, that had been a mistake.

Martin stopped his video and started snapping photos of Remy with the flash. She threw her hands up in front of her face to protect her eyes from the blinding light.

I shook a finger at the imp. "No, no, Martin. Boundaries. You can't just sweep in here with your compliments and make Remy feel bad about not inviting you to this."

"Fine." Martin stuffed his phone in his pocket. "Why didn't you just tell me the truth and save us all of this heartache?" He put a fist to his mouth, stifling a cry.

I resisted the urge to roll my eyes again. I rolled them so much around the imp that at some point they were going to get stuck up there.

"Well . . ." I threw out my hands helplessly. "We didn't know how to tell everyone we didn't want them to come. We didn't want to hurt your feelings, okay? So we figured it might be easier to make something up, spare everyone. Happy?"

Martin frowned. "No, I'm not."

The door burst open again. "What's this about Remy going dress shopping?" Myrtle stood in the doorway now, still in her wolf form, blood dripping from her mouth. "I'm on a hunt and I get a text from the imp about Remy getting fitted at Best Dressed."

I whirled on Martin. "Who else did you text?"

The imp twined his hands behind his back, avoiding eye contact, his pointy ears wiggling. "I might've texted the group chat."

"Are you kidding me?"

That meant he'd told Helen, Gene, Myrtle, Bones, Isaac, and Emerson. They couldn't all show up. Remy didn't want that kind of attention, and I didn't want this special day ruined for my daughter.

Remy groaned from behind me. "I'm like half-naked right now. I don't want Uncle Gene to see me like this." She grappled at her dress, trying to pull it up and cover her bra.

"Don't worry, girlie," Myrtle said as she slinked into the room, her muddy paws leaving prints on the soft white carpet that made the dressmaker look like she might faint. "Busy fighting demons. Helen and Gene won't be able to make it. Is my snout bleeding? Oh, bollocks." Blood dripped from her nose onto the floor, and she let out a string of curses in what I guessed was her ancient Gaelic language.

The dressmaker's face was now a deep shade of purple.

"I'm so sorry," I said, holding out my hands to her. "Just let me deal with this." I gestured to Martin and Myrtle. "And I promise I'll get my best cleaning spell in here to take care of the mud and blood."

The dressmaker didn't say anything, just continued to stare in shock.

"You two, over here, now," I whisper-yelled.

Myrtle approached with her tail between her legs, and Martin strode over, nose high in the air. "I'm sorry we lied to you about dress shopping, okay? But Remy wanted it to be me and her today, so can you two please go? Remy already said you all could come take pictures of her before the Samhain Ball, at our house. Let's stick to that plan."

I looked behind them to see if I should be expecting anyone else. Luckily Isaac was out of town, so we didn't have to worry about him intruding, and I assumed Emerson knew me well enough to know we wouldn't want that kind of intrusion. Myrtle said Helen and Gene were busy fighting demons. So that left . . .

The door opened again, Bones looming tall over us. The half-giant frowned down at everyone, shaking his black bowl cut.

Remy shrieked. "Bones, you can't see me like this!" She dove behind Myrtle, and her dress tickled the werewolf's side. Myrtle jumped about a foot in the air, getting her claws tangled up in a rack of nearby dresses.

Bones's head skimmed the ceiling, and he had to duck to enter further.

"Bones, you idiot!" Martin shouted. "I told you you wouldn't fit inside the shop!"

Bones flicked the imp, easily half his size, and Martin flew back into the mirror, cracking it.

The dressmaker put a hand to her head, her eyes flitting from Myrtle, still tangled in all the dresses, now smearing them with blood and mud, to Martin, laying on the floor as shards of mirror fell all around him.

"Oh god," I said.

"Out," the dressmaker burst. "Out, out, out now!"

"I'm so, so sorry," I said again. "We really didn't mean to make any messes."

"Out," she shrieked, her voice rising three octaves.

"Is that the only thing she knows how to say?" Martin asked.

"Okay." I scurried to Remy and covered her while she shimmied out of her dress, pulled on her jeans, and threw on her T-shirt. Myrtle finally disentangled herself from the dresses, and Bones picked Martin up by his collar.

"Bones," Martin gasped. "You're choking me."

The half-giant paid no mind to the imp as he carried him like a rag doll.

"Get. Out!" the dressmaker yelled, chasing us all from the shop and out onto Main Street.

"Well, that was a little dramatic," Martin said.

We all jumped when the door to the shop slammed behind us, glass rattling in its pane.

Remy sank down onto the curb. "Well, there goes my favorite dress so far."

I sat next to her. "We'll find you another one. I promise."

I shot up a glare at Myrtle, Bones, and Martin, all looking properly chagrined.

"Just go. You three have done enough for one day."

"We just wanted to see the girl," Myrtle said with her thick Irish accent.

"We wanted to participate in Remy's special day," Martin added, kicking at Bones, who finally dropped the imp to the ground.

Bones grunted in agreement. I didn't think I'd ever heard the half-giant talk. I never even asked why he didn't speak, just accepted his grunts and moans like they were a perfectly normal form of communication.

Remy turned. "I love you all, and I always want you to be part of my special moments, but I just wanted to get a dress with my mom today. And now, I don't even know where I can get another one in time for the ball."

"We'll find another dress shop in a nearby town." I nudged her. "It'll be fine."

"Sorry, girlie." Myrtle rubbed Remy with her snout before crossing the street.

"We're sorry, Remy." Martin leaned down to press a kiss to her head, and Bones patted her shoulder with his giant hand.

They walked down the street, disappearing around the corner and out of view.

Remy leaned into me. "I went from having no one but you for two years to having a whole community to love me. And I love Whispering Willows, and I love that everyone cares so much about me, but sometimes it's a lot."

I roped an arm around her shoulder. "I know, I know. I didn't have my mother growing up, and everyone kind of became like a surrogate parent for me. But I forget how smothering they can be. It comes from a good place."

Remy smiled. "I know. It's fine. I don't know if I was really feeling that dress anyway."

A salty sea breeze flowed past us, rustling my shoulder-length brown hair, the exact same shade as Remy's, but while hers was wild and curly, mine was stick-straight.

I raised an eyebrow. "Are you just saying that?"

"No, I think there's something else out there for me. Something that will wow him."

"Uh-huh. You know, you're gonna have to tell me his name before he comes to pick you up for the Samhain Ball."

"What, so you can cyber stalk him to death?" Remy shook her head. "Pass."

I just laughed, then my expression sobered as I studied my daughter. I truly loved that everyone in this town had adopted Remy so easily as their own, but sometimes I just wanted her to myself. More and more, I felt like I was losing her. After this year, she'd be out of high school, out in the world. She might decide to move out, to travel, to go to college.

Remy looked up at me. "Whatcha thinking?"

"That we need to get home for lunch." I stood and pulled her to her feet.

I wouldn't think about that. She was mine. For just a little while longer. And I'd make the most of it.

# Chapter Two

"You got kicked out of Best Dressed?" Helen asked, leaning against the white marbled counter in my shop.

Sun streamed in through the big windows that gave us a view of Main Street, palm trees rustling in the wind, cars parked by meters, shops lining the main road in Whispering Willows. I grabbed a crystal ball sitting on the shelf and bustled behind the counter. A client stood on the other side, darting nervous glances at the little ball that fit snug in the palm of my hand. Sparks of purple and pink shot through the delicate glass, bouncing off the sides with frenetic energy.

"It wasn't my fault we got kicked out," I told Helen, who tugged on her leather jacket, blue eyes twinkling.

"Uh-huh," Helen said, studying her nails, now chipped and broken after the demon fight she got into yesterday. Her phone rang. "Oh, it's Gene. I have to take this," Helen said and left the shop to go outside, running a hand over her bleach-blonde hair.

I set the crystal ball on the counter and grabbed my wand, touching it to the glass as I closed my eyes and felt my magic filling my veins, flowing through me with a rush, the kind of high you might get from riding a rollercoaster. Every time I granted a wish, it reminded me how grateful I was that life led me back to Whispering Willows, back to my life as a witch, to my life as a Witch Granter. Only a rare few witches had the ability to grant wishes, and we took the responsibility very seriously.

"So that's it?" the older woman in front of the counter asked. "You just touch your wand to the crystal, and poof, there's my wish sitting in there?"

I smiled and nodded. "It's an innate ability. The power runs in my blood." I lifted the crystal ball to her. "Now all you have to do to get your wish is whisper what you want to the crystal. That will enact the spell."

"Will it hurt?" the woman asked. "Giving a piece of my soul for the wish?"

The cost of a wish might've been steep, but those who wanted wishes tended to be desperate enough to pay that price.

I laid a comforting hand over hers, crystal ball still balanced in my other hand. "It's different for everyone. It depends on the wish you make, how you react to this kind of powerful magic. For some, it feels like an amazing rush. For others, it might be a pinch." I bit my lip. "And for some, it might hurt worse than that. But it's quick," I said when the older woman stepped back.

"And what happens?" She tugged at her silver hair, chin-length and dusting her cheekbones. Her skin was paper-thin, and I could see the blue veins running underneath, veins that would be filled with a wish soon enough. "What happens?" she asked again. "When you lose a piece of your soul?"

Surprisingly, not many clients asked this question, many of them not wanting to know the details of the price they had to pay for a wish. I didn't blame them. The prospect of giving away a piece of your soul was scary.

I took a deep breath. "I know this is going to be hard to hear, but it really does depend. Wishes are personal, tailored to the person asking for them. That means losing a piece of your soul might not affect you in any way that you can tell." I tipped my head to my shoulder. "Or it could mean losing a passion, an interest, a love." I swallowed. "You have to decide if the wish is worth it."

For most people it was. But I would never force a wish on anyone. As a Witch Granter, it was my responsibility to grant wishes with discernment. Not everyone was the right candidate for receiving a wish.

The woman thought for a moment, then she nodded. "I still want it. My wish."

"Okay." I reached out my hand and she plucked the crystal ball from my palm, then brought it to her lips and whispered her wish. Her head snapped back as the streams of purple and pink left the crystal ball and shot toward her, whirling around the older woman with a frenzy.

The magic circled her, faster and faster and faster until I couldn't see the woman anymore. Then it burst in a bright light and disappeared, leaving the woman, looking woozy, a little dazed.

"How do you feel?" I asked.

She turned her watery eyes on me. "Okay." She put a hand to her chest. "I feel okay. And my wish? It's granted?"

I gave her a big smile. "Your house is protected now. No harm will be able to come to it, and it will stay in your family from generation to generation."

She breathed out a sigh of relief. "I just want to be able to pass it down to my son and my grandchildren and great-grandchildren. A place they can always call home."

"I get it," I said, looking around me at The Wish List, which I hoped to pass to Remy one day, and if she had children, then I hoped it would pass on to them. I knew what it was like to want to continue a legacy.

"Thank you again." The woman grabbed my hands with her frail ones. "I can't thank you enough."

With that, she left the shop, passing Helen on her way out.

"Another happy customer?" Helen shoved her phone in the pocket of her leather jacket.

I nodded and walked around the counter to sit down on the purple couch that sat in the middle of the shop. Helen dropped into one of the purple chairs next to the couch.

"You look happy," Helen said, "and that makes me happy."

The wrinkles around her mouth and eyes crinkled deeper as she smiled big. Helen may not have been my biological mother, but she'd stepped into the mother role after my own had disappeared from my life. Or, rather, after I'd cut her out. Helen had been there for me through the darkest times of my life, and I'd never forget that. And she did it all while figuring out her role as Whispering Willows's resident Demon Slayer.

Now, twenty years later, she was still slaying it. Literally.

"I am happy."

She squinted at me. "You're hiding something from me."

That was the downside to Helen stepping into a mother role—she had this sixth sense about things specifically related to me.

"Everything is fine, Helen," I said.

Okay so not *everything* was fine. I'd possibly forgot to mention that just a month ago, I received a letter from someone who claimed to be my long-lost father. He'd said he was coming to visit. Only he left out one very important detail: when. I had no clue if he was coming in a week, a month, a year. I didn't even know if he was my father. Yes, he thought he was, but that didn't mean anything. My mother told me my father had died. Then again, my mother wasn't exactly known for telling the truth. I'd found out many of her secrets after she died. Ones I didn't feel like reliving right now.

I wasn't sure why I hadn't told Helen. I told Helen everything. I just . . . I didn't feel like the whole town finding out. Not that Helen would go and blab to everyone. But if I told one person, it had this inevitable way of spreading like wildfire. I couldn't handle that right now. Not the speculation. The gossip. The questions. Not to mention, Remy didn't deserve that. She'd just started at a new school a few months ago. She wanted to fit in and make friends, not make waves.

Still, I knew I needed to tell Helen at some point. If he just showed up to town, it would wreak havoc. Everyone would want to know about him, our relationship, his relationship with my mother.

I leaned forward on the couch, arms resting on my washed-out blue jeans. "Actually, Helen, there's something I've been meaning to talk to you about."

"What's up?" she asked, a slight downturn to her lips.

"Well . . . It's just . . ."

But the words never had a chance to leave my mouth. Because right at that moment, a demon came crashing through the windows of my shop.

# Chapter Three

Helen sprang to her feet, a glowing golden sword materializing in her hand, summoned by the presence of the demon now prowling around my shop.

The demon sank down into a low crouch, its talons scraping across the floor. Green slime dripped from its mouth, filled with razor-sharp teeth. Its black eyes bugged out of its head as the demon blinked at us. Then it let out a loud hiss and swiped at Helen, who stalked toward it.

Demons had been getting braver, coming out more during daylight hours when they previously stuck to night. They were coming to more populated areas of the town, too, their goal very clear: take down the Demon Slayer, something I'd never let happen.

Helen raised her sword and charged at the demon. It jumped over her head and landed on the coffee table, perched like a cougar about to pounce.

Okay, Helen didn't need my help. She was badass and fierce and could fight her own battles, but if the day came that she couldn't, I'd be here to back her up.

The demon looked at me and flicked out its forked tongue, and I stumbled back into the counter.

Helen turned to me. "So what were you saying?"

The demon jumped from the coffee table and Helen dodged its attack.

"Saying about what?" I asked from my place at the counter.

"You said you had something to tell me?" The Demon Slayer jabbed her sword forward, but the demon ducked down low, swiping at her and taking her off her feet.

"You want me to tell you now?" My eyes widened.

Helen fell to the floor with a thud, and an audible *oof* escaped her lips. "When else are you going to tell me? I'm always busy. There's always another demon to slay or an emergency with the portal."

The portal to Hell. Which happened to be only a mile from our Main Street.

"Um, okay, well . . ."

Helen jumped up to her feet and grabbed the demon by one of its spikes.

"Uh . . ."

"I'm not getting any younger, Clara," Helen yelled as the demon elbowed her in the stomach and sent her flying backward into one of my shelves of crystals. The crystals fell and dropped to the floor, shattering into a million little pieces. I winced at the mess.

"Okay." I took a deep breath. "About a month ago, I got a letter from my father."

Helen stopped her attack, turning and staring at me, mouth dropping open. "What?!"

The demon punched her in the jaw, and her head whipped to the right. I reached out, then retreated my hand.

Helen cracked her neck, then brought her sword forward toward the demon's gut. It blocked her attempt and knocked the sword from her hand. It slid across the floor and toward the door, making a scratching sound as it glided away.

"Your father? The one you thought was dead? But-but—"

The demon scuttled toward Helen's sword, but she jumped on its back and bashed its head into the floor.

"Maybe we should talk about this later?" I suggested, but Helen cut me a look. "Not on your life. What did he say?"

"That he's coming to Whispering Willows?" I said.

"What?" Helen's screech was so loud the demon covered its ears. She nodded toward her sword. "A little help, here?"

"Oh! Right!" I ran toward the sword and kicked it to Helen. She picked it up, and in one swift swoop, brought the pointy end over her head and down into the demon's. Its body slumped on the floor.

Helen, sweaty and red-faced, chest heaving, stood from the demon, her golden glowing sword disappearing now that its work was done.

The glass shards lifted from the floor and flew back toward the empty space they'd left, piecing together like a puzzle until the glass was whole again.

Helen quirked an eyebrow at it, and I shrugged. "This place is spelled so that it cannot be harmed."

Helen walked back to the purple chair sitting in the middle of the room and sank into it. "Your dad?" she asked. "Your dad." She said it again, like she had to feel out the words. "Your dad is coming here. Why didn't you tell me?"

I sat on the purple couch. "I don't know. Because I don't want the whole town knowing and speculating and making a huge deal out of it."

Helen sat up at that, a trickle of blood flowing from her eyebrow where the demon must've scratched her. "It is a big deal!"

I jumped up to get a wet cloth. Sometimes it was easy to forget Helen was sixty-five years old, but I wondered how much longer she'd keep up her role as the Demon Slayer. I couldn't imagine anyone else doing what she did, but she had to be getting tired. Especially now, with the influx of demons.

I turned on the sink against the back wall and ran cool water over the cloth, then brought it to Helen. She gave me a thankful nod and pressed the cloth to her head. "What if he's evil? Or has bad intentions?"

"There's nothing we can do about it if he is." I sat back on the couch. "He didn't reveal his identity or where he's coming from. I have no way to stop him."

"You could perform a spell . . . on the letter!" Helen nodded. "Yes, that's what you should do. A tracking spell."

"And then what?" I asked. "What am I going to do? Follow the letter where it came from, which could be anywhere. Halfway across the country. Across the world?" I shook my head. "And confront him in a place that's foreign to me where I don't know anyone?"

Helen chewed at her fingernail. "Okay, good point. So we just wait?"

"We just wait," I said.

"Well, I hate that. I don't want to wait around for something that could harm you to just waltz into Whispering Willows."

"The thing is . . . I don't think he's out to harm me," I said.

Helen dabbed at her eyebrow, wincing. "Why is that?"

"It's just a feeling I got from his letter. It didn't seem malicious. It felt like maybe he was excited?"

"Hm" was all Helen said. "Well, I still don't like it. This guy could pop up at anytime, and we wouldn't even know who he was."

"Maybe I look like him?" I asked, taken aback by the hopefulness in my voice.

"Oh, honey." Helen reached over and patted my hand. "You have a dad."

"I have a dad," I echoed.

It filled me with a kind of hope I didn't want. I'd always thought I didn't have any family out there. It was just me and my mom. And then when I discovered my mom was using her Witch Granter powers for evil, it was just me. All alone in the world. I made my own family through Whispering Willows, and they more than delivered. Then, just a month ago I discovered I had an uncle, my mother's twin brother that she'd kept a secret from me. We didn't get along at first, and I might've wished a time or two I'd never discovered him, but we eventually found our way, and now we got along great.

A text lit up my phone. Speak of the devil.

ISAAC

Just saw that picture of you and Remy on Instagram. Never wear those jeans again.

0/10

You failed that fashion assignment

I stuffed my phone in my pocket. Okay, well we were a work in progress.

Either way, I'd lost a parent so early in life, earlier than anyone should ever have to lose such a pivotal relationship. So part of me naturally hoped my dad could fill that role. That he'd appear and we'd just fall into an easy rhythm. That I'd finally have the parental figure my mom could never be.

Helen peered at me. "Just don't get your hopes up? You don't know who's coming to town. You don't even know if he's really your father."

"Well, we'll find out," I said briskly, standing.

Helen took my gesture for what it was, backing toward the door. "Okay, well I guess the demons aren't going to slay themselves. I'll see you later?"

Before she could leave, the cauldron sitting in the corner of the shop started bubbling. Purple liquid foamed up and overflowed onto the floor. I gave a little shriek and stared.

"Are you brewing a potion?" Helen asked.

"No." I stepped forward, peering at it. "I'm not."

The cauldron let out a loud burp, a big purple bubble rising and popping with the noise.

Helen pointed. "So that doesn't normally happen?"

"No, definitely not." I took a few cautious steps forward and arched my neck to peek inside. What in the actual hell? I straightened my shoulders, bristling at the cauldron. How dare someone hijack it and create a spell. In my cauldron. In my shop. No way was I letting this stand. I marched over to it.

"Should you be getting closer to that thing?" Helen asked from behind me.

I came to a stop in front of it, and inside, letters formed in the liquid, right before my eyes. Loops and swirls of white foamed over, creating actual words. Words that sent skitters up my arms.

*You've been summoned*, it read.

"Well?" Helen said from behind me. "What's going on? What is it?"

"A summons." I swallowed thickly. "I've been summoned by the Council."

# Chapter Four

The sounds of bees buzzing and birds chirping filled the field where Preston and I sat, a blanket laying underneath us. In the far distance, the ocean spread out, a vibrant blue under the shining sun. Preston plucked a purple wildflower and tucked it behind my ear, leaning his body close to mine.

I took a drink of wine from the glass Preston handed me, the cool liquid flowing down my throat with ease.

"Easy, there." Preston took a sip from his own glass. "I'm not trying to get you drunk just yet."

His eyes twinkled, and I laughed. Whoops. I guess I drained half my glass already. I set it down. "Better take it slow."

He brought out a bowl of strawberries, blueberries, and raspberries, all ripe and plump.

"I'm going to let you plan our dates more often."

He plucked a strawberry and I opened my mouth as he slipped it inside, his fingers brushing my lips and sending a jolt through my body. "Well, I know you've been stressed lately, with everything going on."

I'd told Preston about both the letter from my father and the summons from the Council, both with no clear date. I could be summoned at any time of the day or night.

"So I did some research," Preston said, "and a summons from the Council isn't always necessarily a bad thing. They have been known to summon supernaturals for accolades, good deeds they want to reward."

I cocked an eyebrow, taking a blueberry and popping it in my mouth. "And you think that's what this is? A reward for my good deeds? I haven't even done any good deeds, nothing extraordinary enough to be summoned."

"I wouldn't say that. You foiled a plan to burn down your shop by the mayor and you released a fellow Witch Granter from a lamp they'd been trapped in for almost fifty years."

Well, when he put it like that . . . I shook my head. "Do you think the Council cares about either of those things? I guess I should've said I haven't done anything that's benefitted the Council."

Preston winced. "Well, okay." He ran a hand over his buzzed hair. "What do you think this is about, then?"

I splayed out my hands. "I have no idea. Maybe something to do with my mother?"

It always somehow had to come back to her. She might not have been part of my life for over twenty years, but time and time again, her presence stayed with me, reminding me that I'd never be free of her.

"Maybe she did something else before she died, and now I have to deal with the repercussions."

Preston took a sip of his drink. "I don't think that's it." His hazel eyes flicked to me. "But I don't want you doing this alone. I want to come."

"You know that's not how it works."

All my life I'd heard about the terrifying concept of a summons. If you messed up bad enough, the Council would notify you, give you a head's up that a summons was coming, but that was as far as their curtesy extended. They didn't tell you when, where, why.

"Remember Ms. Helzdarg?" I asked Preston. "We were in history class one day, and she was lecturing us about the Vampire Act of 1918, when poof! She just disappeared in a cloud of smoke. There one minute. Gone the next."

We found out eventually she'd been summoned. She never returned. Apparently she'd been recruiting students into a cult of dark magic, teaching them how to use blood magic, soul magic, and the Council sent her to the Dark Bluffs, a prison for supernaturals, rumored to be somewhere in Antartica. I shuddered at the idea of being sent there. Surely I hadn't done anything that bad.

"Yeah, the entire school was talking about it. My ex-girlfriend was one of her cult followers."

I took another big gulp of my wine, and Preston wrapped his hand around mine, guiding the glass back down to the blanket.

"You know, let's talk about something else," he said, his fingers walking up my arms and sending tingles through me. "Something good."

That brought a smile to my lips. "Like what?"

He peered at me, his eyes a mixture of green and yellow in the bright sun. "Tell me something that makes you happy."

I gazed at him thoughtfully. "Well, I can think of one specific thing right now. Tall, strong, a man of few words, a hard worker."

His grin grew bigger. "Oh yeah?"

I nodded. "Mm-hmm. And he whips up a killer omelette."

At that, Preston's lips twisted. "I don't think I've ever made an omelette in my life."

"Oh." My hand flew to my chest. "I was talking about Bones. He's been a lifesaver lately, helping me and Remy clean out our attic, lifting all those heavy boxes. Every time I see him, it just makes me happy."

I laughed, and Preston fingers danced to my sides. "You're going to pay for that."

He tickled me, and I laughed hard, falling onto the blanket next to him, squirming under him. Our gazes met, his eyes so intense, boring into me, and suddenly we weren't laughing anymore. Heat flooded me, and I was acutely aware of the way my chest rose and fell with each breath, the way his own warm breath felt on my face.

He swallowed, his Adam's apple bobbing. "Clara, in all seriousness, I need you to know how happy I am that you're back in my life. After we broke up all those years ago, I never thought I'd get a second chance with you. I built a new life for myself, one that was completely separate from the life we'd dreamed up together. Then you came barreling back in, and I realized I could build a thousand different lives, and you'd fit in every single one."

My eyes welled with tears. "Preston—"

He pressed a gentle finger to my lips. "There is no life, no path I could take that wouldn't lead me to you. Every single time."

My heart thudded in my chest at his words, and he leaned forward, his lips slowly coming toward mine. I'd been waiting for this moment for so long, and it was finally here. He wound his arm around my back, bringing me flush with his chest, and I could smell his musky scent, reveled in it.

A groan ripped us from the moment, and we both shot up from where we sat as three demons burst from the trees. Green goop dripped from their mouths, and their slitted black eyes landed on us immediately.

"You've got to be kidding me," Preston murmured, coming to a stand.

I gulped. "Do we have any weapons?"

Preston's gaze flicked to the knife laying on the picnic blanket. The butter knife. I huffed. It was better than nothing. He picked it up and handed it to me while he grabbed a thick tree branch from the ground.

"That's not going to do anything," I protested.

"It's going to have to," he said. "Listen, our aim here isn't to kill. We won't be able to kill those things with what we've got on hand. We just need to distract them enough to get away, okay?"

I stared at the demons lumbering toward us, one of them with bright red scales and a long spiked tail that looked like it might belong to a dragon.

I planted my feet in the ground. I'd been through too much over the last few months to go out this way. I might not have been the Demon Slayer, but I was not going to let these demons go unpunished for ruining what had been a perfectly good date.

One of the demons had what looked like pock marks all over its rough blue face. Pock Marks lunged at Preston, and he shoved his tree branch forward, making the demon fly onto its back.

Meanwhile, Spiked Tail circled me like a lion about to pounce on its prey. The third demon clacked its long talons together, eyes flicking between me and Preston like it didn't know which of us might make a better appetizer. One of its sharp teeth hung over a snarled lip, loose and long, gangly. Its head snapped toward me, and it prowled forward in my direction. So I guess that answered that question.

I jabbed at Spiked Tail with my paltry little knife, and its lips peeled back into a terrifying smile, revealing all of its pointed teeth, crusted with black and red.

"You ruined my date," I gritted out between jabs. Spiked Tail spun around, swiping his tail at me, but I jumped back with a speed that surprised me.

On the other side of the blanket, Pock Marks had grabbed one end of Preston's tree branch and sank its teeth down on it, chomping away and bringing my boyfriend closer to becoming a demon snack. Preston shoved his foot into the demon's stomach and sent it sailing through the air.

I turned my attention back to Spiked Tail and Gangle Tooth, who had now joined the circling of me.

I punched the knife out toward them. "He was about to kiss me." Gangle Tooth hissed as my knife sliced at his arm, black blood sprouting from the wound. "Our first kiss in over twenty years."

Rage flowed through me at that thought. These idiot demons had no idea what they'd just walked in on. Hell hath no fury like a woman stopped from getting her perfect kiss from her perfect boyfriend.

With a cry, I lunged forward and wrapped my arms around Gangle Tooth's neck, then drove the knife straight down into his scaled skin. He let out a scream and threw me off of him but fell to the ground, not moving. Wow, this butter knife was really sharp. I cracked my neck. One down. Preston now had his demon below him, and he straddled him, punching him repeatedly.

Two to go.

I turned my attention on the demon in front of me.

"Do you know what's it like to be kissed by that man?" I pointed to Preston. "It's like the best high you could ever get. Your very own drug, and believe me, it's addicting."

Spiked Tail snarled at me.

"And I was about to get a hit of that drug before you stumbled in and ruined it all. So now, you're going to have to pay." I reared my arm back and sent the knife sailing through the air. It embedded itself right in the demon's gut. Spiked Tail fell to its knees, black eyes widening in surprise.

My head whipped toward Preston, Pock Marks rolling him on his back and now hovering over him, his sharp teeth snapping dangerously close to Preston's neck.

"Preston!" I cried.

His arms shook as he held the demon away from him, but I could tell it was a losing battle. The demon's jaw snapped, centimeters from Preston's bobbing Adam's apple.

I started running but tripped over a mound of dirt, falling forward into the soft ground. My head snapped up as the demon now had its hands curled around Preston's windpipe. Preston's face turned blue under the pressure.

"No," I breathed out, getting up and continuing my sprint toward them, knowing I wouldn't be able to make it in time. "No!"

Just then, a roar erupted. The ground shook under my feet, and a wolf burst from the trees, huge, shaggy, gray fur. It tackled the demon off Preston, and ripped it to shreds in front of us. I hurled myself into Preston's arms, and we watched as the demon became a mess of blood and entrails.

"Preston!" Now that we were safe, I turned my attention to my boyfriend, my hands roaming over his chest, shoulders, arms, torso. "Are you okay?" I asked.

He nodded, chest heaving. "How about you?"

"Yes," I choked out. "Oh, Preston. I thought—"

"I know," he said into my hair, pressing kisses to my head. "I know. But I'm here. You're safe. It's okay."

I buried my face in his chest.

A rustling sound filled the air behind us, then I heard, "Are you two alright?" A deep, soft voice.

I turned to thank our savior. An older man, graying hair, big muscles, square face with a scar stretching form his eye to his mouth.

"Well, I'll be," he said, stepping closer, studying me.

I felt Preston step close behind me. "Thank you for saving us," he said, his voice unsure and questioning. He was no doubt wondering why this man was staring at me with so much focus.

The man shook his head. "I can't believe it. You are your mother's daughter, alright."

"And who are you?" My heart hammered in my chest, so loud I could hear it. I had a feeling I already knew the answer.

The man took a step forward. "My name is Jeremiah, and I think I'm your father."

# Chapter Five

I sat across from my dad at the diner. In silence. We'd been sitting there for nearly five minutes now, though it had felt like an hour. Underwater.

From the little time I'd spent with him, I gathered he wasn't much of a talker. Normally, I had no problem carrying on a conversation, but somehow my throat had closed up, and the words I wanted, needed, wouldn't come. I couldn't do more than stare at him in wonder.

Dad. *Dad*. DAD.

The word rolled through my brain so many times that it started to sound wrong.

He steepled his big hands together. Like many werewolves, he was a large man, stocky, muscles threading his body. I wondered what drew my mother to him. In all the years I'd known her, she never showed any interest in love. Sure, I'd spotted her with the random man over the years, and she'd never shied from telling me the truth: that she sometimes she was lonely, wanted brief companionship, but that she had no interest in an actual relationship. I always figured that's what my dad had been. Just another fling.

Because that's what she'd led me to believe. What about this man made her hide him from me?

"So what's this place called, anyway?" my dad said, shifting on his side of the booth.

I looked around at the faded booths, the worn white- and black-checkered floor, the long laminate counter with a display case that showed off tarts, pies, cakes, and pastries.

"Um." I thought about it. "Well, it doesn't actually have a name. Everyone just calls it the diner. It's one of the only restaurants in Whispering Willows."

Though with the mayor's new development plan, that was changing. We had an ice cream shop, a bakery, and I'd heard rumors that a pizza place might be coming soon, which Remy was very excited about. It was kind of a bummer that we had to drive thirty minutes to the next town over every time we wanted pizza. Or we had to make it ourselves.

"Huh" was his response.

Back to silence. Lyra, one of the owners of the diner, fluttered behind the counter, her translucent wings giving off shimmers of dust every time she flapped them. Wrinkles lined her face, and her silver hair was tied into a bun as she scrutinized us, no doubt wondering what I was doing with this older man. I gave her a small wave, and she just frowned in return. Great. It would be all over town soon enough. Gossip. Rumors about who this man could be. But I also felt a protectiveness from Lyra. My dad was a stranger, after all, and she wanted to make sure I was okay. I nodded at her, and that seemed to satisfy her enough as she fluttered through the swinging back doors into the kitchen.

"How did you find me?" I finally asked, the question bursting out of me. If he wouldn't take the reins on this conversation, then I would.

"That's a long story," he said.

Silence. Again. This man couldn't have been more opposite my mother. She might've been cold, distant to some, but my mother knew how to carry a conversation, how to charm, to weave wonderful tales, to laugh. Oh, her laugh. It was a full-body one that shook her shoulders, lit up her entire face. I loved to make her laugh.

I gestured around us. "Well, we have time."

A waitress came up to us and dropped off a full plate of pancakes for me and a coffee for my dad, no sugar or cream. She scooped up our menus and turned to go.

"You're not eating?" I asked.

He stared at the coffee, perplexed. "How did she . . ." He looked back up at the waitress, now walking away.

Right. I forgot not everyone knew how the diner was ran. "Gerald and Lyra, the owners, employ a lot of clairvoyants. They can't read your thoughts, per se, but they can feel out your intentions, know what you want without having to take your order."

"Right." He took a long sip of his coffee. "Sounds efficient."

"I didn't realize you weren't going to eat," I said, but he waved away my words.

"Please, go on." He gestured at me to dig in, so I did.

Anything to fill this painful silence. I stuffed a big bite of pancake in my mouth.

Whatever I'd imagined when meeting my dad, it wasn't this. I didn't think it was going to be all rainbows and butterflies, but I expected him to at least talk. This strong, silent man in front of me wasn't giving me anything. I couldn't even get a vibe off him, and I certainly wasn't going to introduce him to Remy, to even entertain the thought of getting to know him if he couldn't tell me the most basic information.

I steeled myself to ask another question, to barrage him with questions if that was what it took, but he surprised me by saying, "You look like her, you know." He said it quietly, into his coffee, almost like it was hard for him to produce the words.

He didn't have to speak her name for me to know who he was talking about.

"I know. I get that a lot."

He swallowed, his throat bobbing. "It's almost hard to look at you. All the memories. They just flood back."

And in that moment, I knew he loved her. Whatever happened between them, he wouldn't have hurt her, wouldn't have given her any reason to run. If anything, it sounded like she might've hurt him. Which wouldn't surprise me in the slightest. I leaned forward.

I had a million questions, enough to fill up a lifetime. But I asked the most pressing one first, the one I needed an answer to if I was going to let him into my life, something I was very much on the fence about as of right now.

"Why are you here?"

His eyes met mine, crinkling in a familiar way, and I realized Remy did the same thing with her eyes when she was thinking deeply about something. "To see you, to meet you."

Wow, really couldn't give me more than that?

"But why now?"

He looked away, his jaw locking. "I . . . Well, I wasn't ready until now."

"So you knew about me? You—"

"I learned about you five years ago, when your mom died. But it took me a while to track you down."

I reared back. Oh, Mom. She kept my identity from him, but why? Was she afraid of him? No, Mother wasn't afraid of anything. Plus, nothing about this man seemed frightening, despite me seeing him rip a demon to shreds in his wolf form. Still, that response garnered about a million more questions that formed on the tip of my tongue. What about my mom's death connected to him learning about my existence? I was about to ask when he spoke.

He met my gaze. "Listen, I'm not good at this." He gestured between me and him. "Talking. Feelings. Probably why your mom and me broke up in the first place."

My breath caught at that. At that little piece of information that I wanted to soak up like a sponge. *Broke up.* If they broke up that must've meant they had some kind of relationship. Maybe he could show me a new side of my mother, one I didn't know. The thought sent a thrill through me. Despite spending half my life with her, there was so much about my mother that remained a mystery to me. She rarely talked about her past, so meeting this man, my father, was like finding a treasure chest full of rare and ancient relics. Every tidbit he gave me was like reaching into the chest and pulling out something new and shiny.

I felt his hand on my arm, warm and big and comforting. I glanced up in surprise as he broke through my thoughts.

"What I'm saying is I want to try. I want to get to know you, if you'll let me into your life."

I wanted to say yes, but I'd been impulsive in the past. I thought about just a month earlier when I'd cast a spell that trapped me in a golden lamp. I'd been angry, emotional in the moment, and cast the spell without thinking. It had landed me in my own golden prison, a genie, and it could've ended very badly if I hadn't figured out how to get myself free. I didn't want to do that again, to dive into this headfirst, based on emotion.

"I have to think about it," I said, watching for his reaction.

He didn't show any surprise. He just nodded and released me from his gentle grip. "I understand. I'm staying at the Bed & Breakfast. Run by a very chatty imp and a very big man."

I laughed at that. "That would be Martin and Bones. Don't ask Martin about his garden. He'll never shut up. Do let Bones cook for you. He's excellent."

At that, a smile lifted the corners of his lips. Not a big smile, but it felt like a win, all the same.

"I'll be here a week. Take your time." With that, he nodded, slid out of the booth, then reached into his wallet and threw a few big bills on the table. "You know where to find me."

And then he walked out of the diner, leaving me as confused as I was when he'd walked in.

# Chapter Six

BEFORE

The line of supernaturals stretched as far as Isabella could see. So far, in fact, that the people began to look like little dots in the distance as they stood waiting anxiously, hoping to get a wish from the Witch Granters visiting their small mountain town.

She sat next to her mother, who smiled at each supernatural that stepped up to say what they wanted. It was Isabella's job to give them the questionnaire, to make sure they were fit to receive a wish. Of course, she granted wishes, too, just not today. Today, her mother asked her to come along and do the paperwork, so Isabella agreed, always happy for a chance to escape Whispering Willows, escape her father, and fly through the air to another town.

A leprechaun stepped up, and he fidgeted with his hands, holding his hat in front of him and bunching the fabric tight.

"Hello," Isabella said, her spelled quill poised and ready to take notes as she talked with the leprechaun. "First, I'm going to need some basic information."

She rattled off the questions: name, date of birth, type of supernatural, address, yada yada yada. Then she finally got to the good part. The part that set her soul on fire.

"What is your wish?"

The leprechaun looked down, hesitating.

Next to Isabella, her mother stood, reaching into the bag they brought full of crystal balls and plucking one out, ready to grant a wish to the werewolf who Isabella had interviewed earlier.

"I'd like to fall in love," the leprechaun said.

Isabella's attention snapped back to him as a flush crawled up his neck and to his cheeks. "Love?" she repeated. "We can't make someone fall in love with you."

They got this a lot. Someone had a crush, and they wanted the object of their affection to return their feelings. It wasn't necessarily that it couldn't be done, but first of all, a wish that powerful would take too much of a person's soul as payment. The more powerful a wish, the more it cost, in terms of soul. Second of all, the Council had outlawed granting any wishes that would take away a person's autonomy. They couldn't grant a wish that would make someone fall in love, change their true feelings by force. It was illegal and morally wrong.

"N-no, you misunderstand." The leprechaun held out his hands. "There's not a certain person I want to force to love me. I just want to find companionship, to find a person that would be a good match for me. I'm not looking to make anyone give me their heart. But if there's someone out there who might be . . ." Isabella didn't think it was possible for his face to turn any redder, but his cheeks darkened, all the way to the tips of his pointy ears. "Well, my soulmate," he said in a hush. "Then I'd like to find that person. I know that's not a guarantee. Maybe there's no one out there for me, but if there is, all I'm asking is that I find them."

The quill scratched on the paper next to Isabella as the leprechaun spoke.

"Yes, I think that's something we can accomplish."

She wasn't sure why anyone would wish for love. Love was destructive. Love made you do stupid things. She'd seen what love did to her own parents, how it made her mother into some servant who wouldn't leave her father, no matter how horrible a person he might be. Love made you weak. Something Isabella never wanted to be.

In fact, she'd been looking for an oracle, one she thought might reside in this very town. She wanted to find the oracle and ask if she was destined for love. If she was, she would do everything in her power to keep it from happening. She'd never become her mother. She glanced over at the woman, red hair like her own, soft green eyes, freckles dotting her pale cheeks. Her mother smiled at Isabella and nodded.

She was a kind woman. She loved Isabella. She'd taught Isabella everything she knew about being a Witch Granter. But Isabella didn't think she could ever forgive her mother for not protecting her from her father. A hateful horrible man without magic, who for some unknown reason married a witch when he detested all forms of magic.

Isabella shook her head and turned her attention back to the leprechaun. "You'll have your wish," she said. "If your soulmate is out there, you'll find them within the next year."

His smile grew wide. "Thank you, thank you," he said, moving along to get in a different line, one full of those who'd passed the questionnaire and now were approved to get a wish.

Isabella swiped the sweat off her forehead. Even all the way up here in the mountains, it was hot with the sun beating down. A flash of blonde hair caught her eye in the distance.

A boy. She squinted. No, a man. He stood by one of the shops lining their main street, made of logs like every other building in this town. He wore jeans and a T-shirt that hugged his muscles. He was big. A werewolf if she had to guess. It wasn't often anyone caught her attention, not when she was so focused on her magic, on being the best witch she could be so she could one day take over The Wish List and be a powerful Witch Granter. So she could prove to her father that she wasn't some worthless girl like he constantly told her.

But something about this man drew her eyes. His shining hair, those twinkling blue eyes. He was talking to a vampire, who apologized profusely for something.

Isabella tried to hear what was being said.

"So sorry your order was wrong," the vampire said.

"It's really no problem," the man said in return, his voice so soft and kind.

The opposite of her father, who'd have a tantrum over something like this.

"Excuse me?" a woman said. She was next in line.

Isabella shook her head and tried to focus. But her gaze kept flitting back to that man.

She took a deep breath. "I'm sorry," she said to the woman. "We're going to have to stop for the day."

The man made her antsy, and she wanted to go look for the Oracle before it was too late.

"I'm sorry?" the woman said.

Isabella gestured to the line of people who'd already been approved for wishes, which had at least twenty supernaturals by now. It would take her mother forever to get through them.

"We'll be back," Isabella assured the woman. People in these towns were desperate for access to Witch Granters when they didn't have one of their own, so Isabella and her mother traveled frequently.

She stood, as if to end their conversation, and turned to her mother. "Mother," Isabella said. "I'm going on a walk. Is that alright?"

Her mother nodded absently, focusing on the little crystal ball in her hand. "Yes, dear, just make sure you're back by the time I'm done."

"Okay," Isabella said, knowing exactly where she needed to go to find this oracle.

She marched off with a purpose, looking behind her to see that the blonde-haired man was gone. Something like disappointment welled up in her, but she pushed it back down. Why did she care about some random werewolf in a middle-of-nowhere town? She didn't. Besides, after she found this oracle today, she'd find out whether love was in her future, and if it was, she'd make sure she never succumbed to it.

# Chapter Seven

Sun streamed through the window onto the dust-covered floorboards of the attic. A fan whirled above us, circulating the stale, hot air.

"So remind me again why we're here instead of at The Brewery like I suggested?" Emerson asked, sitting amidst a pile of opened boxes, blonde hair piled on her head in a messy bun that somehow looked classic and elegant on her head. Everything Emerson did looked classic and elegant with her long legs and tanned, smooth skin. In another life, she could've been a model.

I took another book from a box and set it in a pile of books to the side. "I really need to organize this attic. It's time. I've been putting it off for too long." I stood and dug into the box, bringing out a dried-out pen. "See? Look at this. Just useless stuff up here that needs to be thrown out or donated."

Emerson squinted at me. "Uh-huh. And this has to be done on a Friday night because . . . ?"

I thought about my meeting yesterday with my dad, the meeting I hadn't stopped thinking about since it happened.

I bristled, throwing the pen in a trash bag. "Like I said: it needs to be done."

Emerson held up her finger. "Or something has happened that's bothering you and you're stress cleaning."

I gaped at her. "What are you talking about?"

She rolled her eyes and crossed her arms. "Oh, come on, Clara. I know you. This is what you do when you get stressed. Remember senior night? Everyone else was going out partying, celebrating, and you were so stressed about some fight with Preston that you insisted on staying home and reorganizing your potions cabinet?"

I scoffed. "That . . . that . . ."

Emerson smirked and I threw up my hands. "Okay, fine. I'm stress cleaning."

It was disconcerting at times how well Emerson knew me despite just recently having come back into my life. We hadn't talked for nearly twenty years after we both left Whispering Willows—for very different reasons—but Emerson came back a month ago, and our friendship picked up right where it had left off, like no time passed at all. And apparently, she still remembered all my quirks and bad habits. Wonderful.

Emerson picked up an old pair of underwear from a box, wrinkling her nose and throwing it toward the trash bag. "So why are we stress cleaning instead of stress drinking? I think the latter is much healthier."

I gave her a look. "My dad came back in town."

She gasped. "Your dad?"

I'd told her about the letter shortly after I told Helen. There was no point trying to hide it now. Everyone would find out soon enough, and Emerson was important to me. Now that she was back in my life, it was a tricky balance picking up where we left off while also trying to find our way as middle-aged women. We'd been friends so long ago, wild teenagers who made bad decisions and weren't nearly as mature as we were now.

Who was I kidding? I still made bad decisions. But still. It was new territory to navigate, and I trusted Emerson and didn't want her finding out from some random person off the street instead of hearing it from me.

"Your dad?" Emerson repeated, then leaned forward. "So what's he like? Tell me everything."

I lifted another heavy book from the box. How many books did my mom own? I wonder if she even read any of these.

"I don't really know," I said, studying the book cover. *How to Cast the Perfect Spell Every Time.* Yeah right. There was no such thing. I tossed it aside. "That's the thing. I think we spent an hour together total and he maybe said ten sentences in that entire time?"

"Ooh." Emerson tapped her chin. "You know, I can see why your mom would go for that. She was this larger-than-life personality and your dad was the strong-but-silent man, in the background. Giving her what she needs—"

"Okay stop." I pointed at her. "You need to cool it with the romance novels."

"I'm just saying, it makes sense to me."

"Really?" I asked. "Because it doesn't make sense to me! I don't know how they met, what my mom saw in him, if it was just a fling or something more serious . . . I kind of get the feeling it wasn't a fling, though. Which would mean Mom lied to me. Again."

It would only be the hundredth lie I uncovered of hers over the past twenty years.

Emerson's face softened. "I'm sorry, Clara. I know it's so hard finding out all this stuff about your mom. She must've had her reasons for keeping this from you."

"That's the problem. That's why I don't know if I should let him into my life. Introduce him to Remy. What if Mom had a good reason for keeping him from me?"

I thought about my uncle Isaac, Mother's twin brother, who I'd just met a month earlier. Isaac might've been annoying and definitely a little extra, as Remy would put it, but she never should've kept his existence a secret from me. It wasn't fair to Isaac and it certainly wasn't fair to me or Remy. We should get the choice whether we want a family member in our lives. My mother made that choice for us, all because she was scared Isaac would take The Wish List from her, take away her heritage. So what about my father frightened her? What was she scared he might take away from her? Or from me?

My phone lit up with a text. From Isaac. Why was it that every time I thought of him, it brought a text. He was out of town right now, visiting family, and planned to be gone for a month.

**ISAAC**

> Did you wear my favorite cashmere sweater? Because I saw picture on Remy's Instagram of you in a certain maroon De La Roche, and I just know that couldn't be mine because I padlocked my closet before I left and expressly forbid you from entering.

My cheeks flushed. Guilty. Isaac happened to be close to my size and had excellent taste. Though I'd never tell him that. His head was already big enough.

I texted him back.

**CLARA**

> Nope. Not your sweater. I definitely didn't find the key to the padlock and unlock your closet and steal one of your sweaters. Couldn't be me.

**ISAAC**

> I knew it! You better not have spilled anything. And no more wearing my clothes!

> That color was all wrong for you.

> And you wore the sweater wrong too. It's off the shoulder. Ugh. God. You're such a peasant sometimes.

I rolled my eyes and put the phone away.

Emerson tapped her chin. "You know, your mother always talked about how much she valued her independence. Maybe your dad scared her for reasons connected to that? Maybe she was afraid to let herself fall in love."

I reached into the box and pulled out another book about bugs and their medicinal properties. Trash. "That could be. But what if it's something more sinister? I mean the guy could barely tell me anything. Maybe he's hiding something."

"Or maybe he's a nice guy who's never been a father and feels awkward and overwhelmed but is doing his best. Oooh." Emerson pulled a lacy bustier from the box she sat in front of. "Now this might be worth keeping. A little sexy surprise for Preston?"

I snorted. "He hasn't even kissed me yet, so I think we're a long way from lingerie."

Emerson's mouth dropped open. "Still no kiss? Not even after your romantic picnic date?"

I'd totally forgotten to mention the demons that ruined that particular date. My father showing up and saving our lives had kind of overshadowed that whole thing. I sighed but kept the attack to myself. I didn't feel like getting into it.

"We got interrupted," I said. "I think he was close to kissing me."

Emerson set the bustier aside. "I hope so. That man better kiss you soon or I'm going to burst." She fanned herself. "If Cruz made me wait like that . . ." She winked. "You need some of my romance novels. They'll tide you over. And if he doesn't make the move to kiss you soon, then you're going to have to be the one to do it. Just lay one on him."

The thought had crossed my mind. But Preston wanted our first kiss since we got back together to be special, and I didn't want to take that from him. Oh well. The bustier would have to wait. But maybe Emerson was right and I could borrow a romance novel. Or two.

I frowned at the book in my hands, this one with a shiny rose gold exterior but no title or author. "That could be it too," I murmured, studying the exterior.

No, not a book. This was a journal. I opened the first page, blank. Then flipped through some other pages. Also blank. A journal that had never been written in. A hope I didn't realize I'd had deflated like a balloon. For a fleeting moment, I thought maybe I'd stumbled upon my mother's diary, a piece of her that I could claim. A way I could learn more about her, something that wasn't just more bad news. Another evil dealing by my mother. Sometimes, it was hard to remember that she was more than the bad things she'd done. She'd been a good mother, loved me, but those good parts were starting to fade in my memories, and I desperately wanted to cling to them. I sniffed, turning the journal over in my hands, something keeping me from putting it in the trash pile.

"What's that?" Emerson asked, arching her neck as she pulled a corset-looking thing from the box.

"A journal, I think," I said. "It's never been written in. I might as well keep it."

"Yeah, you know, journaling could do you some good. Be a great way to get your feelings out. Write all the things you want to say to your mom and your dad." Emerson snapped her fingers. "And maybe all the things you want to do to Preston. Then slip the journal into his desk and let him read it. That'll motivate him to kiss you." She waggled her eyebrows and I threw a pen at her. She ducked, laughing.

"Okay, okay," she said, still laughing. "But seriously, I think journaling about your mom and dad could be good for you. Help you work through your unresolved feelings."

I opened the journal again, staring at the blank pages, that disappointment welling in me. If only my mom had written in this. Given me something. Anything. She couldn't. No one could show me a good side of her. No one except . . . I thought about my dad. He clearly had feelings for my mom once upon a time. I could tell from the few things he'd said, the way he'd talked about her. The same thought I'd had in the diner popped into my mind again. He could tell me about her. If I could get him to talk. But surely that would come if we built a relationship.

"Uh oh," Emerson said. "That's your determined face. What are you thinking?"

I looked up at her, clutching the journal tight. "I think I'm going to tell my father I want him to stay." I could get to know my dad and reclaim a piece of my mother I'd lost when I discovered she was evil. I could have it all, and my dad would be the key to getting it.

# Chapter Eight

The boat floated in the sparkling blue water, sun shining overhead, slight breeze. In other words, it was the perfect Southern California day. I lifted my face toward the sky as I lounged back on the widespread deck, letting the rays warm my face.

"So what do you think?" Preston asked from next to me. "Better than Martin's rowboat?"

I snorted, realizing I'd never actually been in a boat other than Martin's. And boat was a poor descriptor for that thing. All three times I'd ventured out in it so far, I'd feared for my life.

"How did you even get a yacht?" I looked around at the pristine white ship, shiny and sparkly clean.

"I have a few connections." Preston grabbed the bottle of wine from the ice bucket sitting in front of us. "One of my students' parents owns a few of these and rents them out."

My eyebrows raised. "And what's the occasion?"

Preston's gaze turned wicked, and he leaned over, nuzzling my neck. "To spoil my girlfriend."

His voice was rough, low, and heat flooded my core. I thought about what Emerson said, about the bustier, suddenly wishing I'd worn something a little sexier under the jeans and blouse I was sporting. This was it. Today had to be the day Preston finally kissed me. You didn't just rent an entire yacht for you and your girlfriend not to kiss her.

The ocean spread out around us for miles, no one, not a thing, in sight. The perfect place to steal some kisses, and maybe more, without any prying eyes.

I grinned at Preston as he poured me a glass of wine, and we clinked our glasses together.

"To us," Preston said.

"To us," I echoed, letting the gentle waves of the boat rock me into a lull. In this moment, everything felt perfect. Just me and Preston and the open sea.

"What's Remy up to today?" Preston asked.

"She's out with Emerson, dress shopping for the Samhain Ball."

I shot him a look, gauging his reaction. Remy had told me Preston would be chaperoning the ball, and part of me thought he might ask me to be his date. Chaperones often brought their spouses or significant others to enjoy the night. But he had yet to mention to anything. Not a peep from this man. Maybe he didn't want a date for the ball. It was a work event, after all, and not all teachers wanted their partners involved in their work lives. I understood if he didn't want to bring me. But part of me hoped he'd ask.

I thought again about Emerson's words, about taking control, making the first move. Just because I was going to let Preston make the first move in kissing me didn't mean I had to wait for him to make the first move in every aspect of our relationship.

"Preston," I said, meeting his gaze.

His brows furrowed at the seriousness of my tone.

"Yes?"

"Will you be my date to the Samhain Ball?"

His eyebrows shot up, and he laughed. "I was going to ask, you know."

I bristled. "Well, I guess I beat you to it."

He leaned forward, his nose touching mine, and my breath caught in my throat. "I'd love to go to the ball with you, Clara Joanna Westfold."

I started at that. He'd known me as a Westfold, but I was technically still a Burgmont, hanging onto my husband's last name because I didn't want a different one than my daughter. I hadn't actually had that conversation with Remy, asked how she'd feel if I dropped that name and adopted my Westfold one again. As Preston grazed his lips against my cheek, down my neck, to my exposed collarbone, thoughts of my name fled, and I was pretty sure this man's kisses might very well make me forget my name entirely.

"I still remember when I got to take you to our first ball together," he said into my neck as I mmm'd, his flutter of kisses making my toes curl. He retreated, taking a sip of his wine nonchalantly, like he hadn't just set my entire body on fire. He stared out at the ocean with a smirk, and I knew he was enjoying this far too much.

I remembered the ball like it had happened yesterday. It had been the shock of a lifetime when he'd asked me to go with him. The Preston Hammond? Star soccer player, witch extraordinaire, future lead witch detective of the Whispering Willows Police Force. He'd been the most popular boy in school, and I never thought he noticed me. I spent half my days staring at him, daydreamed about what it might be like to be his girlfriend. We'd talked here and there, me stumbling over my words and blushing furiously.

One day, I'd found him struggling over a spell he needed to create for a school assignment. I might not have been confident in my abilities to catch the attention of the most popular boy in school, but if there was one thing I was confident in, it was my abilities as a witch. I'd agreed to help him with his spells, tutor him in the art of magic. We'd spent months together after school, hunched over a cauldron, gathering ingredients, writing spells.

One day I'd been dropping ingredients into the cauldron, then instructed Preston on how to move his wand, what intentions to set for the spell, and hovered behind him as he waved his wand back and forth in a zig-zag motion. Before our eyes, the cauldron had lit up, the spell activating, and Preston was so excited he spun around and lifted me in the air, whirling me round and round. When he set me down, he stared at me for a long moment, those intense hazel eyes boring into me and burst out, "Will you go to the Samhain Ball with me?"

And the rest was history. Well, not quite. There were a few hitches on our way to becoming a couple, but we got there eventually. I snuggled into his chest, turning my body so it molded right into his, a perfect fit.

Gentle waves lapped around the boat, the occasional call of a bird echoing through the calm day at sea. Every once in a while something splashed in the water, a mermaid tail or a fish or a seagull. Preston drew lazy circles on my back with his finger.

Perfect day.

"Do you remember our first kiss?" he asked after a while.

I choked on my wine. Did I remember our first kiss? It was only seared into my brain, seared onto my lips. Nothing had ever topped the way Preston kissed me. I liked kissing my late husband, of course. But I knew what I had with Greg. It was stability. Love, yes. But not the passion I'd felt with Preston. I touched my lips absently, then darted a glance at Preston, deciding to do some teasing of my own. Two could play at this game.

"Yeah," I said breezily. "It made the top one hundred."

Preston's eyes bugged. "Top one hundred? Kisses?"

"Mm-hmm. You just cracked the list at ninety-nine." I shot him a mischievous grin.

His laugh rumbled, and he leaned closer. "Well, I think it's time to fix that. I need to make the top ten, at least." He flipped me onto my back, hovered over me, his lips so close to mine.

My breath hitched. "Yes," I said, all the teasing gone from my voice. "I definitely think we need to fix it. And you're going to have to work very hard."

This was it. My moment. Finally. I lifted my head, my lips aching for his, other parts of my body aching too.

"Oh I plan to." Preston dipped his head down.

"Ahoy matey," a voice called out from down below and we shot apart.

Preston's chest heaved along with mine, his eyes wide and dazed like he'd been ripped from a dream. A very good dream. I sat up and arched my neck to look down below. Whoever just interrupted us was about to get an earful. No, scratch that. I might actually commit murder on this boat today.

I stared down at the intruder, and there sat Martin in his rowboat with . . . my mouth dropped open. My father. Apparently, since he'd missed walking in on my make-out sessions as a teen, this was his chance to make up for lost time. Preston looked from me to my father, scratching at his head, his shirt lifting to reveal a shock of his golden-tanned skin.

I reluctantly dragged my eyes from his figure back to Martin and my father. The imp smiled, his ears wiggling. It was in an imp's nature to be mischievous. They just couldn't help themselves, and from the way Martin was smiling big, I could tell he was enjoying this far too much.

"What are you two up to?" Martin asked innocently.

I glared at him. I was a grown woman. I would not be embarrassed by the fact that I was about to make out with my sexy boyfriend. My dad sat in the boat next to Martin, quiet, studying the two of us. Okay, I was a little embarrassed. No matter how old you were, you didn't want your parents walking in on you and your partner. Especially not your estranged dad. Your estranged dad whom you hadn't talked to since the diner meetup. I'd planned to go see him later today, after my and Preston's date.

I narrowed my eyes at the imp. "What are you two doing out here?"

Martin raised his nose in the air. "I'm taking your dad on a little excursion out to sea. Only a five-star experience for guests at my B&B."

The rickety boat they sat in begged to differ. My dad's hulking form looked ridiculous in the tiny vessel, boards with chipping paint, cracked wood. The thing looked like it might fall apart with the slightest breeze.

I crossed my arms as Preston came to a stand beside me. "Uh-huh. Well, it was nice seeing you two. Um." I looked at my dad. Jeremiah. "Jeremiah, maybe we can talk later? I was planning to come see you today."

Preston and I had some business to finish. And I was determined to get my kiss before we both started another long week of work.

My dad gave a small nod. "That works for me."

"Oh, but Jeremiah, you were just telling me how you planned to go on a hunt tonight, with the local pack." Martin smiled like he was helping the situation, when he was very much doing the opposite. He was wrecking my plans with my boyfriend.

"Is that true?" I asked my dad, frowning. I didn't want to impede on his plans. He'd mentioned he was a lone wolf, and wolves didn't generally do well alone.

The only other lone wolf I knew was Myrtle, who was an exception to basically every rule out there. If he had a chance to connect with other wolves, I didn't want to stand in the way of that.

"No, no, it's fine," my dad said, but I could tell it wasn't.

"No," I argued. "I don't want to interrupt something like that."

"How about this?" Preston stepped up to my side. "I'll go back to shore with Martin, and your dad can spend some time here, with you, on the yacht?"

I stared at Preston, hoping he was receiving my message: *Don't you dare ruin our date. Take it back. Take it back. Make up some excuse. Anything.*

Before anyone could speak, he started to climb down the ladder on the side of the boat. Message definitely not received. I heaved a sigh. My dad, clearly uncomfortable with the whole situation, avoided my gaze and fidgeted with his hands. I'd never met such an awkward person in my life. Preston got to the bottom of the ladder, and my dad stood in the boat, his huge form rocking it wildly. Martin flew to the side, letting out a strangled yell. I hoped the boat capsized and took the imp with it. This was all his fault.

Instead, he just squirmed as waves sloshed on him, and he got a mouthful of seawater. That, at least, gave me a little bit of satisfaction.

My dad reached out for the ladder and Preston hopped into the boat, both of them switching positions. Well, there went that plan.

Goodbye perfect date.

Goodbye perfect kiss.

Hello awkward conversation with my long-lost father.

# Chapter Nine

"Sorry," we both said at the same time as my dad settled next to me on the deck of the boat, ice bucket now full of water, wine lukewarm.

I grabbed the bottle and took a swig anyway, watching Preston and Martin row away into the distance.

"I didn't mean to intrude on your date," my dad said. "Martin saw your yacht and insisted on rowing over to say hi, even though I said I didn't know if it was a good idea."

"Sounds about right," I muttered. "Martin loves to push buttons. My buttons, specifically."

My dad let out a quiet laugh. "Well, either way, I'm sorry. So I guess you don't have the same fear of the ocean as your mother?"

I stopped at that, offering the wine bottle to him. He grabbed it and took a deep gulp.

"You knew about her fear of water?" I asked, curious now.

He nodded, drawing his knees up and hooking his arms around them as he gazed out at our surroundings, nothing but blue for miles all around. "It was stupid, really. One time I decided to surprise her with a date at the beach. I hardly knew her, should've asked before bombarding her like that. She didn't take it well," he said, going quiet.

"A date?" I asked. "You and my mother dated?"

He glanced at me, his eyes wide at my shock. "Well, yes. Before we got engaged, of course."

"You and Mom were engaged?" I screeched, and he winced at that. "Sorry. I just, Mom never mentioned you. Didn't say a thing about you."

His face fell, and regret stabbed me. He must've cared for her, and it couldn't be easy to hear this.

He set the bottle down with a clink. "What did she tell you about me?"

"Nothing," I said truthfully. "That you were a one-night stand and she never saw you again." I didn't know if this was the right time to reveal that she'd also told me he was dead. Probably to ensure I'd never go looking for him. I needed to gauge how he felt about my mother before revealing that kind of information.

"Right." His voice was full of disappointment.

In the distance a fin peeked out of the water. Then another. And another. A dolphin burst through the surface, its sleek gray body twisting in the air as it splashed back down.

"They're beautiful creatures," my dad said, letting out a sigh. He paused, opened his mouth, closed it, opened it again. Then he pushed a hand through his thick gray hair. "I'm sorry I'm not better at this."

He handed the bottle back to me, and I took a good long gulp before wiping my mouth. "You don't have to keep apologizing to me, not for who you are or the way you present yourself. You're here, and that's enough." I bit my lip. "But you do have to be more forthcoming. If I'm going to let you into my life, into my daughter's life, then you need to tell me the details of your relationship with my mother. How you met, how long you were together, what your relationship was like, why she left you. Or did you leave her? I don't even know." I flung out my hands. "I want to know everything."

He swallowed hard, like that might be a difficult thing for him, then he turned his wide gaze on me, and I noticed the small flecks of yellow in his green irises, the exact same flecks I had, that Remy had. "You have a daughter? I have a granddaughter?"

His voice wavered, and I smiled gently.

"Yes, and believe me, you want to know her. She's the most wonderful person in the world. She'll dazzle you with her smile, she'll entertain you with her wit. Just beware, you'll fall in love with her. Everyone does."

He chuckled and shook his head. "I don't doubt that." Then he took a big breath. "Listen, I'm not much of a talker, which you've probably gathered by this point. And I've never talked about my relationship with your mother. Not to anyone. Not because it was a secret but because it's . . . painful. Everything that happened between us. I have a lot of regrets, and if she were still alive, I know she would too."

"So you know she died?" I asked, and he nodded.

"Yes. Your mother wasn't exactly incognito in the supernatural world. A lot of people wanted her to pay for her crimes, and I heard rumors about all the things she'd done, abusing her powers."

"Did she do that stuff when she was with you?" I asked.

He shook his head, and my shoulders sagged in relief. So I was right. Maybe he could give me some insight on my mother, remind me of all the good parts of her, the parts I so desperately wanted to cling to.

A father. I stared at this man sitting in front of me. I had an actual living, breathing father, and he seemed . . . decent? Maybe I could finally have that parental relationship I never did with my mom. My mother loved me. I knew she did. She might have never said it, but she showed it in everything she did. She made bad choices, yes, but that didn't strip away what we had. Still, it would be nice to have someone in my life, in Remy's life, who could say those words I wanted to hear. That my mother never said. Three little words. So simple. But so, so complicated at the same time.

I cleared my throat. "Okay, then."

My father looked at me. "Okay?"

I nodded, firm. "You can stay, meet Remy, get to know us. If you still want that?"

"Yes," he breathed out. "Yes, I want that." He looked around. "This place brings back so many memories." His eyes shone.

"Wait," I said, holding up my hand. "You met my mom in Whispering Willows?"

He shook his head. "No, no. I met her when she came to my town one day to grant wishes. She came with her mother, a kind woman."

That took me aback. As with everything, Mom didn't speak about Grandmother often, and I'd never quite been able to get a picture of the woman in my head. Anything my mom did say was always kind, and her voice took on a sorrow when she spoke of her own mother, so I gathered the woman was good, loved my mom, and raised her with that love.

"You met my grandmother?"

He nodded. "Many times. She . . . she really wanted your mother and I to have our happily ever after. We got along very well, actually."

I wanted to ask why they didn't get their happily ever after, to ask what could've possibly stood in their way, but I also didn't want to push him. He'd already said this was painful for him, and I wanted to respect the boundaries he set. So I would give him time. Let him reveal his relationship with my mother in bits and pieces until I finally had a full picture of her, instead of the broken fragments that filled my mind. It could help Remy too. I'd told her very little about my mother because in some weird way I was still protective of my mom. I didn't want Remy to think the worst of her grandmother, but I didn't know how to show her all the good. Maybe my dad could do that.

He grabbed the bottle of wine and took another drink, then chuckled and nodded his head toward the beach in the far distance. "A few weeks after I'd met your mother, I asked her to meet me here for what would be our disastrous first date. I lived a few towns over."

I noted the use of "lived" and wondered where he lived now.

"So this was the date when you surprised her?"

He nodded. "I was so desperate to see her again after we met that I sent her a note. I honestly didn't think she'd show. Surprise of a lifetime she did."

That surprised me too. My mother hated the ocean, didn't want to go anywhere near it if she could help it. She must've really liked him. Which made me like him more. My mother was a lot of terrible things, but even with all that, she was a good judge of character. I didn't have the same radar—clearly—but something in my gut told me I could trust this man.

"So what happened next?" I asked.

That brought a smile to his face, softening those hardened edges, making that long scar running from his eye seem less intimidating. "She stood back, away from the water. I'd set up some chairs, a little table closer to the shoreline. She wouldn't come near it, and I couldn't figure out why. She wasn't very forthcoming."

"It was because of her father," I said softly. "My grandfather. He wasn't a nice man. Her trauma surrounding the ocean came from him."

My dad nodded. "I found that out . . . eventually. But not that night. Instead, I kept asking her to come sit at the table I'd set up, while she refused, saying she'd go somewhere else with me. I got frustrated. She got frustrated. And we got in a screaming match on what was supposed to be our first date."

I choked on the wine, coughing and sputtering, until I finally found my voice. "How in the world did you ever get a second date? Mom held grudges, and if you moved to her bad side, good luck ever crossing back over again."

My dad laughed. "I actually think that fight is what made your mom like me more. She knew she couldn't just bowl me over. I think she also realized I was trying to do something nice for her and that I didn't know any of her history with her dad. So the next time we met, she was the one who planned the date. Took me flying on her broom. Most terrifying experience of my life."

"She loved that broom," I said.

Brooms were archaic now, rarely used, but my mother refused to engage in any other mode of transportation when she was alive.

"So what date did she plan for you two?"

He smiled. "Took me to a small town up the coastline where she was going for the day to grant wishes. She gave me forms, told me I would be responsible for gathering information from potential wish seekers, interviewing them, making sure they were eligible to receive a wish."

I snorted. Of course work was my mother's idea of a good date. My father didn't seem annoyed though. Instead a wistfulness filled his voice.

"I think that was the day I fell in love with her."

Love. So he did love her, at one point in time at least.

"It made her so happy, granting wishes for all those people, making literal dreams come true."

I felt the same, and as soon as my dad said it, memories flooded me of watching my mother grant wishes at the shop, watching the way it invigorated her.

"Thank you," I said softly. "For sharing that with me."

He reached his hand out, then seemed to think better of it and retreated it back into his lap. "Like I said, I'm going to try."

That was all that mattered. Today hadn't exactly gone how I expected. I peered at my dad as he stared at mermaid tails splashing in the distance. But somehow, the day had turned out to be a good one, anyway.

Now I just had to introduce him to Remy and hope I wasn't making a huge mistake.

# Chapter Ten

Remy hunched over a paper, scribbling with a quill, scratching out words, adding new ones, muttering to herself. I finished placing the last cleaned crystal on the shelf after a day of wish granting. "You okay there, Remy?"

"I can't get the spell right," she said and straightened. A cauldron sat behind her, waiting to be filled with ingredients so a spell could be cast. Every time I saw that cauldron, it made my skin crawl, thinking about the summons, about the fact that I still hadn't appeared in front of the Council and that it could happen at any moment. I shook my head, focusing my attention back on my daughter.

Remy tapped the end of the quill against her chin. "I want my first spell in our family grimoire to be worthy of the Westfold legacy."

I leaned down on the counter, resting my elbows on the cool marble. "You do remember that I didn't put my first spell in our family grimoire until I was forty years old because I'd worried about the exact same thing." I bopped her nose with my finger. "Don't be like me. Don't overthink it. Whatever spell you create will make a wonderful addition to the Westfold grimoire."

The book in question sat closed on a tall stand next to the cauldron, its cover wrinkled and leathery, a big star in the middle signifying our family crest.

Remy bent over again like she hadn't even heard me, muttering to herself as she wrote out something, then immediately drew a line through it. Well, she'd have to learn in her own time. There was only so much wisdom I could impart on my daughter. Some lessons she needed to live through to really understand.

The bell to the shop rang, and my father stepped in, his big frame filling up the doorway. "Hi. Hello," I said, suddenly feeling nervous as I darted a glance at Remy, who now had set the quill down, gaze snapping to my dad, her big green eyes studying him with interest.

I nodded at him, and he took a few steps inside, the door clicking shut behind him. I'd told Remy her grandfather had arrived in Whispering Willows but not much else. She'd been eagerly awaiting the day she could meet him. I knew it was time. I couldn't keep them from each other, didn't want to. I had a feeling they were going to get along great.

I bit my lip as my father took a few more tentative steps forward before Remy threw herself into him and began peppering the man with questions. He fumbled over his words, but his voice stayed quiet and calm while Remy bounced on the balls of her feet. She was so excited to meet him, and I was excited for her.

"Mom?" Remy asked. "Hello?"

My head snapped up. "Sorry, what was that?"

"I asked if I can show Jeremiah what I'm working on," she said, gesturing to the spell she'd been writing. "He just asked about it."

"Oh!" I said. "Yeah, of course." Remy led my father around the counter and he studied the paper where she'd been writing the spell, as well as the ingredients laid out.

He chuckled. "I haven't seen spell casting since . . ." He glanced up at me. "Well, since your mother cast a spell for me. That was the first and last time I'd ever seen witch craft." He scratched his head, ruffling his thick gray hair. "To be honest, I've forgotten how all this works. Care to show me?"

He was offering out a branch for Remy, something for her to grasp onto so she could show her strengths, show him something she was clearly proud of. That small gesture, him showing interest in her life, warmed my heart, and I felt a renewed sense of peace over all of this. I'd done the right thing by choosing to let my dad into our lives.

I wanted to ask him what spell my mother had cast for him, but

Remy had already began rattling off what she was doing. "Okay, well since you might not remember, spells are all trial and error. A good witch knows what ingredients are best for certain spells. Some plants are better for cleaning spells, some types of animal skin might be better for healing salves, and so on."

My father nodded thoughtfully. "Makes sense."

"So knowing that, you start off with ingredients you think will best support the spell you're trying to cast." She gestured to the ingredients laying out before her: squid ink, a broken pen, diopside crystal, and a tablespoon of turmeric. "I'm trying to create a spell that will keep my pens from drying out. I'm sick of going to school and constantly having to find new pens because they all run out of ink so fast."

My dad smiled. "Now that's a useful spell. One I'd use."

Remy nodded, frowning down at the paper. "I know! I just feel like I might be missing something."

"Well you can't know until you try, right?" my dad asked.

Remy scratched something else from the paper and rewrote the line. "I think I'm getting the wand movement wrong. It feels off." She scribbled something quickly and my dad watched, fascinated.

"I forgot so much of this," he murmured. "You have to write the spell to activate it." He looked down, shaking his head. "Your mother had forgotten her quill and ink when she wanted to cast a spell for me. She was so frustrated and I had no clue why. I didn't understand the importance of it all until she explained how spells work, until she showed me."

Remy nodded, satisfied at her work. She began dropping the ingredients in the cauldron one by one while both my dad and I stared. She'd been working on this all morning, and she'd tried the spell at least four times now with varying results, none producing the magic she wanted.

She grabbed her wand, oak with light blue silk threaded through it and unicorn hair sprouting from the top, then she moved it in a circular motion, her brows furrowed while she concentrated on her intention.

The cauldron glowed a bright pink, brighter, brighter until the color burst like a balloon, zapping away. My father blinked a few times, and Remy reached inside the cauldron, pulling out a single pen.

She squealed. "It worked, it worked! But do you think this is the spell I should put in our family grimoire?" she asked, looking from me to my dad. "It feels so trivial."

"I can't tell you that, Remy," I said in my singsong voice as she stuck out her tongue.

My father scratched his jaw. "Well, if your mother can't tell you, I certainly can't either. I do know your grandmother loved this grimoire." He ran a finger down its spine in what felt like an intimate gesture. "She loved writing spells for it, said those spells were her legacy." His expression grew thoughtful. "But she didn't care about the power behind the spells. She talked about how she just wanted to leave behind spells that would be useful for generations to come, no matter how small a use they may be."

That brought a smile to my face. It sounded like my mom. So practical of her. At the same time, I wondered when she became less focused on helping others and more focused on gaining power. My father's words were a good reminder that she hadn't always been power-hungry. I wish I knew what had changed within her. What suddenly made her decide power was more important than anything else in her life, more important than me.

Remy tapped her chin with her wand. "I'll think about it. But for now, I have a pen that won't completely suck."

She high-fived me, and I laughed, my dad chuckling along.

Remy's eyes glittered. "So are you here to tell us stories about Grandma? How'd you meet? How'd you fall in love? Why did you break up? Did you know about my mom?"

I could see the panic flashing across my father's face, the way his skin paled, and his hands clenched and unclenched at Remy's endless barrage of questions. I'd told her to take it easy, which she clearly had forgotten about in the midst of all this excitement.

"Okay, hon. That's enough. Give the poor man a chance to breathe."

He cleared his throat. "That's what I wanted to talk to you about, actually."

I put an arm around Remy. "Go on?"

"Well, I was thinking that I know you must be frustrated by the lack of answers I've given so far, by how it's been hard for me to talk about this part of my life." He swallowed. "So I thought maybe I could show you."

My nose scrunched. "Like you want me to create a spell, draw out your memories?"

That sounded invasive, and my father was a private man, so it surprised me he'd be willing to do something like that. But also, I didn't just have a spell like that on hand. It would take quite a while to gather those kinds of ingredients, to figure out the right wording for magic that powerful. Plus, I didn't want to find out about my mom and dad that way. I wanted to hear it from him. I liked the picture he painted of my mom, the way I could see her so clearly through his eyes the times he had spoken about her.

He shook his head. "No, no, not exactly. I thought I could take you to all the most significant places in our relationship. Maybe being back in those places will make it easier for me to talk about them, give you the answers you want about your mother. Plus, we can spend time together, which I'd really like."

My heart ballooned. Yes, yes, that sounded like exactly what I needed.

Remy's eyes lit with excitement, and she pressed her hands together. "Yes!" She turned to me. "This will be perfect. We can take fun little day trips, get to know Jeremiah better, learn about Grandma. I'm in."

I rolled my eyes. "I guess that's a yes," I said to my father, reining in my excitement more than Remy had, but in reality, it sounded wonderful. Not only could I spend time with my father, but I would actually get to see the places my mother and him spent time together. I would be learning about an entire part of my mother's life that had been closed off to me. A part she hadn't been willing to share. I wouldn't think about that for now. About why she wouldn't tell me about Jeremiah, not when he seemed like such a good, down-to-earth guy.

"So when do we start?" I asked.

He spread out his hands. "How about now?"

## Chapter Eleven

The road wound in front of us, up, up, up further into the mountains. We'd been driving for two hours, Remy telling my dad all about the Academy where she attended school, my father listening intently, the smallest hint of a smile on his lips as Remy talked about her schoolwork—and all the latest gossip.

"And then," Remy said, "my science teacher gave us a pop quiz. Everyone had to figure out what kind of chemical reaction would turn the penny green."

My mind wandered. I'd already heard this story anyway. It ended with Remy getting distracted by her vampire crush and accidentally turning the penny blue and failing the assignment. She still hadn't said yes to her vampire, and at this point, I had no idea what she was waiting for. He hadn't asked anyone else, was clearly still pining after her. That girl must've been taking a page out of Preston's book, making the vampire sweat.

Very similar to what Preston was doing to me. Well, to be fair, Preston had tried to kiss me several times now, but we kept getting interrupted by demons and imps and my father. We had another date scheduled in a few days, and lord help me, if that man's lips didn't end up on mine, I was going to positively lose it.

"So you like him, and he likes you," my father was saying, "but you still won't accept his offer to take you to this ball?" He scratched his head, just as confused as I was over the whole situation. Good luck trying to understand the inner workings of a teenage girl's mind, buddy.

"Well, I'm not sure I want to go with him anymore." She paused. "He's pouting, and it's not a good look on him."

"You did say no," my father said. "He's probably allowed to pout a little about that."

I looked in the rearview mirror, seeing Remy's expression turn thoughtful. "I suppose that's true. I just feel like everything is so tense between us now, that it would be weird for me to say yes. Maybe not enough at this point? I said no and embarrassed him in front of a lot of people, and since then, I've just been ignoring him. I feel like I've screwed everything up too much to fix it all."

My father shook his head. "Believe me, you haven't. You know, your grandmother and I briefly broke up right after we first started dating?"

"Shut up," Remy exclaimed.

My dad's lips pressed together, and he clearly wasn't sure how to proceed.

I patted his arm. "It's okay, she says that when she's really excited about something. Continue." I tried to keep the eagerness from my voice, but I wanted to hear this story just as much as Remy did.

"Yeah." My dad scratched his head. "I'd accidentally stood her up for our second date."

I looked over, narrowing my eyes.

"I know, I know."

"How do you accidentally stand someone up for a date?" Remy asked.

"I was on my way, and my car broke down. This was before the invention of cell phones. She was so mad she wouldn't answer any of my calls, give me a chance to explain myself. I thought we were done."

"But you weren't," I said, stating the obvious.

"No," he agreed. "But, to be honest, it took us a while to find our way back to each other. I thought she was being overdramatic with the whole thing, thought it wasn't fair she wouldn't even give me a chance to explain why I hadn't showed up to our date. I put some distance between us because of that. But fate intervened and we ran into each other at some farmer's market, of all places. She listened to me, and once I explained what had happened, her anger melted way. Just like that, we were back on track." He turned to look at Remy. "Never would've happened if she hadn't listened. Just from what you told me, I can tell your vampire would still take you to the ball. Maybe you just have to give him the opportunity."

"Hm . . ." Remy's voice was hopeful. "You're a natural at this, Jeremiah."

"I don't know what *this* is, but I'm glad I could help, at least."

I met Remy's eyes in the rearview mirror and she just smiled big at me.

"So where are we going?" I asked, the car continuing up the windy road, each zig and zag making my stomach turn. I didn't get car sick, but these narrow sharp turns were making my stomach heave.

"We're actually going just a little further," my father said, pointing past a worn wooden sign with letters scratched on it that I couldn't make out. "Turn there."

I slowed the car and turned onto a dirt road that plunged into the mountain forest. The thick canopies blocked out the sun, stray rays breaking through in spots otherwise surrounded by shadows.

It just now hit me that I was driving myself and my daughter to a remote location in the middle of nowhere with a man I didn't actually know all that well. I really hoped my gut feeling was right and that my father was a trustworthy man. We drove deeper into the forest, our surroundings only becoming darker the further we went. I gulped at the jagged shadows jumping out at us, the stray branches scraping across my car, the eyes peeking out from the darkness stretched between the trees.

"Okay." My father leaned forward. "Now take a sharp turn here."

He pointed to an even narrower road, and I followed his directions, turning the wheel and slowing down, the car creeping along.

"We're almost there," he said.

I drove further, the trees now opening and letting in more light, much to my relief, until my father ordered me to stop before the little road abruptly ended, a huge cluster of bushes and tangled vines hanging in front of us.

"We'll have to walk from here." My father stepped out of the car, and Remy jumped out after him before I could signal to her to be careful.

I stepped out of the vehicle and followed as my father held back the long stringy vines and Remy ducked under.

"Remy, wait!" I called after her, but she disappeared behind the curtain.

"Go ahead." My father gestured, and I crouched lower, following my daughter.

When I straightened, my breath caught in my throat. A towering waterfall thundered down before us, the water crashing into a small pond.

The canopies parted far overhead, and the sun shone down on the crystal blue water, which sparkled like diamonds.

Remy's hand lifted to her mouth as I came to a stand beside her. "This is so beautiful," she breathed.

I felt my father's heavy presence behind me. "My hometown is only a few miles down the road, but that's not technically where I met your mother." He pointed to the waterfall. "This is."

My eyes widened, and I turned to him. "You met her here? But what was she doing?" I asked.

My father smirked and gestured to a few large, flat rocks that bordered the pond. Remy and I each sat on one, and my father settled on another, looking out over the waterfall with a fondness shimmering in his eyes.

"Rumor says this water has special healing properties. I can't say whether or not that's true, but my mother had been sick with a cold for a few weeks, so my father asked me to make the trek out here to retrieve some for my mother to heal. We didn't have the kind of money required for a wish from the revered Witch Granters who were visiting that day. So out here I came to get the water, and when I walked into the clearing, there sat Isabella. Crying."

"Crying?" I echoed.

My father gestured. "She sat right there on that rock where you're sitting, Clara."

I looked down, as if I would see my mother here, next to me. But all I had was the image my father was painting with his words.

"I was young, stupid. An eighteen-year-old boy who'd dated a handful of girls and had no idea how to treat one."

Remy snickered at that.

"But I knew your mother was special. With that flaming red hair, those captivating green eyes. I knew the moment I laid eyes on her that I was in trouble."

"So what happened?" I asked.

"Well, I asked her if she could move."

My mouth fell open and Remy barked out a laugh.

My father held up his hands. "I told you I'd only dated a handful of girls. I had no idea what I was doing. Of course, now I know the smart thing to do would've been to ask her why she was crying, but at the time, I couldn't think of a single thing to say."

"So you asked her to move?" I said in disbelief.

He gestured to the waterfall. "Well, so I could get to the water. Her legs were stretched out between the rocks."

"You could've chosen anywhere else to access the pool of water!" I said again in disbelief.

He chuckled and shook his head. "My brain wasn't working that well, not after seeing her."

"What did she say?" Remy asked, probably thinking the same as me, that my mother would've likely given him an earful over the entire thing.

"She glared at me and said that I didn't own this waterfall and she could sit where she damn well wanted to."

That sounded like my mom, alright.

"Embarrassed, I ducked past her and gathered up the water in my bucket. That's when I finally had the sense to ask your mother why she was crying. She said she'd come out here in search of answers, but she didn't find what she'd been looking for. So I did probably the smartest thing I'd done so far that day: I sat down and listened as she talked. She was upset because she'd been searching for an oracle, a powerful one who had the ability to give someone an answer to any question they had."

I reared back. I'd heard of these oracles. They weren't common in the supernatural world, about as rare as Witch Granters.

"If you could find one of these oracles and pay their price, they would answer a single question, and your mother thought the oracle was here, at this waterfall."

"Why?" I asked, heart beating hard in my chest.

"Because she'd been told the oracle lived near Whispering Willows, in a place where water caged her. Your mother assumed that meant she lived behind the waterfall. She'd gotten her hopes up."

A place where water caged her. How vague. I could see the logic behind it, though.

"I later found out she'd wanted to ask the oracle if she would ever find love."

I nearly fell off the rock and into the water. "Love?"

I couldn't believe my mother cared about such a thing, especially knowing how much she hated my own relationship with Preston when I'd been a teenager.

My father just stared at the waterfall, immersed in his memory. "She had gotten into a fight with her mother, who wouldn't leave your grandfather. She couldn't understand why your grandmother would stay in such a relationship. She was worried she was destined to repeat your grandmother's mistakes. She never wanted to be in a relationship like that."

I shook my head. "Wait, so she wanted the oracle to confirm that she wouldn't find love?"

My father chuckled. "Exactly. She wanted to find this oracle and to know that she'd never be in a position like that, that she'd never fall for someone and be that vulnerable. She was afraid that she'd fall in love and lose all good sense, just like her own mother had."

That made so much sense. My mother never would've wanted anything to have power over her, including love. She often talked about her mother, my grandmother, how weak of a woman she'd been when it came to my grandfather. She refused to leave him despite how awful he was, and that took its toll on my mother.

My father continued, "We talked for hours after that, and by the time your mother realized that she had to go, she wasn't crying anymore. She also wasn't as concerned with finding the oracle. I asked when I could see her again, and she just smiled and told me it was my turn to visit her. I don't think she realized how seriously I'd take her words, that I'd show up in Whispering Willows in a few weeks, ready to take her on our very first date." He snorted. "The terrible one on the beach."

I let his words about my mother sink in. And just like that, it felt like a tiny piece of the puzzle that was my mother was revealed to me, a precious gift that no one could ever take away.

# Chapter Twelve

Martin pushed the oars of his rowboat through the ocean, his green skin luminous, which made me slightly jealous. That man had his skincare routine down. Ocean water spilled over the sides of his boat and pooled into the bottom, and the tang of sea salt filled the air.

I stared out over the horizon, at the way the sun glittered on the water's surface.

Martin scoffed. "I cannot believe I let you talk me into this."

Oh, please. I didn't have to talk the imp into anything. All I mentioned was that I'd like to borrow his boat, and he jumped at the chance to take me on my little mission. He clearly missed Isaac and wanted something to take his mind off his boyfriend, who was still halfway across the country visiting with his mother.

"Missing Isaac?" I asked, brow raised.

Martin just rolled his eyes. "Not everything has to be so dramatic, Clara." I gave him a look, and he threw out his hands. "Yes, okay? I miss him. I'm afraid he's having so much fun with his mother that he's going to want to leave and never come back."

Martin burst into tears.

"Oh, Martin." I reached over and patted him as he sobbed. "Isaac has every intention of coming back to Whispering Willows."

It had been a shock when I'd found out Martin and Isaac were dating, but even I had to admit, they were the perfect pair. I'd never seen Martin this besotted with anyone. The imp was a notorious player, and relationships were never his thing . . . until he met my uncle, possibly a bigger diva than the imp.

Martin sniffed, wiping his nose, and continued rowing. "You're right. Isaac is going to come back. I'm just ready for him to be home."

"Well, at least it sounds like he's having a good time with Greta?"

Martin nodded. "Oh, yes. They're reconnecting, and your theory was right. It was your grandfather who asked Greta to take Isaac far away, told her she needed to protect him. Poor Greta didn't know your grandfather's evil intentions."

Isaac hadn't told me that. My grandfather hated magic, and I never knew why he married my grandmother, a witch, when he clearly resented her power so much. He'd hoped his children would be born without magic, but when his twins were both born with magic, he'd taken Isaac and given him to Greta, a nurse at the hospital, telling the witch to run far, far away with the baby and never come back. Then he lied to my grandmother and told her one of her babies had died shortly after she'd given birth. I couldn't even imagine the kind of pain that imparted on my grandmother.

Sometimes I wondered if my mother would've turned out different if she'd grown up with her twin brother. By the time he finally found his way back to Whispering Willows, it had been too late for them to have a relationship, and she'd cursed Isaac to a life stuck in a golden lamp, worried that if anyone found out about him, her legacy, her heritage would be at stake.

Poor Isaac. Yes, he was annoying and dramatic and way too into reality TV, but he'd been through so much. And I was glad he and Greta were reconnecting. He'd need a mother figure going forward.

"You know, you really should be spending more time with your father," Martin said.

"What? Why do you say that?"

He gave me a pointed look. "The poor guy's miserable at the B&B. Spends all his time in my gardens staring forlornly at the flowers."

"Forlornly?" I echoed.

"Yes. For-lorn-ly," Martin said slowly. "Instead of spending time with him you're out here with me, doing . . . what again? Are you going to tell me why I had to bring you out here?"

Martin's words flushed me with guilt. "Volunteered," I coughed out, pushing the guilt away.

He cocked a thick black eyebrow. "I'm sorry?"

"You volunteered. I didn't force anything."

He sputtered. "As if I'm going to trust you with my boat."

No matter that the boat in question was rotting, needed a new paint job, and creaked ominously every time the ocean rocked it. Martin had an unhealthy attachment to this thing.

"So?" Martin asked, continuing to row. "Let me guess, we're visiting the mermaids. Oh wait, no. We're going to be sung into a trance by a siren. Or we're going to be forced to listen to a seagull sing show tunes that will make my ears bleed."

I shook my head. "No, smart ass, none of those things. I . . ." I hadn't told anyone about this little trip today. "Well, okay. There's an oracle—"

Martin groaned. "I knew it. I knew this wasn't just a nice row out to sea like you made it seem."

I might have told Martin I just wanted to take a relaxing ride in his boat.

"What does the oracle do? What do you want with it?"

I knew the question I wanted to ask. What I wanted to know more than anything in this world. What made my mother turn evil? What made her do all the bad things she decided? What was the turning point for her? I needed to know. The question burned into me like a fiery brand. If I could just get that answer, maybe I'd finally be at peace with the whole thing.

"I just want to ask the oracle a question," I said.

Martin harrumphed, like he didn't believe me. Technically, I didn't know that the oracle wasn't dangerous, but I had no reason to believe she would be. Yes, we hadn't had great experiences in the past with these adventures, and we almost died in this boat a few times, but that wasn't what was happening here.

"So I heard that this oracle lives in the coves, the ones near that shipwreck."

Oracles tended to live in secluded places, both because otherwise people would constantly be seeking them out and because many of them could read minds, and it was too hard to live near society, where the voices would be loud in their head, hard to manage. My mother had told me of an oracle who made the mistake of coming to town, and people flooded her, the voices in her head coming so fast she couldn't stop them. She'd ran straight into the portal to Hell, so overwhelmed by it. She'd never been seen again.

Martin's gaze snapped to me. "I'm sorry, you want to travel out to the coves to hunt down some oracle that might or might not be there so you can ask a question?"

My plan, or lack thereof, was suddenly starting to feel very silly. "Well, you know oracles live in secluded locations that they don't advertise. But if we can find the oracle, then they'll answer any question you have."

"And you honestly think an all-powerful oracle is going to live in the coves? By the shipwreck? Have you lost your mind?"

I think I might have. It did sound really dumb. Still . . .

"Now that we're out here, we might as well go check it out . . ."

Martin just glared at me. "I have been wanting to see the shipwreck, so count yourself lucky I'm agreeing to this. Also you're going to have to take some pictures of me in front of the wreck for my Instagram."

"You have an Instagram?" I said.

"Remy set it up for me, thank you very much. Also, you're welcome."

"Once again, I wanted to do this by myself. You're the one who insisted on coming."

Martin ignored me and stayed on course, rowing the boat through choppy waves that made my stomach lurch each time the boat tipped up or dipped back down in the crash of the sea. As Martin rowed, we fell into a silence, the sound of the ocean surrounding us. In the distance a group of seagulls sat on the water until a whale sprang from the depths and arched into the air. My breath caught in my throat as I watched the massive creature burst forth, scattering the birds in all directions. The whale flopped back to the water, disappearing down below.

"Wow," I breathed, and then I saw it. It was still a ways in the distance, nearer to the coves, but I couldn't tear my eyes away: the stern of a ship poked out of the water, the ship's body partially erect as waves washed up over it and then receded. Martin turned his rowboat in that direction, and even though it must've only been twenty minutes, it felt like it took hours to finally reach the shipwreck.

This was a particularly dangerous place for boats to come near because the waves could easily pull you in and not let go. Before you knew it, the ocean was smashing your ship against tall cliffs and sharp rocks before spitting you out to the sandy little beach.

The massive ship rose up, and my eyes widened as I took it in.

Martin got the boat as close to the shore as he could, and we both jumped out, pushing the vessel ashore.

Wet, cold, and tired, once Martin and I had our feet planted on solid ground, we both collapsed into the sand. "Well, I certainly don't see an oracle here, do you?" Martin peered at me, and I made a face at him.

He was right. I didn't see any kind of powerful seer who might be able to answer a question about my mother.

"I'm sorry," I said. "It's just, I really wanted to find this oracle so I could maybe finally get an answer about my mother—"

"Your mother." Martin gasped. "I should've known this had to do with her. And when your mother is involved, nothing good ever comes of it."

Well, I couldn't really argue with that, as much as I wanted to.

"No, it's not like that. There's no evil or ill intentions here, there's no horrible mystery to solve. There's just a question about my mom that I—You know what? It's not a big deal. Really."

"Why?" Martin shook his head, his thick salt-n-pepper hair shaking with the movement. "Why on earth would you need an oracle to answer a question about your mother? She's gone, Clara. What could you need to ask this badly?"

"Because . . ." I gestured weakly. "Because I just do."

I guess I really didn't know why it mattered so much. It just did.

Martin wiped at his brow, sand now crusting his forehead. "I cannot believe you lured me out here like this under false pretenses."

I stared at the ship, my eyes catching a part of it where water washed over the lip, a lower compartment underneath opened and protected from water washing inside. I gasped. Even if an oracle wasn't at the coves, it would still be fun to go see the ship. How often did one come across a shipwreck like this? I'd never been to the coves before, and this whole area looked so rugged and abandoned. Might as well explore while we had the chance.

"It's not like I'm asking you to help me fight some sea monster," I shot back. "Now, c'mon..."

My voice trailed off as eight large tentacles crept out of the water, curling and undulating. I gulped.

"You were saying?" Martin stood, shooting me an accusing glare.

"I'm sure it's a friendly giant squid." I squinted at it. "With sharp pointy teeth and—is that blood coating its mouth?" My voice didn't sound nearly as confident as I'd hoped it would.

"No, it's absolutely not a friendly squid."

"How do you know? Are you a giant squid expert?" I asked as the creature rose out of the water and covered the ship with its body.

"Because I'm with you, and nothing is ever so simple when you're involved."

Well, that was rude. But also kind of true.

We both backed away as the squid eyed us with its soulless black eyes. This definitely did not look like any kind of squid I'd ever seen.

"Just stay calm," I said out the side of my mouth. "And do not run."

"Really?" Martin squeaked. "Because running seems like a good idea right about now."

Without warning, the squid shot out one of its arms, grasping me tight around the waist. I shrieked and Martin grappled for my arm, but I slipped from his hold right as the squid pulled me with it, straight into the inky depths of the sea.

Down, down we went. My lungs burned, and I choked on sea water. Darkness surrounded me, the squid's tentacle wrapped tight around my waist, pinning my arms to my sides so that my only recourse was to kick. I flailed wildly, but it had no effect on the squid, who continued on its path.

I tried to yell, but the only thing that escaped my mouth was bubbles. My vision started to fade, and all I could think about was Remy. This could not be my end. I couldn't leave Remy like this. The only comfort I took in the moment was knowing that Whispering

Willows would take care of her. They all loved Remy as much as I did, and she wouldn't be alone.

My lungs squeezed tighter, pain erupting through my body as the squid raced through the darkening depths of the ocean. Everything grew cold, and my body became limp in the creature's tight hold. I wanted to fight, but I was so tired and in so much pain from the pressure of the creature's tentacles.

I shook my head. No. No. What was I doing? I couldn't give up. Remy needed me. So I did the only thing I could think of in the moment. I bent down and sank my teeth right into the squid's soft flesh.

Yuck.

But it worked. The squid screeched, and its hold loosened on me just enough that I could wriggle free. The squid shot toward me, and I kicked out a foot, right into its eye, disarming it enough that I could swim away. I kicked like crazy, pumping my arms and swimming back toward the surface.

I didn't feel the looming presence of the squid behind me.

Light filtered through the water, and I knew I was close.

I pushed hard until I broke the surface. Green hands pulled me from the water and to shore.

"Clara," Martin said, voice panicked.

My vision doubled, stars dotting my eyes.

"Martin," I responded. "There's two of you."

"What are you talking about?" he asked. "Clara! Clara!"

And then I passed out.

# Chapter Thirteen

BEFORE

"Jeremiah, where are we going?" Isabella asked, his big hands wrapped around her eyes, his body behind her as he guided her forward.

Isabella's stomach twisted. She didn't often like to give up control like this, but Jeremiah said he had a surprise for her, and she didn't want to ruin it by refusing to go along with his plans.

Leaves and grass crunched underfoot, a breeze tickling her face.

"You'll find out soon enough." His teasing voice rumbled in her ears.

The faint sounds of birds chirping surrounded her, coming from above. That must mean they were in the forest, in the hills surrounding her beach town, where the birds resided. But why. Why were they in this forest?

She was just about to tell Jeremiah she couldn't stand the secrecy anymore when they abruptly stopped. Jeremiah loved surprising Isabella, and she didn't have the heart to tell him that she hated surprises, not when it made him so happy to plan romantic outings, gifts, dates. He showered her with love, and she couldn't bring herself to reject it, even if it scared her a little sometimes.

He unwound his large hands from her eyes, and she spun around to face him. She blinked at their surroundings. So she was right. They stood in a forest, surrounded by thick, tall trees with towering canopies. Leaves and twigs scattered across the ground, and birds chittered from their perches on branches overhead.

She pointed a finger into his chest. "You have some explaining to do."

A smile quirked his lips. "Do I now?"

She gave him a pointed stare, and he took her by the shoulders and slowly turned her around, where she came face-to-face with one of the largest trees she'd ever seen. Its base spanned nearly as big as The Wish List, and carved into it was a little door, a door that led into . . . what?

She'd never seen anything so magical, so whimsical, like something out of a book. That was saying something for a woman who granted literal wishes.

Jeremiah stepped up beside her, and he looked down at his hands, folded in front of him, suddenly seeming so shy and unsure. Her sweet, gentle man. They'd only been dating for a few months, but she could already tell he was different from any other man she'd ever met. Soft spoken, willing to say sorry, to admit he was wrong, not power hungry or needing to prove himself. The exact opposite of her. But he complemented her well.

"Jeremiah?" she asked. "What's going on?"

"I . . . well, I hope it's okay that I did this, but I, uh, I found an oracle."

She sucked in a breath. Oracles were notoriously hard to find. They hid out in the middle of nowhere, their powers so strong and unpredictable, they tended to fare better alone. If you were lucky enough to come across one, though, they'd share their visions with you. For a price.

Isabella didn't have that kind of money. Not when her greedy father took everything they earned from Isabella and her mother.

"I'm not sure I have the money for this," she said to Jeremiah.

His breath caught. "Did he take from you again?"

She nodded.

He swore under his breath. "Isabella, why don't you leave? Come live with me. In the mountains. We'll open your own shop, we'll—"

"You know I can't leave her."

Jeremiah stilled. She wouldn't leave her mother, stupid as the woman may be for staying with that awful man, she was all Isabella had, and she couldn't just leave her to her father's angry whims.

Jeremiah cleared his throat. "Well, I've got the money for the oracle. You don't have to worry about that. I know how much you wanted to find that oracle the day we met."

Isabella had been so disappointed when she hadn't found the oracle under that waterfall. She'd been so sure she would get the answers she wanted. She'd never told Jeremiah the question she wanted to ask. She peered at him, frowning. Not sure now that she still cared to know if she'd find love. After all, her entire plan had been to prevent it at any cost, but . . .

Jeremiah frowned. "What's wrong? Oh hell, I messed up, didn't I?"

She grabbed his hands and led him away from the little green door. "No, you didn't."

They sat down on a long log that stretched between two trees.

Once they were settled, Isabella spoke. "This was so kind of you, Jeremiah. It was . . ." She spread out her hands. "Well, I can't believe you did this for me."

"Of course I did. I'd do anything to make you happy."

"I know," she said, and her heart squeezed.

Why didn't she want to go see the oracle? To find out if she'd find love? She stared at Jeremiah, at the face that she knew so well. Those blue eyes, that sandy blonde hair, the mole he had right below his left ear, the freckles that came out when he stood in the sun. She could be plunged into darkness and still know that face, maybe better than her own.

She gasped at the realization that hit her. She didn't want to see the oracle because she didn't need to know if she'd find love. She'd already found it, and she didn't want to prevent it.

"I love you," she said to Jeremiah, a little breathless.

He went so still Isabella thought maybe he'd turned into a statue.

"Jeremiah?" she asked.

He leaned forward and pressed his lips to hers, urging them open, slipping his tongue into her mouth. She groaned into him, reveling in the feel of his muscled shoulders under her hands. He sat back, a grin on his face.

"Does that mean you love me too?" she asked.

"I've loved you since the first day we met," he said simply. "Just didn't want to say it too soon and scare you away." His eyes crinkled. "So what does that have to do with the oracle?"

She took a deep breath and told him about what she'd wanted to ask, hoping he wouldn't judge.

But of course he wouldn't. He was Jeremiah, the best man she knew.

He took her hands in his. "Hey, I understand why you'd be scared to fall in love, especially with the father you have. But I will never hurt you."

Isabella stared into that face and believed him, but a small seed of guilt churned in her gut. She hadn't told him the other reason she didn't want to fall in love: that she was afraid love might hold her back, force her to make compromises. It wasn't just that she was afraid of repeating her mother's mistakes. It was so much more.

Her and Jeremiah walked away from the forest, hand in hand, and Isabella never thought about the oracle again. But if she had walked into the oracle's lair that day, she would've learned that love wasn't going to be her downfall, in the end.

That would be something else entirely.

# Chapter Fourteen

My eyes blinked open, harsh fluorescent lights shining over me, the sound of a machine beeping near my ears in a steady rhythm.

"Well, this might just top the stupid cake of all the stupid cakes you've eaten," a voice said.

My mind, still groggy, had trouble identifying the voice. I blinked more, vision blurry, mind slow.

"Really? Even over trapping herself in that lamp?" another voice countered, this one with an Irish accent.

"Let's just agree that Clara has done a lot of stupid things."

I groaned and slowly sat up to see Myrtle, Helen, and Gene sitting around me. I glanced at the room. White tile floors, machines hooked up to me. I looked down. A hospital gown. I rubbed my face. I was in the hospital?

"What happened?" I croaked.

Helen narrowed her eyes at me. "Well, you almost got eaten by a squid and Martin had to drag you to his boat and row you to land, then call for help. An ambulance brought you here. And then Martin called us."

"And Remy?" I sat up straighter.

"Still at school," Myrtle said. "Doesn't know what happened."

Yet.

I relaxed back into the bed, wincing as sharp pains shot through my sides.

"Why would you ask Martin to take you out to some shipwreck?" Helen asked, crossing her arms.

It was all starting to come back to me: the boat ride, the shipwreck . . . that horrible squid.

"I was trying to find some oracle," I said miserably, "The oracle has the power to answer one question for you, any question—and I wanted to ask her what made my mom turn evil."

Helen's eyes shone with pity. Her husband just cocked an eyebrow, his gelled bleach-blonde hair particularly shiny under the hospital lights.

Myrtle barked out a laugh. "Why does it always lead back to your mother? Clara, really."

Gene huffed a sigh. "I can't believe I'm saying this, but I agree with the werewolf."

"That's because I'm not just beauty and brawn like some vampires I know." Myrtle shot an accusing glare at Gene and tugged at her pink tracksuit that matched her pink hair . . . and pink rectangle glasses. "I got brains."

"You're right. You don't have beauty or brawn," Gene shot back.

"Okay." Helen stretched out her arms between the two of them. "Enough."

Those two had a centuries-long grudge against each other they still hadn't solved.

I pointed at them. "You know, this feels a lot like the pot calling the kettle black. You two want me to get over my mother, who just died five years ago, yet you've had two hundred years to work out your issues and—" I gestured at them as if that was proof enough.

That effectively shut them both up.

"Why do you want to know what made your mother evil?" Helen leaned forward. "What's so important about it?"

My eyes rolled upward. I wish I knew. "I just—my dad has been sharing stories about my mother, good stories, ones that make me remember why I loved her so much. After over twenty years of hearing nothing but bad about my mom, it's refreshing. And lately." I shifted in my bed. "I've been wondering what caused my mom to make that shift from good to bad."

"Oh christ," Gene said. "Have you ever considered that nothing caused it? That that's just the way your mother was? Not everyone has to have some huge, life-altering event to make bad decisions. Trust me, I'd know."

Gene, aka the Serpent, was Whispering Willows's most notorious vampire once upon a time. Then he met Helen and she turned his entire world upside down. Fifteen years later and those two had one of the strongest marriages I'd ever seen.

"I know, I know." I sighed heavily. "It was stupid. I just wanted to find the oracle, and I wasn't really using my brain."

"That's obvious," Myrtle muttered.

Helen paused. "I know it was hard leaving your mom at nineteen, cutting her out of your life. And then even harder when you found out she died five years ago. But you do have another parent, another opportunity."

My eyebrows drew together.

"Your dad," Helen reminded me.

"Actually seems like a decent guy," Gene added. "And I don't usually say that about werewolves." He shot a glare at Myrtle, who flipped him off.

The ancient werewolf frowned, accentuating the wrinkles and deep folds of her skin. "And I thought he was telling you all about your mom. Isn't that what you wanted?"

"Yes." A headache grew behind my temples. "It is what I wanted. What I still want. He's opening up a whole side of my mother I never knew about. I just thought this oracle might give me another insight. I guess I got greedy."

Gene nodded while Helen shook her head no. She looked at her husband and elbowed him, and he coughed. "Um, no, you're not greedy."

I just rolled my eyes.

"It's not greedy to want to know about your mom, Clara," Helen said gently. "It's understandable now that you're learning about her past that you would want more, but you have to draw a line somewhere. And that line is a freaking shipwreck that a giant squid happens to be guarding."

Myrtle adjusted the glasses on her nose. "No more chasing after this oracle. And absolutely no more trips out to sea in Martin's boat."

"Okay, you're right. I won't chase after the oracle anymore." Disappointment welled up in me, but I knew they were right. It was a fool's errand, and I'd almost gotten myself killed, left Remy without a mother. I couldn't take those kinds of risks anymore.

They started to stand. "Where are you guys going?" I asked, a whine in my voice.

Helen stepped forward and kissed my forehead. "You need to rest. Remy will be by after school, and if you think we were bad . . ."

I winced. Remy was going to have a fit once she found out what I'd done. And who was I kidding? I deserved whatever she had to say, no matter how harsh.

Everyone said their goodbyes and left the room, and I fell into a restful sleep.

∽

"Seriously, Mom? A squid?"

My eyes fluttered opened to see Remy's frowning face as she leaned over me. I felt like a kid about to be grounded.

"Remy—" I started.

"No." She paced back and forth, hands clasped behind her back. "This was such a monumentally stupid thing to do. And you didn't even tell Martin where you wanted him to take you!"

"Remy—"

"An oracle? You wanted to find a freaking oracle? As if you don't have enough on your plate already."

"Okay, but—"

Remy started ticking off her fingers. "A shop to run, a daughter to raise, a long-lost dad coming back into your life, a boyfriend. Not to mention you've been summoned by the Council, and you have no idea when they're going to whisk you away."

"Remy!"

"What?" She whirled around, eyes blazing, chest heaving.

"You're right," I said softly and patted the bed.

She eyed it warily. "I am?"

I nodded, laughing. "Yes, you are."

She raised her nose. "I know."

"Come here." She sat on the bed and I roped her into a hug. "I shouldn't have gone searching for that oracle. It was stupid and I promise I'm done with all that."

"Okay," Remy said into my chest, her voice muffled. "You really need to stop almost dying. It's kind of getting old."

I laughed again.

"Also"—Remy leaned back—"we need to talk."

"Oh." I sat up straighter, heart stuttering. "Okay. What's up?"

My daughter's eyes grew serious and she tugged on one of her curls. "I think we should invite Grandpa to come stay with us. I mean, Isaac is going to be gone for at least another month, so Grandpa can stay in his room. We have plenty of room, and that way we can really get to know him . . ."

Huh. I was not expecting that to be what came out of her mouth. But it actually . . . made sense?

"I think he's lonely at the bed and breakfast, and Martin says he sees him spending a lot of time alone in the garden. It makes me feel bad."

"Remy, I completely agree."

Her eyes widened. "Really? Because I have an entire powerpoint prepared."

I arched an eyebrow. "A powerpoint?"

Remy shrugged. "What? I was ready for you to say no."

I thought about my stupid trip out to sea, how close I'd been to death, to not having the chance to get to know my dad. "But I think it's brilliant. Let's do it."

Remy squealed in delight, and suddenly I was feeling much better. Now, I just had to see what my dad thought about us officially becoming roommates.

# Chapter Fifteen

We stood in my mother's old room, Isaac's room now, evident by the cheetah print blanket thrown over the chair in the corner and the zebra-striped comforter on the bed. Paint swatches were taped to the wall, glimmering gold and shimmery silver. Isaac had employed Emerson to help him redecorate this room and make it go from, in his words, "drab to fab."

My father scratched his head, looking around. "Um, wow, I didn't think this was your mother's style."

Remy smirked from beside me.

"It's not. It's her . . ." I almost mentioned Isaac but didn't think now was the time to reveal mom's twin brother and that entire sordid mess to my father, who wouldn't know about Isaac.

I'd tell my dad the story soon, before Isaac returned home, but now didn't feel like the right time.

"We're redecorating," Remy said brightly, understanding I didn't want to divulge Isaac and all the drama that had come with his arrival to Whispering Willows just a month earlier.

"Huh" was all my dad said, continuing to stare. "Okay, then. I appreciate you letting me stay here."

"Of course," I said.

I'd chosen the guest room for myself and given Remy my old

bedroom when we moved in here. I thought about taking my mother's room, but too many painful memories arose at being in here, and I couldn't bring myself to sleep in the same bed she'd slept in, use the closet where all her clothes still hung. It was too much, but maybe one day I'd get there. For now, I was letting Isaac live out his chic dreams and make this room into whatever he wanted.

My toes curled into the soft shag rug under my feet. Even if Isaac's style didn't exactly match my own.

I gestured around the room. "I know it's not your style, but I hope you can feel at home here."

His eyes shined. "You know, I actually have been here before."

My eyes widened. "Really?"

He nodded, a sheepish grin coming to his face. "Your, uh, mother snuck me in here a couple times." Now his cheeks reddened.

"Oh my god," Remy said. "Go Grandma."

I pointed at her. "Do not get any ideas."

"Why did she sneak you in?" I asked.

He scratched the back of his neck. "Well, I don't know how much you knew about your grandmother, Clara."

Not a lot, admittedly. Mother never talked much about family, shockingly. I'd seen pictures, of course, dreamed up stories in my mind of Grandma and what she might've been like to raise someone like my mother, but I'd never been able to conjure a complete picture of the woman.

"But she was obsessed with finding your mother someone to marry."

My eyes widened even further at that.

"Seriously?" Remy asked, walking over to the chair with the cheetah print throw and flopping onto it. "Like 1950s-style you-must-have-a-man-to-survive kind of thing?"

My father nodded. "Exactly like that."

"Wow." I sunk onto the bed, processing this information. "So what did that have to do with you?"

"Well, your mother didn't want to marry, to be taken care of by a man. She'd seen the kind of damage that had done between her own father and mother."

I winced. I guess I should've realized how much my grandfather and his verbal abuse would've affected my mother. She would've seen the terrible relationship my grandfather and grandmother had, seen how my grandmother refused to leave my grandfather despite how horrible he was. Of course she wouldn't want to be in a relationship when she'd grown up witnessing a toxic one.

"Your grandmother feared for your mother, feared that she'd be alone with no one to take care of her. She didn't realize that your mother was perfectly capable of taking care of herself. Your grandmother hounded Isabella daily. She even set her up on a few blind dates, surprised your mother by inviting men to dinner randomly." He chuckled. "One time, your grandmother had suggested she and Isabella take a stroll through town, and she'd secretly planned to run into one of her friends and their son, who was Isabella's age."

Remy just shook her head in disbelief. "I can't believe my great-grandma did all of that."

My father nodded. "Oh, yes. And it infuriated your mother. The more your grandmother insisted she find a husband, the more Isabella resisted the entire idea. So when we met and actually hit it off, your mother wanted to keep me a secret, afraid that her mom would ruin what we had by pressuring Isabella to marry me, start a family right away. Things that Isabella wasn't even sure she wanted."

I swallowed. I knew he didn't mean to hurt me with his words, but it stung knowing that I might not have been wanted by my mother, that she might've viewed me as a burden of some sort. Had I held my mother back, kept her from achieving all her dreams?

"Anyway." My father shifted from foot to foot. "It was a long time before Isabella finally introduced me to her mother. So I spent a lot of my days climbing that tree outside her window."

He pointed to a huge oak tree with sprawling branches that nearly reached the side of the house.

I couldn't believe my mother had been so bold, so in love with my father that she was willing to sneak him into her own house, risk it all for him. Again, I was struck by how much she must've cared for him.

I shook my head and stood, bustling over to the closet. "Well, I haven't had a chance to clear out this space yet, but you're welcome to put your clothes in here." I opened the door, the musty smell of old clothes hitting me.

My father's eyes glazed over, like he'd been put in a trance. He moved forward slowly, reaching out and touching random articles of clothing. Some of my mother's dresses and nicer pieces of clothing were still in clear bags, preserved and pristine.

"Wow," my father breathed, and Remy appeared at my side as we followed him into the space. "Your mother wore this when we'd been on a picnic and got rained on." He ran a finger down a bright red blouse with gold buttons running up the front. He touched a black sweater. "She wore this when she took me on my first broom ride. Terrifying. I never rode a broom again after that." He moved further into the closet. "She wore these striped pants when she got an award for her amazing work as a Witch Granter. I was so proud of her that day."

I didn't even realize my mother had gotten an award. The OSAAs (Outstanding Supernatural Academy Awards) were hosted every year in Los Angeles, a huge ceremony that drew in supernaturals from around the world who were awarded for their amazing work in the community. Wow. My mother had gotten an actual OSAA and never told me about it?

"And this." My father stopped in front of an emerald green dress, still in a bag. "She wore this when we went to a ball together."

"Wait a minute." Remy rushed forward and grabbed the dress, taking it out of its sleeve.

"Remy, what are you doing?" I asked. She held it up to me, humming and furrowing her brows, her mind clearly made up about something. "Yes!" she said. "This is perfect."

I shot a look at my dad, who just shrugged. "What's perfect?"

"This dress. For you. The Samhain Ball."

I'd completely forgotten about the ball, which was rapidly approaching.

"You haven't even gone dress shopping yet."

"Well, I have been a little busy."

"Exactly." Remy held up the dress. "This is it, Mom. This is the dress for you."

"I can't wear my mother's . . ." I trailed off, studying the dress.

It was floor-length, silky smooth, spaghetti straps, the back plunging and open. It was beautiful and would hug every curve on my body.

Preston might actually drop dead from a heart attack after seeing me in it. Remy was right. It was perfect.

Still . . .

"You should wear it," my father said. "Isabella would love to see her daughter wearing this dress. She only ever wore it once, never had another occasion to put it on, but I remember her saying she wished she could wear it everyday, that it made her feel beautiful." His eyes shone, some memory I couldn't see playing out in his mind. "Remy's right. This would be perfect for you."

I reached out and grabbed the dress from Remy's outstretched hands.

"Okay, then. I guess I've found my dress for the Samhain Ball."

Preston was not going to know what had hit him by the time I was done with him.

# Chapter Sixteen

I approached the old town square, cobblestoned ground spread out before me, old fountain in the middle of the square, a statue with its head missing right in the middle of the fountain. And there was the portal to hell, red and bubbling, but mostly closed, kept in check by the Demon Slayer. A few stray embers rose from it into the air.

"Hello?" I asked to the silent and still courtyard.

Preston had sent me a cryptic text to meet him here, and I was starting to wonder if some demon had kidnapped him and stolen his phone, sending me this text to lure me here. Though I had no idea what a demon would want with me, so maybe that suspicion was a little far-fetched.

I stepped further into the square, old shops lining the area, broken windows, chipped paint, chairs and tables turned over. This used to be the hub of Whispering Willows, the place everyone came to socialize and shop. Long before I was born. Then someone went and opened this portal, and demons poured out, destroying the square and infesting Whispering Willows with demons for more than a century before Helen finally came along and accepted her position as Demon Slayer. She put the demons in their place and Whispering Willows was now thriving again.

I gulped and peeked into the fountain. A spark of lava leapt from it and I jumped back. Helen might have things under control, but I didn't particularly want to be near the portal if I could help it.

"Preston?" I asked again. Maybe I was right. This was getting weird. "Has a demon kidnapped you? Scream if you need help? Hello?"

Then I saw it. A table sat by an old shop, covered in a checkered tablecloth with a little vase of flowers sitting on top. Two shiny plates lay on either side of the table, silverware set, sparkling crystal glasses already filled with wine waiting to be drunk. A demon probably didn't have quite this much finesse.

I smiled and moved toward the table, sitting down. A menu lay next to the plate with three options:

Spaghetti marinara with meatballs

Pistachio pesto with chicken

Fettuccini Alfredo with shrimp, oysters, and scallops

I gasped. Did Preston do all this for me? I looked around, trying to find him. This was ridiculously adorable. He was really stepping it up with our dates lately. If he wasn't careful, I was going to get too used to these extravagant date nights.

"Well, hello." Preston appeared at my side, wearing a plaid button-up that hugged his muscles. "I see you've had a chance to peruse the menu."

I set the paper down and smiled. "I've had a few minutes, yes."

"And has the lady decided what she'd like?"

"Hmmm." I shot him a devious grin. "Now, aren't oysters an aphrodisiac?"

His eyes glittered. "I believe they are."

"Then I think that's the way to go."

"Excellent choice." His voice rumbled as he took the menus and disappeared into one of the older restaurants. From the pictures of fish sketched on the window, I assumed it used to be a seafood shop of some kind. I arched my neck. Was Preston actually cooking in there? Now that was something that had changed. Preston couldn't cook to save his life back when we were dating in high school.

He reappeared with two heaping plates of fettuccini, plump shrimp, oysters, and scallops sitting atop the pasta. He sat down and put his cloth napkin over his lap.

"Why, Preston Hammond, how did you make that so fast?"

He took a sip of his wine. "I might've prepared all three dishes in advance so I could bring out whichever one you picked right away."

My breath caught in my throat. That was so adorable. So sweet. So unbelievably romantic. I wasn't sure what I'd done to deserve this man, but I had no intention of ever letting him go.

"You know," Preston said, "it feels like we have a lifetime of memories, even though we only got two years together before you . . ."

Before I left him.

"Before I left," I finished for him, and he nodded. "Preston, I know we haven't exactly talked about that, well resolved it, I mean. I don't know if you're harboring any feelings about the way I left, our break-up—"

"Clara," he started, but I held up a hand, needing to get this off my chest.

"The truth is that after I left Whispering Willows, I was always so afraid a kernel of my mom lived within me. That whatever evil took root in her would find its way to me, and therefore, I needed to stay away from all magic, because if I did that, I could avoid becoming like her. At first, I wanted to believe I could leave magic behind but still keep you."

Preston's eyes welled, and his jaw locked.

I grabbed his hand from across the table. "And the thing is, I knew if I asked, you would've left Whispering Willows, but I couldn't do that to you. I realized that if I ripped you from your life here, I'd be just as selfish as my mother, only thinking of myself."

Preston shook his head and started to speak, but I quickly went on.

"You loved your life here. You had an entire future planned, and I couldn't take that from you. So I broke up with you instead of just talking to you about it like I should have. I took away your choice in the matter and that wasn't fair to you."

"No it wasn't," Preston said quietly, wiping at a stray tear. "But I don't blame you. I understand why you pushed me away."

I nodded. "I just want you to know that I won't run anymore. Not ever again. And if I do have to run, I'm going to give you the choice to run with me. You're an adult, and I know you can make your own decisions."

He smiled and lifted my hand, pressing a kiss to it. "Thank you for that. Just so you know, I'll run with you anytime. Anywhere. I'm with you. Always."

He stood and grabbed our plates, putting them on a nearby table. Then he grabbed our glasses and silverware. I lifted a brow in question, but he just smiled, lips holding secrets that I wanted to explore.

"What—"

He put a finger to my lips. "Do you remember our first kiss?"

My nose wrinkled. "Well, yeah. At the Samhain Ball—"

He shook his head. "Wrong. That was our almost first kiss."

I thought back to the ball, scouring my brain, realizing he was right. "Oh my god. You were so close to kissing me at the Samhain Ball when my mother—"

"Appeared. Furious you lied to her."

Despite how embarrassing and horrifying it had been at the time. I smiled. "She was so angry. We were on the dance floor, swaying to whatever song played." I couldn't remember the music, but I could remember the way my body fit against his, our cheeks pressed together, the way he smelled like sandalwood and briny sea air. The way I felt in that moment as he held me. I'd known then that was it for me. No one else could compare to Preston Hammond, and no one else ever would. He'd leaned his head in, lips so close to mine, and that's when the doors to the gym burst open, my mother standing in the doorway, smoke practically pouring from her ears. She'd dragged me right out of that room and grounded me for a month. I'd been so humiliated I avoided Preston for two weeks after that, convinced he'd want nothing to do with me. I couldn't have been more wrong.

"Okay." I shook the memory away as Preston stepped closer. "That wasn't our first kiss, so what was?" I wracked my brain through all our kisses—there had been many formative ones—trying to recall which had been our very first.

Preston swiped his arm across the table, clearing off the table cloth, which fell to the ground at our feet.

"Preston!" I squealed as he lifted me up and pressed me to the table.

I could get used to this.

"Right here. In this very courtyard."

I gasped, his words conjuring a vivid memory of me running into Preston a full two weeks after the Samhain Ball. I could only avoid him for so long in this small town. I'd seen him on Main Street and ran blindly, not paying any attention to where I was going. He'd chased after me, finally catching me here, in the old square. After a lot of tears, confusion, and some yelling, he'd pulled me into his arms and planted a kiss right on my mouth, surprising the hell out of me. That had been it. I was done for after that.

Preston hovered over me, gaze pinned to me as I recalled our first kiss.

"You remember?" His arms caged me, his gaze intense.

I nodded, heat curling through my body as he pressed himself against me. My hands reached up and I ran my fingers through his hair as he leaned down, nuzzling my neck, pressing kisses right at the sensitive spot at my collarbone. I gasped, my hands bounding down, fists curling into his shirt.

"You may have forgotten that first kiss," he rasped, "but I'll make damn sure you don't forget this one."

My body clenched in anticipation, wanting his lips on mine, wanting all of him. Turns out I didn't need those oysters after all. I just needed him.

"Clara, Preston?"

I shot up straight, my head connecting with Preston's nose. He took a few forceful steps back, his hand covering his face, blood seeping through his fingers as his eyes widened.

"Helen?" I screeched, sitting up on the table, hair probably mussed, shirt wrinkled and askew.

The Demon Slayer emerged from the shadows, glowing golden sword in hand. She monitored the portal carefully, especially with the surge in activity lately, but I hadn't expected her to just show up in the middle of our date.

Pink tinged her cheeks right as a demon jumped from the shadows onto her back. "Sorry about that," she shouted, the demon rolling off her back.

My eyebrows pinched together. "Wait a minute. Remy is supposed to be with you. Where..."

Remy stepped out of the shadows next, a sheepish smile on her face. Oh for the love of god.

She gave a little wave as the demon pulled Helen's hair and she let out a yell.

"We didn't see anything," Remy said. "Except maybe we saw everything and I might be scarred for life. We were trying to sneak away quietly, but the demon cornered us. I'm learning a lot about demon slaying."

I looked at Preston, who stared at Remy in horror, and I groaned. Dried blood now covered his face, the bleeding having stopped. I cannot believe I hit him in the nose. With my head. Who said romance was dead?

Helen threw the demon off her back and it flew across the courtyard, back cracking on the edge of the fountain. She stalked toward it with sword in hand.

Well, this was my worst nightmare. Not the demon. My daughter. Here. Witnessing a very private moment between me and my boyfriend, who happened to be her teacher.

Preston stepped forward. "Remy, listen, I know this has to be awkward."

She held up her hand. "It's fine, Mr. H. I mean, I better not walk in on you and my mom doing"—she gestured to the table—"that again. But you make her happy. Like happier than she's ever been in her life. Just, next time, keep it behind closed doors maybe."

I grimaced and scrubbed a hand over my face right as Helen drove her sword through the demon's gut.

"You know," I said to Helen, "when I said to hang out with Remy, this isn't what I meant."

Helen turned, wiping her brow as the golden sword disappeared from her hand. "Oh, I'm sorry I just saved you two from becoming that demon's meal."

I just gave her a look, then turned to Remy. "Are you okay?"

"My eyes have seen better days, but yeah."

I snorted as a sound of horror escaped Preston's mouth. "I meant are you okay after that demon fight?"

"Oh yeah." Remy waved her hand. "That's not what's going to scar me for life." I pinched her, and she smirked. "You two continue your little date. It's actually kind of sweet Mr. H did all this for you."

Preston looked like a deer in the headlights. There'd be no salvaging this. "You know, I think our lunch is probably over."

Disappointment welled in me. Well, there went another date. Another chance to kiss one Preston Hammond.

"Let's go home," I said when the ground began vibrating underneath my feet.

"What's happening?" I looked around in panic. "Helen?"

She shook her head. "This isn't the portal, Clara."

I looked down to find the source of this. An earthquake, maybe? My feet started disappearing, unraveling like a rug.

"Mom?" Remy's voice had gone from teasing to scared. "What's happening to her?"

Preston rushed forward, trying to grab me, but his hands swiped through me.

It hit me too late what was happening, but before I could get the words out, I disappeared from their sight.

# Chapter Seventeen

My feet slammed into a hard tile ground, and I fell to my knees, wincing at the sharp pains that shot through my joints.

"Oh, well I expected you to wear something a little more professional." The smacking of gum followed that statement.

I slowly got to a stand, and my eyes adjusted from the bright light of day to the dim lighting of whatever this place was. I stood in a hallway with sconces attached to the walls, flames flickering inside that lit the narrow space. White tiles covered the floor, and at least ten doors lined both sides of the otherwise bare hallway.

The woman standing in front of me tutted as she observed me. "Can you maybe . . . ?" She mimed pulling up my shirt, and I looked down to see the plunging neckline of my blouse revealing a little too much cleavage. Well, it was actually the perfect amount of cleavage for my date with Preston, but not so much for what I was about to face.

The woman, red hair piled on top of her head in a messy bun, blew out a bubble with her gum that popped loudly. She held a clipboard in hand and gestured to a lone chair sitting against the wall.

I attempted to pull up my blouse to no avail and sank onto the chair, my stomach twisting.

"Okay, hon," the woman said, looking at the paperwork in front of her, tapping a pen to her chin. "Looks like you got summoned today because . . ." She trailed off. "Ahhh."

Was that a good or a bad *ahhh*? I couldn't tell. I fiddled with my hands while she continued perusing the document in front of her.

"Huh," she said.

I blew out a breath in frustration.

Her eyes snapped up to meet mine. "What's going on here? Am I actually meeting with the Council today?"

"'Course you're meeting with the Council today. I'm here to get you registered before your appointment." The thick Jersey accent was really throwing me off here.

"Right," I said as if that answered all the questions running through my mind. I sank back into my chair, then straightened. "Okay, but how exactly do I get registered? And how long is this whole thing going to take? I was in the middle of a date—"

The woman looked down her nose at me.

"Right. Probably not important."

It wasn't like it mattered at this point anyway. The date was clearly over, and so was my chance at kissing Preston. But, looking up and down this empty hallway, I realized that was the least of my worries at this point. My stomach knotted even further.

The woman now scribbled something on the paper, muttering to herself, and I thought I heard her say "not taking this seriously."

"No, I am!" I burst out. "I am taking this summons very seriously. I want to rectify whatever problem the Council seems to have with me."

"It's not about you, personally," the woman said. "The Council doesn't hold vendettas against people. They uphold the supernatural law."

"Right, that's what I meant. I know they're not out to get me, specifically." I cocked my head. "My only teensy little concern is that they are associating me with my mother, whom I'm obviously nothing like." I stretched out my arm as if that might convince this woman of my argument.

She peered at me. "Who is your mother, exactly?"

"Isabella . . . Westfold?"

The woman's eyes widened, and she began scribbling furiously again, blowing out a huge bubble of gum that popped and receded back into her mouth.

I arched my neck to see what she was writing on that paper, but she kept it close to her so that I couldn't see.

I raised a finger. "Like I said, I'm nothing like my mother. Couldn't be more different. I actually ran away from home at the age of nineteen and went into hiding, all to avoid my mother." I leaned forward. "Are you getting all that down? Is the Council going to read whatever you're writing?"

"Daughter of Isabella Westfold," she mumbled as she continued to move the pen.

I worried at my bottom lip. This already didn't seem like it was going very well. Clearly I wasn't making a good impression on this woman. I took a deep breath, trying to remind myself it wasn't the woman I needed to make a good impression on. It was the Council, who probably wouldn't even read whatever she was writing.

"Okay." The woman brought the clipboard to her chest. "Time for your appointment, hon. C'mon now. The Council doesn't like to be kept waiting."

I wanted to point out that I was not the one running the show, here, but thought better of it. No need to piss off the lady whom I needed directions from.

I stood on shaky legs and followed behind her as we passed unassuming door after door, stopping at the third one on the right. She gestured to it. "Here we are. Just step inside, and the signs will show you where to go."

Okay, easy enough. I opened the door to pitch black. I turned around to ask the woman what signs, exactly, I was supposed to follow, but she no longer stood in the hallway. I leaned out and looked back and forth. She'd completely disappeared. Weird.

I turned slowly and took a tentative step forward, falling straight into nothing.

My body tumbled into a free fall, and I screamed as I fell down, down, down. My life flashed before my eyes, all of the best, and worst, moments replaying in my mind while I careened toward the ground.

The first time Preston kissed me.

When I found out my mother was using her wish granting powers for evil.

When I had to run away from the only home I'd ever known.

Breaking Preston's heart.

Meeting Greg for the first time and feeling a spark of hope.

Greg proposing to me, cementing in my mind that I'd made the right choice by running away from home, from magic.

That first moment I held Remy in my arms while she squawked and wriggled her tiny little body.

When I found out Greg died and my life fell apart for the second time.

Deciding to come back home to Whispering Willows and bring Remy with me.

All of the moments spun through my mind like a wheel of memories.

My throat felt raw and hoarse from yelling, but I couldn't stop, the involuntary sound bursting from me. My hair whipped around my face, clothes billowing, harsh air pushing all around.

Finally, my body slowed, feet gently touching the ground, and I let out a sigh of relief. I was alive.

Then I shot a glare at my dark surroundings. "Signs?" I yelled to no one. "Seriously? You could've warned me I was about to plunge through the air. I thought I was going to die!"

My voice echoed in the darkness.

I shook my head. "Signs," I muttered. "More like house of mental torture."

All of a sudden, big lights around the room turned on one by one, each flash brighter than the last. I shielded my eyes from the glare and waited a few minutes before I lowered my arm, letting my eyes adjust.

I stood in a cavernous room, the domed ceiling high above, stadium-type wooden bleachers circling me, empty of any spectators. I wondered what the bleachers were even here for. Surely they didn't allow audiences for summonings like this.

Someone cleared their throat, demanding my attention. I turned my gaze from the stadium seating to the middle of the room, where six individuals sat behind a long, raised podium so that they towered over me.

I swallowed, my throat thick, tongue heavy. The Council. They stared down at me, their faces severe, which only made me more nervous, and it wasn't until I had turned fully to face them that I realized one of the faces was familiar, from the curve of the nose to the large and bushy eyebrows to that thick gray hair.

The floor rocked from underneath me.

My father.

My father sat with the Council members.

My father *was* a Council member.

# Chapter Eighteen

I stood before the Council members, feeling small and insignificant. My father's mouth dropped open as he stared at me, shock written clearly across his face.

He was as surprised to see me as I was him. But how? Surely as a Council member he knew all those being summoned, and—my dad was a freaking Council member. Had he always been one? Did my mom know he was a Council member? Did the Council know he was my father? That he'd been Isabella's fiancé? What in the actual hell?

A man with a long nose and long black hair that hung past his shoulders stared down at me. "Case number 67921. Please state your name for the Council."

I cleared my throat and folded my hands in front of me, trying to keep my gaze from straying to my dad. "Clara Westfold."

Everyone rifled through the papers in front of them, studying my case, I assumed. I had an urge to reach up and snatch one of the papers from them, figure out exactly what was being said about me.

"Ah," the man said. "The Witch Granter."

The rest of the Council straightened at that, a woman on the far end with dark skin and braided hair glancing at me before looking back down at the paper in front of her.

I stepped forward. "Can I ask—"

"You will speak when you are spoken to," the man with the dark hair said.

"Regus," my dad said. "There's no need for that."

Regus sighed heavily. "You've been summoned because of some disturbing activity at your shop."

"Disturbing?" I echoed, racking my brain for what he could be talking about.

"A destroyed wish?" Regus asked, and everyone shuffled in their seats at the words.

A destroyed wish was unheard of, and I should've known that would get me in trouble. It had been a month ago, after I discovered that stupid magic lamp in the basement of The Wish List. The lamp had malfunctioned, shooting out dark magic that destroyed a wish I was in the middle of granting.

I'd fixed it eventually. Not by granting another wish, but by making it right with the person whose wish had been destroyed.

"Yes," I said. "I know that sounds really bad."

"It should be impossible," one of the older Council members said from beside Regus, a woman with long and wispy silver hair. "Wishes can't be destroyed. Were you performing some kind of dark magic?" She looked over at Regus. "We should perform a forensic analysis on her shop immediately, see if we can find any traces of foul play."

My dad shifted in his chair. "I don't think that's necessary." He looked at me. "Let's at least give Clara a chance to explain herself."

Six sets of eyes focused on me. I steeled myself, straightening my back and clearing my throat. I had left my home when I was nineteen years old. Rebuilt my life from scratch. I'd lived through my husband dying. Rebuilt my life again. And now I was living out my dream granting wishes. I was not going to let some Council who didn't know me or my life come in and threaten to take it all away. "This is all a misunderstanding. You see, the wish was destroyed by dark magic—"

A few of the Council members gasped, and I held up my hand to silence them.

"Not because of anything I did. It was dark magic created by an ancient artifact that has since been disposed of."

Kind of. By disposed of I maybe meant I gave it to a mermaid, but that was a long story and not one I particularly felt like sharing with the Council at this point in time.

Regus's eyes narrowed. "So you admit to having dark magic in your shop?"

I stepped back. "No! That's not—there was dark magic, but it wasn't *my* dark magic."

"Like mother, like daughter," a vampire muttered, his fangs glinting in the bright lights that shone down.

My dad's head snapped to the commentator. "Really, Brian? Was that necessary?"

So that's what this was really about. I wasn't summoned because of a destroyed wish. I was summoned because I was Isabella Westfold's daughter, and I'd moved back to Whispering Willows and opened my mother's magic shop—something that apparently threatened the Council.

I met my dad's gaze, and I gave him a slight nod as if to let him know I could handle this, then trained my gaze on the rest of the Council members. "Okay, let's clear the air for a minute. Yes, I am Isabella Westfold's daughter. Yes, my mother committed unspeakable crimes, ones that I cannot answer for. I don't know why she decided to use her powers for evil. But I do know that I am not her. I love being a Witch Granter, and I have no intention of following in her footsteps. I have everything I could want in life. Why would I ruin that? Furthermore, why would I be stupid enough to bring dark magic into my own shop and then not even try to hide it?"

The Council members gave each other looks, a silent conversation happening between them that I couldn't decipher.

Regus looked back to me. "Consider this your warning. One misstep and the Council will reserve the right to strip you of your Witch Granter status."

Well, that seemed ominous. "Okay," I said, not sure what else there was to say about that. It seemed pretty final, and from the look on the Council members' faces, I gathered that maybe I should be grateful that was all I was walking away with.

Regus banged his gavel down. "Dismissed," he yelled, and then the floor dropped out from underneath me.

I was falling. Again. Unbelievable. Did they not have any other mode of transportation around these parts than this? We had cars, buses, planes, brooms—but letting people free fall through the air was really the best they could come up with? My limbs flailed, hair whipping wildly around me, and wind rushed at my face so fast and furious it lifted my cheeks. Then, it all stopped.

Unlike last time, my feet didn't hit the ground. I floated in the air, looking around at the dark expanse surrounding me. Nothingness. As far as the eye could see.

I gulped. "Um, hello?"

Jagged cracks formed in the black expanse, rays of yellow, green, and blue seeping in and filling the space.

"What in the fuck is happening?" I asked, still floating as more black cracked away, falling down below into the black abyss, each piece that dropped revealing more of the real world.

I squinted. Blue skies, green lawns, a bright yellow sun. I nearly cried in relief. It looked like home. I glanced down at my feet, and they were back on solid ground as the last of the black chipped away.

I wrinkled my nose, staring at my surroundings. I stood in a courtyard with soft grass, pruned bushes and shrubs, a big stone fountain with a statue of a dancing fairy in the middle, her wings spread wide. A massive building surrounded the courtyard, stone gray with twisting spires rising into the air and intricate flowers, vines, and leaves carved into the sides of the building. It was beautiful.

"Hey," a voice said, and I whipped around to see my father standing there, hands shoved into his pockets.

"What am I doing here?" I asked him. "Where is here?"

He waved his hand. "It's just the courtyard at the Council headquarters. Instead of sending you home, I asked you be sent here so we could talk?"

I crossed my arms as he gestured toward a bench. "Yeah, we definitely have a lot to discuss, Councilman."

He winced like I'd thrown a dirty word at him. "Please sit?" He gestured next to him.

I huffed and threw up my arms. "Fine." I walked over and sat down, then turned to him. "How could you not have told me you were on the Council? That's kind of a big deal."

His hands clenched at his sides. "I didn't realize you'd been summoned. I've been a little busy, what with being in Whispering Willows and all."

Right. Of course he had.

"The last thing I would want is for you to feel misled or lied to. I told the Council, by the way. I was going to tell them anyway at some point, but I just let them know the conflict of interest. I don't want you getting into any more trouble because of me. I'm really sorry, Clara. About all of this."

"No, I'm sorry," I said, and he lifted his face, confusion written between his furrowed brows.

I looked at the way he hunched over like a chastised schoolboy, his foot tapping on the ground like he was so anxious. It's no wonder he hadn't told me about this. Over the last few weeks since his arrival, I'd shown very little interest in getting to know him at all. I'd been so focused on learning more about my mother, I forgot all about my father. How terrible that must have been for him, to finally get to meet your daughter and then she doesn't even care about getting to know you. I thought about my stupid trip out to sea to find that oracle, to find answers, how I'd almost gotten myself killed. And now this. My own father didn't even tell me about his profession. No, I hadn't even bothered to ask.

I shook my head. "I've taken things too far these last few weeks. Did you know I went to try and find an oracle?"

His mouth dropped open in surprise. "I didn't know that."

"Yeah. It was stupid, and it almost got me killed." I gestured to him. "And here you are. My father. I have an actual father, and you're kind and caring and willing to divulge everything you know about my mother, despite how painful it must be. And here I am, not showing any interest in getting to know you."

Wow, I'd been so selfish up to this point.

"Clara." My dad put a hand on my arm. "Of course you want to know about your mother. I don't fault you for that. You deserve to know about her, and I want to tell you everything I can. I hope I've been able to show you parts of her you never saw, ones that show you how I saw her."

I nodded. "You have, and it's been wonderful, but I want to get to know you too. It's important to me that Remy and I know you."

He stroked his chin. "You can get to know me *and* still learn more about your mother."

"I'd like that," I said.

A few goblins in business suits walked past us, sipping their coffees.

"So where do we start now?" he asked.

I jabbed a thumb back at the Council headquarters. "Well, this would be a pretty good place to start. How long have you worked for the Council? Did my mother know you worked for them?"

She was never a fan of the Council, hated the way they placed restrictions on supernaturals and the use of their own powers.

"It's complicated." He bobbed his head from side to side. "You know, something I loved about your mother was how determined she was to go after what she wanted. If she set her sights on something, I had no doubt she was going to get it. That's just who she was. That's never who I was. I didn't have a lot of motivation to do much, to be honest. Thought I'd stay in the little town where I grew up, join my pack, maybe work my way up the ranks, but I didn't have high aspirations or anything. I was never going to be the pack leader."

"Why not?" I asked, already feeling myself being drawn in by his words, suddenly wondering how I could have not wanted to get to know this man. He had an entire life I knew nothing about.

He shrugged. "I guess I didn't believe I could do it. I didn't have a ton of confidence. Not until Isabella Westfold barreled into my life. Suddenly, I had aspirations, goals, and your mother inspired all of them. The Council was one of those goals. I worked for them a long time ago, and yes, your mother knew about it. I quit after serving on the Council for five years, but they recently asked me to come back. I'd been feeling restless, so I agreed." He spread out his arms. "And here we are."

"Wow." I blinked a few times, trying to process everything he'd said.

"And for the record." He held up a finger. "Not at any time was I trying to keep this from you. I just hadn't had a chance to tell you yet, and I had no idea about this whole summons thing." He wrinkled his nose. "You found a golden lamp in your shop?"

I waved away the question. "Long, long story."

He smiled. "We have time."

"Yeah." I nudged him. "We do."

My mother had hidden entire parts of her life from me, had kept secrets upon secrets, had built walls. I didn't want that kind of relationship with my dad. It wasn't like I expected him to tell me every single thing about his life, but I wanted to feel like I was a part of it, not like an outsider looking in, which was how I'd often felt with my mother. Why I was now so desperate to know her.

I tapped my chin. "Okay, so from now on, how about we work on communicating a little better. Both of us."

He stroked his chin. "I would like that."

"Great." I looked around. "I'd like to go home now. As long as it doesn't involve the world's scariest sky dive?"

He laughed and held out his hand. "Come on, then. Let's go home."

# Chapter Nineteen

Remy and I walked through a field with wildflowers that grazed our hips as we waded through them, after my dad. I let my fingertips brush against the delicate petals of the flowers and closed my eyes to soak in the nature surrounding us.

"What are we doing here?" I asked my dad.

The sun shined down, warming my face, and the sounds of birds and other critters rose up around us. It was the perfect day.

After I insisted I wanted to get to know my dad more, he'd suggested an outing, so here we were. Wherever here was. We'd packed up into his car and he'd driven us up, deep into the mountains surrounding Whispering Willows. We'd hiked for about thirty minutes and finally came upon this field that seemed to stretch on forever.

"You'll see," my dad said from up ahead, and I could hear the smile in his voice.

Remy looked in wonder at a little caterpillar that inched its way up over a thin reed. "Aw, hey little guy," she said.

"We never really spent much time in nature, huh?" I asked.

Remy looked at me. "No, not really. You and Dad never wanted to go out on the weekends. Dad was always too tired, and you liked to stay home."

I opened my mouth to say something, but Remy cut me off.

"It's okay, Mom. If you're about to apologize, just stop. I know why you didn't like going out. You were afraid that Grandma would find us, or something stressful would happen and your powers would manifest. I get it. I really do."

"But we should do more stuff like this." I hooked an arm around her shoulder as we continued through the field. "These outings with my dad have been pretty fun, huh?"

"Yeah, they have. He's shown us so many different areas outside of Whispering Willows that we'd never even seen. It's pretty cool, actually." Remy gasped and skipped ahead. "Maybe we can go camping?"

"Like at a hotel?" I asked.

Remy gave me a look. "No. Real camping with a tent and a fire and looking up at the stars."

"Okay, okay, let's take one thing at a time. First, let's get more used to nature and the outdoors, and then we'll slowly work our way up to a camping trip. Maybe you could sleep in the tent and I'll just go back home for the night, then I'll come back in the morning in time for you to wake up?"

Remy just rolled her eyes. Up ahead my dad rounded a narrow path that led between two tall hillsides. They arched over the path, creating a tunnel.

He ducked slightly to get through the little opening, and we followed. When I came out on the other side, I gasped. The field continued, but now it was filled with horses. Wild horses.

"Oh my god," I said. "This is amazing."

My dad chuckled. "We patrolled these mountains a lot growing up. Always looking for demons or other evil activity that might be a threat to our small town. Me and my brother, we loved to explore, and one day, we came across this field full of horses. We were in our wolf forms, of course, and the horses were spooked by us, definitely not happy with our presence. In fact, many of them startled and began to run. But my brother and I weren't going to prey upon these beauties." My dad's eyes shined. "Actually, we were afraid that others in our pack might not be so generous, so we made it our goal to protect these horses, to keep others from finding them and their little sanctuary."

I could tell Remy was having a hard time processing the fact that werwolves might actually eat wild animals, and I patted her on the shoulder.

"We came here almost everyday," my dad continued, "to see the horses and just watch them in their natural habitat."

"You never shifted to human form when you visited them?"

"No." He gazed out at them as they ate and lounged. "Something about being in my wolf form, being in their presence as another animal, it just felt right. One time, a few mountain lions came upon them, ready for a feast."

My chest tightened at the thought. "What happened?" I asked.

"Me and my brother fought off the mountain lions. Got a few broken bones and deep cuts, but not a single horse was harmed. After that, the horses trusted us, would actually come right up and sniff us, the fear no longer in their eyes."

"Wow," I breathed, seeing the way the horses eyed us right now, clearly not comfortable with our presence, but not scared enough to run away, especially when they were eating.

"This kind of became our place," my dad said. "As you can imagine, my family, we were never great at talking or communicating. Didn't hug much, didn't use words like *I love you* or *I'm proud of you*. My brother and I had fallen into that trap. We were never very close, until we found this place."

He scuffed his foot in the dirt.

"Something about being here, with the horses, working together and just knowing we were both going to protect these animals no matter what, it created a bond between us."

He looked up at the sky and shielded his eyes from the glaring sun.

"Soon, this became the place we'd go when we wanted to talk. Mind to mind in our wolf form. We'd watch the horses and he'd tell me about how he was struggling because he wanted to leave the pack, to do something with his life other than what my dad clearly wanted for him. While I told him about how I was the opposite, afraid I wouldn't amount to anything. This was the place I first told him about your mom. I hadn't told anyone. But I told my brother."

A lump formed in my throat. "Where is he now?"

My dad shook his head. "He passed away a few years ago. Cancer.

Left behind a wife and two sons, Bryant and Brody. Brody has three daughters." He nudged Remy. "I'd love to take you two to visit them."

"I have cousins?" Remy asked, eyes bright.

"Well technically, they're my cousins." I frowned. "I don't actually know what they are to you. Second cousins? First cousins twice removed?"

"I don't care," Remy said, "I just think it's so cool we have family out there to meet."

My dad smiled. "Oh yeah, and Charlotte just turned eighteen. She's the oldest, and then you have Sarah, who's fifteen, and Marlee, who's eleven."

"Oh my god, I want to meet them," Remy said, her voice taking on a whine.

"Of course we can go meet them. I'd love to," I said.

I looked back out over the horses, my heart expanding. I'd always wanted a big family. Growing up, it had just been me and Mom. Now, I questioned if there were others out there whom I'd never met, that she shielded me from for her own purposes. Either way, it was nice to know I had actual cousins. An aunt.

"I'm sorry for your loss," I told my dad. "I'd love to learn more about your brother."

"Oh, I have a whole album of pictures. Embarrassing ones."

"Like what?" Remy plucked a flower and twirled it between her fingers.

My dad positioned his hands around his head. "I had a bowl cut when I was ten."

I gasped. "You didn't."

"Oh yeah, I did. Matched my brother's. We also went through a leather phase."

"Oh my god," I said through laughter. "I'm definitely going to need to see those pictures. And meet your family, when you're ready."

A horse approached, and we all stilled. My dad put his arm out to guard us. "Just stay where you're at," he said. "No sudden movements, and we should be fine."

But the horse didn't seem threatened. It shook its shiny black mane, streaked with white, and trotted closer, until it stood right in front of us. The horse leaned its head down and put its snout right into my dad's outstretched palm.

"I think it knows you," I said.

My dad's eyes widened. "I've never visited in human form."

"But it must sense it's you. Have you come back here often since your patrolling days with your brother?"

He nodded. "I make it here at least once a month, in my wolf form"

"This is so cool," Remy breathed, both of us entranced by the horse standing in front of us.

It dipped its head one more time and then trotted away.

"Thank you for sharing this place with us," I said.

Now that I'd gotten just one piece of my dad's life, I couldn't help but want more, and I only hoped he'd keep opening up to us.

# Chapter Twenty

BEFORE

It hadn't been Isabella's intention to meet with her father. She hadn't seen him in years, not since she finally got the courage to cut him out of her life, thanks in part to Jeremiah's encouragement. It hadn't been easy, not when her mother insisted on staying with him.

She and her mother still worked together at The Wish List, after all. And though her mother had barely spoken to her for almost a year after Isabella moved out of their house and told her father she never wanted to see him again, she'd slowly come around. At first it was with a word or two, then with a soft gaze, and finally, Isabella knew her mother would forgive her when she asked if her daughter had been eating enough, then proceeded to bring Isabella's favorite meal— spaghetti and meatballs—to the shop for her to take home to her apartment.

The apartment she could afford because she insisted on getting pay for the work she did, refused to let her father take her money any longer. When he protested, she'd threatened to use magic on him.

Of course she'd never actually do that. The Council would send her a summons within minutes. And Isabella couldn't have that, not when she'd just gotten engaged to the man of her dreams and had an entire future ahead of her.

Jeremiah didn't know about this meeting with her father. No one did. Isabella wasn't even sure why she was here, in this dark alleyway, an overflowing dumpster on one side of her and a feral cat on the other side, who kept hissing and swiping at her with its claws.

She looked both ways down the alley and finally saw his thin form appear. He stalked toward her, limp gray hair hanging around his face, bony shoulders poking out of his white tank. If possible, the frown on his face deepened upon seeing her as he came closer, stopping a few feet away.

Isabella crossed her arms, shrinking away, a reflex that she hated she still had after all this time away from. *He has no power over you*, she tried to remind herself. "Well?" she asked. "Why are we here? If it's money you want, then you're wasting your time."

He turned his head and spit. "It ain't money I'm after," he said.

Isabella quirked an eyebrow. "Then what is it?"

"Just thought I'd let you know I'm taking your mother and leaving this godforsaken town."

Isabella stepped back, into the wall. "What are you talking about? You can't just take her. You can't—"

"I can do anything I want. Your mother may have magic, but she doesn't have any power over me."

Anger flared, hot and explosive, inside Isabella. Because she knew he was right. Her mother wouldn't want to leave her only home, the shop she so dearly loved. But she would. She'd leave here with him.

"Why are you telling me this? Why make me come here so you can . . ."

He stepped closer, the smell of whiskey and cigarettes wafting from him. "Because I can. Because I know this will hurt you. You think you're so smart, leaving home, demanding pay for granting your little wishes, but you forget that I'm untouchable."

She wouldn't cry in front of him, wouldn't let him see how his words rattled her. She was a grown woman, but he had a way of making her feel so small and insignificant.

"Why did you ever marry her? Why have children with a witch when you hate magic so much?

His gaze went misty, a far-off look in his eyes. "I didn't always hate magic," he said. "Not until I realized it was something I could never compete with. Married your mom and realized too late she loved magic more than me."

Isabella shook her head, mouth hanging open. "That's why you became this hateful, horrible human being? Because Mother loved magic more than you? That's why you spent years tormenting me, making me feel this big." She pinched her fingers together. "Because of *jealousy*?"

For fuck's sake. She hadn't expected this, of all things.

He simply snarled at her.

"And why are you choosing now to run away?" she asked.

"Because all your mother wants to do is spend time at The Wish List, with you. It took her a while to forgive you for leaving. I thought she'd finally be all mine again. But no, now she can't wait to leave the house and scurry off to her little magical life at her magical shop with her magical daughter."

"You're disgusting," Isabella said.

He bared his yellow teeth in what she realized was supposed to be a smile. "Yet I'm still going to walk away with your mother, and there's nothing you can do about it. No matter how much she may love you or magic, she'll never leave me. She'll stand by my side like the good little wife she is."

It was all true. Isabella saw it time and time again. Her mother crying, swearing she was going to leave, then falling for Father's pretty words and staying. Over and over and over.

"I'll be seeing you around." He paused. "Well, actually I won't. In fact, I look forward to never seeing you again."

With that he sauntered away, and Isabella collapsed against the brick wall behind her. She couldn't let this happen. She couldn't let her father leave with her mother.

Her shoulders straightened, a determination settling deep in her bones. She'd protected her family once, long ago. A secret she'd kept all these years. She'd bound someone dangerous to a golden lamp; she'd kept the threat from hurting her or her mother. And she'd hated herself for it.

But she could do it again. Only this time, she didn't have some magical golden lamp. She didn't have anything to bind her father to. Besides, magic like that was highly illegal. And she didn't just want to bind her father. She wanted him to disappear. For good. For that, she'd need true power. She'd heard of a way to gain that kind of power, the kind where you didn't even need ingredients or a wand or a cauldron. The kind where you could snap your fingers and whisper your intention and a spell would be at your fingertips. It required taking souls. It required dangerous magic. But sometimes dangerous magic was needed to deal with dangerous people.

A darkness took seed in her heart. Just a kernel. But that was all that was needed to set her on a new course, one that would forever change her life.

# Chapter Twenty-One

It was another busy Saturday night at The Brewery, Whispering Willows's one and only bar. Emerson and I sat at a hightop table while trays zoomed around us, carrying shots that people reached out and grabbed. Fairy lights were strung around the whitewashed brick walls, giving off a soft glow. We sat near the hearth, a roaring fire crackling inside, a cauldron brewing some new potion that floated into the air. Orange and cinnamon mingled together, and I wondered what potion the owner was cooking up.

"Okay." Emerson took a drink from her skull-shaped cup. "What is going on with you and Preston? It's been like forever since we talked, and I still don't see a ring on that finger."

I glanced down at my bare hand, frowning. A ring? I just wanted a kiss. I wasn't even thinking about a ring. Though now that she mentioned it, the thought of being Preston's wife sent skitters down my arms.

"You're getting ahead of yourself." I took a sip of my own drink from a witch's hat. The fruity mixture of pomegranate and blueberry exploded on my tongue. "I'm still reeling from finding out I have a father, one who actually wants to be in my life and who has this entire history with my mother I never knew about."

Emerson made an eesh face. "Yeah, um, how's that going?"

"Good, actually. He's completely normal. No lies." I thought about my past relationship with the mayor and how he'd lied to me our entire courtship, which ultimately was what caused its demise. "No drama." I thought about Isaac and how much trouble he'd caused when he first came into our lives. "He's just this nice, normal man. It's really refreshing."

Emerson raised her glass. "To nice, normal men."

We clinked glasses.

"So, speaking of nice, normal men . . ." Emerson moved her hands as if to prompt me to speak.

I groaned into my drink. "I don't know what's going on with me and Preston. He's planned all these wonderful, beautiful dates for me, and every single one has been ruined by something. Demons, my dad, Helen and Remy. And Preston's so busy teaching and coaching, and I'm so busy running a business and raising a daughter, we can't seem to find time to see each other."

Emerson pointed a long, manicured nail at me. "You need to step up your game."

I brought a hand to my chest. "Mwah?"

"Yes, mwah." She shook her head, her perfect blonde waves barely moving with the motion. "No more of these little afternoon dates. Find someone to spend the night with Remy, book a hotel, and you give Preston the best night of his life."

My entire body lit up at that. At the thought of having Preston in a hotel room, all to myself. Absolutely no distractions. Just him and me . . . and . . . warmth pooled between my legs.

"Girl, you need an ice bucket right now." Emerson smirked. "Whew, I want whatever you're planning."

"I'm not planning anything," I said, cheeks flushing, but even as I said it, I thought about where Preston and I could go. The only place to stay in Whispering Willows was Martin's B&B, which was a hard no. I could only imagine how that might go, showing up hand in hand with Preston, Martin and Bones breathing down our necks.

But we could easily drive a town or two over, where no one knew us and we'd have complete privacy for an entire night. My body ached at the thought of it.

"Okay, seriously, do you need to go for a swim in the ocean?" Emerson asked.

I swatted at her from across the table. "Preston and I just haven't had a lot of alone time together, and like I said, every time he's planned something, we get interrupted in the worst of ways. I guess I'm tired of waiting."

Emerson slapped the table. "Then take charge. It's time to stop waiting for life to happen and to grab it by the horns and, you know, take it for a ride . . . while you're taking Preston for a ride." She winked at me, a rueful smile on her face.

I had to admit, everything she was saying sounded pretty damn good. But Preston had told me he wanted to kiss me, to choose the moment, and I didn't want to take that from him. It was clear he'd been trying to plan something special for the big moment: the picnic in the field, the yacht ride, the date at the place where we first kissed. I wondered what else Preston had up his sleeve at this point. How many more romantic dates could the poor guy plan at this point before we finally got our kiss? Maybe he was tired of all the extravagant planning but didn't want to disappoint me after his promise that our first kiss would be unforgettable. Maybe he'd appreciate me taking that off his plate, taking the reins, riding the bull. Him being the bull.

Behind us a raucous group of leprechauns broke out into laughter, cheers'ing with big mugs of beer that sloshed over the sides of their glasses and splattered to the black epoxied floors.

"What's going on in that head of yours?" Emerson asked.

"Okay, maybe you're right." I stirred my drink with my straw. "Maybe I should plan a date, take the lead with this whole kiss thing."

Emerson's face soured. "You're not going far enough."

"I can't propose to him, Emerson! I don't even know if he wants to get married!"

She raised an eyebrow. "You guys never talked about that?"

I threw out my arms, accidentally smacking a vampire making her way through the crowded bar. I shot her an apologetic smile as she flashed her fangs at me. Yikes.

"Of course we talked about that. Like twenty years ago. We haven't had a chance to talk about it recently. Yes when we were teens he wanted to get married, to have kids. And I know he wants to be with me. I'm not doubting that. I'm not doubting anything about our relationship. He loves me and I love him. But that feels like a huge leap to plan a whole proposal when I don't know if his views on marriage have changed over the last twenty years."

Emerson leaned down to take a sip of her drink. "Well, if they have, would that bother you?"

I thought about it. It wasn't actually something I'd considered. If Preston didn't want to marry me, would that be a dealbreaker? No, never. "I've done the marriage thing already. And guess what? Just because I was married, it didn't mean I was living some happily ever after."

Emerson shifted in her seat as a group of fairies flitted past us, clutching onto their tiny drinks that were as big as my pinky nail. I guess I hadn't really told Emerson much about my marriage to Greg, or Greg at all. After all, Emerson had left Whispering Willows shortly before I did, but unlike me, Emerson cut off all contact with everyone. I hadn't even known she was going to leave. She'd just up and vanished one day, no trace of her at all. I'd been heartbroken for years, not understanding how my best friend could just leave like that. But she'd recently come back to Whispering Willows with her own demons to fight, and we reconnected, both of us needing closure over past wounds. Now it was like we hadn't spent any time apart, picking up our friendship right where it left off, even if we both were different people now. I still didn't know what had happened that had forced Emerson back home, still didn't know exactly why she'd chosen to stay, chosen this life here in Whispering Willows over her extravagant one in LA. It was a story she wasn't ready to tell yet, but I'd be patient and wait.

Emerson nodded, like she understood, and I knew she had been engaged as well in her time away from Whispering Willows, an engagement that didn't end well.

"So it wasn't a fairytale marriage?" Emerson asked.

I barked out a laugh. "Not exactly."

Sometimes it didn't feel right, talking about Greg like this after he'd died. But he knew what we had between us as much as I did. "One time, a few years after we got married, Greg took me out on a date. The first date he'd taken me on in a long time, and he said he was so glad he found a wife that could support him, support his career, and be stable."

Emerson's eyes crinkled at the corners, but she stayed silent.

"And that hit me in the moment. We didn't have some great love. He knew it. I knew it. We both needed something from each other, and we fit that need. I don't think Greg ever knew exactly how much that marriage saved me after I ran away from home, but he knew enough. He knew the bare details, that I was running from something, and he was my safe haven." I shrugged. "Marriage doesn't always mean love."

Emerson nodded. "I know. You're right, and I'm sorry. I'm not trying to pressure you into something you're not ready for."

I shook my head. "I would marry Preston in a heartbeat if he asked me to. What we have . . . I'm more sure of it than I've ever been about anything in my life. Which is definitely saying something since I'm a generally indecisive person."

Emerson took a deep breath. "I get it. You don't need a wedding to validate your relationship. That's healthy. What you have with Preston is healthy. I know you're just frustrated right now at the slow progress."

I took a big slurp of my drink. "That is an understatement. If that man doesn't plant his lips on mine soon, I'm going to combust."

Emerson's lips curved into a wicked smile. "Girl, you came out with the right person tonight. Because I have some ideas about that."

# Chapter Twenty-Two

I locked up The Wish List after another day of granting wishes. Today, a seer had asked that I help him find happiness after his wife died, an imp asked that she find clarity between two difficult career choices, and a vampire asked that he could find peace with his new immortality.

I turned around and came face-to-face with my father, who stood with his hands shoved in his pockets, a small smile on his face. "Oh good you're here! Ready to go?"

He nodded. "Definitely."

I gestured to my car that was parked outside the shop on the street, a clunker of a sedan that badly needed to be replaced. "We can swing by Remy's school and pick her up."

My car was so old, I had to manually unlock it. No pressing buttons for me. I stuck the key in and turned it, then got inside and pressed the Unlock button so my dad could get in. Despite the cool air outside, the inside of my car was sweltering. My dad's huge form filled up the passenger seat, and he shifted like he was uncomfortable.

"Sorry," I said. "I know it's a little cramped."

"No." He shook his head, which almost skimmed the top of the car. "Well, yes."

I laughed and started the car, which sputtered pathetically, but revved to life. We drove the short distance to Remy's school and arrived in the circle drive out front right as the loud bell trilled out its sound, signaling the end of another day. Suddenly, students flooded the front lawn of the school.

My dad chuckled. "You know, your mom snuck me in here one time."

My head snapped to him at that. "What? But you two started dating after she graduated. I thought . . ."

He held up his hand. "We did, we did. I told her about my tiny one-room school that was more of a shack than a place of education. You know, I never thought myself much of a scholar. Didn't really think much of education, to be honest. But she brought me here after I told her what my experience had been like in school. I couldn't believe a place like this existed." He turned his head, studying the three tall brick buildings with black pointed peaks, the gray balconies and ledges with gargoyles hunched and guarding the school.

Legend had it that those gargoyles had once existed in our world but had tried to wage war against other supernaturals and lost, now cursed to guard magical places all around the globe. I had no idea if that was true, but it was a fun story to tell.

"So what'd you think?" I asked, remembering my own experience sneaking into school with my mother. She loved this place. It had been a reprieve from her own home, from her terrible father.

"I loved it," he said, a little breathless, then turned back to me. "I thought it was possibly the most magical place I'd ever seen." He tilted his head. "No pun intended."

That got a smile out of me.

"When she snuck me through the doors, and I saw the sweeping staircases, the enchanted ceilings, the classrooms, the projects lining the glass cases—I wanted to turn back time and beg my parents to move to Whispering Willows so I could experience something like this."

The smallest hint of bitterness lined his voice, and I laid a hand on his arm. "But look at you now. You're a councilman. I mean, that's an amazing accomplishment, especially if you didn't get a leg up at a place like this."

"Thanks, Clara. I guess I never realized how much of life I was missing out on until I met your mother. She really opened up my eyes to what was out there. In my small mountain town, all I knew was my pack. Of course I knew other supernaturals existed, knew of the Council, knew of fancy schools like this. But I didn't really *know*. Not until Isabella introduced me to this whole new life."

I looked over at him. "You know, I'm really glad my mom introduced you to all these new things, but you were enough before you met her. I hope you know that."

I thought I saw his eyes well with tears, but just at that moment Remy opened the door and jumped in the backseat. "Hey guys!"

He turned with a smile. "Hey, kiddo."

I put the car in drive. "Alright, let's go find out where Jeremiah is taking us."

I pulled up to an empty parking lot and what looked like an abandoned restaurant. Shingles hung from the roof, dangling precariously. Boards covered the windows, graffiti scribbled across the wood.

My dad took a big breath, staring at the place in awe. "Believe it or not, Isabella made me the happiest man on earth right here in this spot."

We got out of the car and looked around, and I wrinkled my nose. "Really? Because this kind of seems like the place you go to murder someone or dump a body."

My dad just laughed and shook his head. "No. It's where she proposed to me."

My eyes nearly bugged out of my head. "I'm sorry, she proposed to you? My mother asked you to marry her?"

"Oh snap. Go, Grandma." Remy leaned against the car, crossing her arms.

My dad held up his hands. "To be fair, I was going to ask her. I had it all planned out. Was going to take her back to that waterfall, the place we first met. I had a picnic packed, even bought a little basket, a checkered blanket. Hell, I even had wine."

I chuckled at that, and Remy smirked, still leaning against the car.

"So how did you end up here?" I asked.

"Well, your mother was not one for being patient."

That much I knew.

"We were actually driving to the waterfall, where I had my amazing proposal planned," he said, eyes misting. "And then my car broke down. We managed to get it to this parking lot, and I wanted to work on it, get her to the waterfall, to the proposal. Instead, it started pouring down rain."

I gasped. "No."

He nodded. "Oh, yes. I'm under the car. Mind you, my father was the town mechanic, and I spent every day in his shop, watching from him, learning from him. So I knew a thing or two. But I didn't have the parts I needed to fix the car. So I came out from underneath, and there was Isabella, twirling in the rain and laughing."

I couldn't even picture such a thing. My mother? She was a lot of things, but carefree was not one of them.

He stared out at the parking lot on this perfectly sunny day, and I knew he was somewhere else now. Reliving a memory. His voice was soft as he spoke. "I started laughing, too, then. What else could I do? She took my hands and round we went until my vision was spinning. We stopped, falling into each other's arms, and she looked up at me and said, 'Marry me.'"

My heart swelled. It all sounded so whimsical. I could just picture the scene, picture the way my mother said the words, so firm and sure of herself. She was sure of herself in everything she did.

"And I said yes."

Remy wiped at her eyes, and I couldn't tell if she was as emotional as I was or just dealing with allergies.

"That's really romantic," Remy said.

My dad nodded. "It was one of the best days of my life. Well, most days with your mother were the best days of my life."

"Did you ever get to show her your amazing proposal?"

He shook his head. "There was no need. Hers was better. I didn't want to overshadow that moment, or even redo it. I just wanted to keep that memory exactly as it was. I did give her the ring, though."

We fell into a silence, staring at the empty parking lot and the decrepit building. "So a mechanic, huh?" I said, coming to stand beside him and elbowing him. "Think you can do something with my car?"

He stared at the sedan, probably in worse shape than the restaurant. "I don't think anything can fix that car."

Remy barked out a laugh, and my dad just shook his head, smile on his face, as we made our way back to the car.

# Chapter Twenty-Three

The Whispering Willows Magic Academy auditorium had undergone a complete transformation. A thick mist covered the floor, and the ceiling above had been spelled to look like a starry night sky that glittered overhead.

"Would you like some punch that some of the seniors likely spiked?" a low voice said from beside me, and I turned to see Preston holding up a red drink.

"Spiked?" I asked. "Say no more." I grabbed the cup from him and took a sip, then my mouth twisted.

Preston cocked an eyebrow. "Just how much alcohol did they put in there?"

"Not the alcohol," I coughed out. "The sugar. God, that's a lot of sugar."

He laughed and swept me into his arms, taking the cup and setting it on a nearby table. "Glad you agreed to be my date?"

I stared up at him, getting lost in those hazel eyes that darkened as he held me. "Absolutely."

Students filled the auditorium in sparkling dresses ranging from silky and long to poofy and shimmering. Yet I didn't see the one person I was looking for: my daughter.

Remy had told me she wanted to get ready at Megan's house, and I was a little sad to be missing out on pictures at home, but she reminded me I'd be chaperoning and would be able to take as many pictures as I wanted when she arrived. She'd found her dress weeks ago but wouldn't let me see, saying she wanted it to be a surprise. I stood on my tiptoes, arching my neck to get a good look at the door. I couldn't wait to see her.

"God, this is going to be a long night," a voice said from beside me.

I looked over at Gene, who scowled, and Helen, who beamed at the room. "This is going to be so fun," Helen said. "You know I got stood up for my senior prom?"

My mouth dropped open as Preston excused himself to go unentangle two students who were currently groping each other on the dance floor. "You got stood up?"

"What's his name?" Gene growled. "I'll go bite him."

Helen gave her vampire husband a shove. "You do remember your wife is the Demon Slayer and I have an actual sword I can use on him if I wanted to?"

Gene flashed his fangs. "No, you fight bad guys all day long. I get to fight a few every once in while—especially if they hurt you."

Helen's eyes sparkled, and I knew even though they'd been married for fifteen years she loved the way Gene championed her, had her back no matter what. She patted at her strapless black glittering dress, the little sequins catching bits of light that reflected on the floor.

"It was actually my ex-husband," Helen said.

"Piece of shit," Gene muttered. He looped an arm around Helen's waist and drew her into him. "Can't believe that idiot let you go."

My mouth was almost on the floor at this point. "Your ex-husband stood you up at prom, and then you still went on to marry him?"

Helen gave a guilty shrug. "I was young and stupid and believed he was sorry that he got too drunk at the pre-party to show up to our dance."

"That's why you wanted to come to this so badly?" Gene asked, the features of his hardened face softening. "You've never told me this before."

Helen gestured around the auditorium full of dancing students. "Well, being here is bringing back all the memories. How sad I was standing there alone while everyone danced around me, and I had no date. I just stood in the corner the whole night crying."

"Damnit," Gene said, then held out his hand. "Let's go dance."

He didn't wait for an answer as he pulled Helen out to the dance floor, her bleach-blonde gelled hair glimmering under the starlight.

Preston returned to my side, and I looked at him. "I can't believe Gene and Helen actually came to a high school dance."

Especially Gene, who looked so out of place and uncomfortable among all the teenagers surrounding him. I laughed as a gangly boy bumped up against the vampire, who flashed his fangs and growled, making the boy fall onto his butt and scamper away as fast as he could. Helen swatted Gene, who turned his attention back to his wife.

"I gotta say." Preston grabbed my hand and brushed my knuckles against his lips. "I don't think I ever would've guessed anyone could tie down the Serpent."

I arched a brow. "Is that what you think that is?" I gestured to Gene and Helen, who spun around, gazing adoringly into each other's eyes. "You think that's tied down?"

Preston shifted from foot to foot, and I realized I was treading into territory we hadn't covered. What I'd told Emerson was true: I was confident in my and Preston's relationship, but I had absolutely no idea how he felt about marriage. His comment just now didn't make it seem like he held it in the highest esteem.

He brought me into his chest, and I leaned back against him, loving the way my body molded against his hard planes, snug and tight, like we just fit together.

"Maybe tie wasn't the right word," he said into my ear, his voice low and growly.

Oh no. I recognized that voice, and we were entering a different kind of dangerous territory. I spun out of his grip and faced him. "Is that how you really feel about marriage, though? That you'll be tied down?"

An uncomfortable look flashed across his face, and I couldn't discern what he wasn't telling me, but it quickly passed, and his expression eased back into its usual casual appearance. "What's making you bring up all this marriage talk, anyway?"

The doors to the auditorium banged open and my eyes snapped to the entrance, heart beating in my chest. My excitement quickly waned when I realized it wasn't Remy standing there, but Myrtle. I shook my head.

"Myrtle?" What was the werewolf doing here? It was already weird enough that Helen and Gene were here to help chaperone, but now Myrtle had agreed to come as well? She didn't even like kids—except Remy, of course. But that was a given. Everyone loved Remy.

Her silver tracksuit made her look like a walking disco ball as she strode into the room, everyone's eyes on her. She pushed her sparkly rectangle glasses up her nose. "What's everyone looking at, then?" she asked in her Irish accent, always thicker when she was annoyed.

A new song blasted over the speakers, and everyone went back to dancing as Myrtle approached us.

I crossed my arms. "You're a chaperone now? Really?"

Myrtle grabbed a glass of punch from the nearby table and took a sip. "What can I say? I had FOMO."

"You know what FOMO means?" I asked.

Myrtle grimaced as she took another sip of the red drink. "Remy taught me. Fear of missing out," she added, like she wanted to make sure I believed her.

"Okay." Preston clapped his hands together. "You know what? I think it's time we dance."

I shook my head. "No, no, no. I can't until Remy gets here. I don't want to be dancing and miss her entrance with her beautiful dress, and . . ."

The doors opened again, and I trailed off. There she stood. My baby girl. Well, not a baby anymore. My hand fluttered to my chest.

"Wow, what a sight," Myrtle said, coming to a stand beside me.

Remy wore an A-line periwinkle blue dress with a tight bodice that flowed into a poofy skirt. Glitter sparkled and shimmered with each movement she made, her skirt fluffing out at her ankles. The light blue brought out the subtle shimmers of red in her hair that I usually only noticed in the sun.

Megan stood by her side, stunning in a silky pink dress with a slit up to her knee, her dark skin luminous, her black hair twisted into braids that made up an intricate bun.

"Oh my god," I said, tears welling in my eyes. "She's so perfect."

"Yes she is," Preston said, and that's when I realized she had no date on her arm. No handsome vampire to walk her in.

"Where's her date?" I asked, frowning.

Remy walked toward us, smiling bright, her brown curls tamed into an elegant updo.

"You like it?" she asked, and I nodded, speechless.

"Emerson did our hair and makeup." Remy gave twirl and Megan did a curtsy.

Remy nodded at her friend, who skipped off toward the dance floor, immediately joining in with the students moving along to the song playing.

I pulled Remy in for a hug. "You look stunning."

"Thanks, Mom." She pushed me out at arm's length. "You're not so bad yourself." She touched my hair. "You look beautiful. I bet Grandma would've loved to see you in this dress."

She groaned as I made Myrtle take a picture, then I changed my mind and realized Myrtle was likely cutting of our heads or putting her thumb over the camera, and I handed my phone off to Preston. He snapped a few pictures of us, each one eliciting more complaints from Remy, until I reminded her that she promised I could take pictures once she arrived.

"Hey, where's your date?" I asked.

Remy looked away. "About that."

"Remy!"

"I decided I just wanted a fun night with my friends. I promise it's not a big deal." She started backing away. "And now is not the time to talk about it." Her eyes flicked to Preston as a slow song started to play on the speakers.

Remy disappeared into the crowd of students, and I threw my hands up in the air. "Well, that was confusing."

"Welcome to being a parent of a teenager," Myrtle said, lifting her cup in my direction.

"And you know a lot about that?"

"Well, I do now that I have Remy."

"Uh-huh."

Myrtle stepped closer. "You know, we didn't have prom in Ireland growing up. But had village dances. We'd gather under the full moon, the fiddler would strike up a tune and we'd spend the night spinning under the stars." She nodded her head toward the starry sky above. "This reminds me a bit of that. Some nostalgia."

I didn't often hear Myrtle talk about her time in Ireland, before she fled the wars between vampires and werewolves and landed here, with no family, no pack. But she'd made Whispering Willows her home over the last couple centuries and found her way.

"Do you want to dance?" I asked Myrtle and ignored the way Preston stiffened beside me. I knew he wanted to dance with me, but how could I not ask Myrtle after that story she'd just shared?

"No, no. This old girl?" She waved her hand. "I'm going to drink my punch and make sure no one's engaging in any kind of hanky panky. Not with me here." Her gaze locked on a couple, and she yelled, "Hey, knock it off! If I have to come stand between you two I will."

Preston grabbed my elbow and led me to the dance floor. "May I have this dance?" he asked, holding out his hand.

Finally. I nodded, and he pulled me into his embrace.

We swayed to the slow lull of the song. "I can't believe Myrtle is here." I gazed up at him. "What a weird night. But at least Remy seems happy." I nodded to my daughter, who danced with a group of girls, all of them laughing. I settled into Preston's arms, laying my head on his shoulder. "Now I'm ready to just focus on us."

"I would love that." His head rested against mine, his hands pressed into the small of my back. "You know," Preston said, "the Samhain Ball was when I realized I was in love with you."

I stopped dancing at that, pushing back a little to look at him. "You never told me that!"

He cleared his throat. "You'd, um, you'd gone to get some punch. Purple that night, but just as heavily spiked."

I laughed.

"And I watched as you grabbed a cup, then bumped into someone and spilled the punch all over your dress and the floor."

I remembered the moment. I'd been humiliated. But I hadn't wanted to ruin the night, so I'd gone into the bathroom, cleaned myself up as best I could, and gone back out to the dance, head held high. Still, that was not the moment I'd been expecting Preston to say he knew he loved me.

"That's when you figured it out?" I asked in horror. "After I'd done something completely mortifying?"

He stroked his jaw. "I guess I'm not explaining this right."

I squinted. It was dark and hard to see, but I could've sworn the man was sweating. "Are you okay? Are you sick?"

"No." He shoved a hand into his jacket pocket. "Clara, I—"

Just then a woman squealed from across the room. "Oh my god, John, yes I will marry you!"

"You've got to be kidding me," Preston mumbled.

Another teacher, Remy's History of Supernaturals teacher, knelt down with a box held up to a red-haired vampire, who jumped up and down, her heels clacking against the floor as the music slowed to a stop and everyone turned to stare.

"That's so sweet," I said, looking back at Preston, a slight pang in my chest.

It was okay if he didn't want to get married, I reminded myself. It was okay if I never had that moment where he knelt down in front of me. I didn't need it.

"Yeah," Preston said, voice tight. "Hey, you wanna get out of here? There's something I want to show you."

"Is that okay? We're supposed to be chaperoning, right? I don't want you to get in trouble."

He gestured to Helen and Gene, whose arms were wrapped around each other, and to Myrtle, who had physically pushed herself between two students dancing too close for her liking. A group of people now surrounded the engaged couple, admiring the woman's sparkly ring.

He had a point.

He held his hand stretched out, and I grabbed it. "Let's go."

## Chapter Twenty-Four

Preston pulled me along through the hallways of the Academy.

"Where are we going?" I asked, but Preston didn't answer.

We passed glass cases, full of student projects and various trophies, shiny and glinting under the slats of moonlight shining in through the windows.

"Preston, seriously, where are you taking me?"

It wasn't toward his classroom; that was in the opposite direction.

We stopped in front of a full-length painting of the very first headmaster of the Academy. She'd been a seer, and she foresaw a great school coming to Whispering Willows and realized she was the one meant to build that school. So she did. Along with help from plenty of other supernaturals.

It started off small, from what we'd always heard as students. Just this one hallway with six classrooms. But it grew over the years until it had become one of the best schools on the West Coast.

I stared at the woman, her severe face, the tight bun on her head, the glasses perched on her nose. "I've seen this painting a hundred times," I said to Preston.

"Yes, you have." He backed me up into it. "One particular time I remember I had you pressed up against it."

I smiled. "Ah, yes. That was a great study session."

"We got a lot of studying done."

Of each other's mouths, mainly.

"So why are we here?"

He stepped away, taking his delicious warmth with him, but that didn't stop the heat spreading through my body. "Do you remember the night we broke into school to go on a scavenger hunt? Me, you, Emerson, Cruz, and a few others?"

I nodded, my nose wrinkling. "Yeah, we were looking for the rumored underground tunnels that students have been trying to find since the school opened."

Apparently the tunnels were haunted, full of unexplained noises, echoes, moans that worked their way up into the school. But no one could ever find a passage that led to these tunnels, including us. No, all we'd gotten for our little night break-in was a detention. Well, me, Preston, and the other students from our school got a detention. Emerson and Cruz were spared since they never attended the Academy —they'd been students at the public school in Whispering Willows.

Preston reached around me, and I was wondering what this was all about when I heard a soft click. I spun around to see the painting swinging open, revealing a stairway that led into a dark abyss.

"What the hell is this?" I asked.

Preston took a step down. "So turns out the rumors are true, but you only have access to this passageway once you get tenure here."

Preston had been teaching at the school for ten years, and he had gotten tenure just a few months earlier.

My mouth dropped open. "It's real?" I joined him and gingerly stepped down. Then I swatted him. "And you didn't tell me?"

"It's supposed to be a secret!"

We walked further down, and Preston took out his phone and turned on the flashlight, shining a beam on the broken concrete stairs.

"So why are you telling me now?"

"Just thought it might be a fun surprise. Something special for us to experience together. That was the night I finally told you I loved you, you know."

Oh, I remembered. The security guard who caught us, a goblin with a big belly and a huge flashlight that he reveled in shining straight into our eyes, had been screaming at us. He took the other students out to start questioning them individually while we waited for the headmaster to arrive. Once they left the room where he'd detained us, Preston and I had burst out laughing. I still remembered it so well, how Preston had straightened, his face sobering as he looked me straight in the eye and told me he loved me.

"Oh, Preston," I said as we delved deeper down, the stairs becoming more uneven. The warmth from the memory quickly turned cold at our surroundings. "Um, are we supposed to actually go down here?"

Preston shrugged. "It's not forbidden or anything. But has anyone actually descended into these tunnels? I'm not sure. We just learn about its existence and then go about our day. No one's been down here for years, as far as I know."

I gulped. "So maybe we should just go back up?"

"Oh, come on. Where's your sense of adventure?"

I gave him a look, even though it was pitch black and he wouldn't be able to see it.

"I think I've had plenty of adventures these last few months, enough for a lifetime, actually, and I don't want to invite any more."

"Fair enough."

Our feet hit solid ground, and I heard the rustle of Preston's movements as his light shined down on the cracked cement ground.

"These tunnels were used during the Demon Wars, over a hundred years ago. Soldiers needed an efficient way to transport weapons, goods, food to those fighting the battles, so they built these tunnels to quickly get important goods to those who needed it most. They were also used as a hiding place for civilians in Whispering Willows when things got really bad."

When the demons almost won and took over Whispering Willows. Then the very first Demon Slayer had arrived, a man who fought back the demons but unfortunately died about a decade later. The demons never grew so powerful that they took over again, but their presence had always been a problem in Whispering Willows—until Helen arrived and claimed her role as the Demon Slayer. She'd managed to keep everything in check for twenty years now.

I shivered, my gaze catching on a huge cobweb with an equally huge spider crawling up it. "Preston, can we go? This place is kind of creepy, and I was actually enjoying the dance?"

"Shit," he said, a hint of embarrassment in his voice. "Yeah. I'm sorry. I don't know why I thought bringing you here would be a good idea. I just . . . I'm trying so hard to make this special."

I realized what he was talking about immediately. So that's why he was taking me to all these memorable spots. First kiss. First time he realized he loved me. First time he *said* he loved me. Maybe Emerson was right and it was time I took over. He was so desperate to make our first kiss memorable that he brought me down to some secret underground tunnels.

I reached out toward his voice and touched his arm.

"I just wanted everything to be perfect." Now his voice held a trace of sadness.

"But everything is perfect. I'm having an amazing night, Preston."

"Good, that's what I wanted."

I heard him take a step toward me, and the flashlight on his phone shined bright in my eyes.

"Ah, sorry." He averted it to another corner, and I gasped and shrieked, jumping into his arms. "Is that a . . ."

"A skeleton," he finished. "Yeah, maybe we should get out of here."

This was definitely not where I wanted our special kiss to happen.

A shriek echoed through the tunnel, bouncing around us, inhuman almost. "What was that?" I asked when something caught my eye. A flicker of red, hot and angry. Like an ember.

Without thinking, I moved toward it, my hands out in front of me as I felt my way along.

"Clara, what are you doing?"

A thought flitted through my mind, and once it took hold, I couldn't shake it. "What if there's something dangerous down here? Under the school where my daughter attends? Where you teach?"

Preston's footsteps fell in line behind me. I felt my way around a corner and my mouth dropped open. Preston came to stop beside me, his phone clattering to the ground.

"Oh my god," he said.

Sitting before us was a giant angry hole, full of red bubbling lava, screams escaping it.

"That's . . ." I pointed weakly.

"It's another portal," Preston said.

Another portal to Hell.

# Chapter Twenty-Five

Angry chatter rose up in the diner, practically the entire town of Whispering Willows stuffed inside, everyone talking about the portal Preston and I had discovered the night before.

The mayor stood on top of the long counter, trying to calm everyone down. "Now before we get ourselves into a frenzy, let's remember we have a very capable Demon Slayer who's kept these demons in check for over twenty years." Daniel nodded toward Helen, who stood in the back corner with Gene.

Helen nodded, lips flattened into a thin line.

Everyone erupted again, yelling over the mayor. This was the closest I'd been to him since we broke it off after he basically dated me so he could get me to sell him my shop and then he could destroy it. All because of a century-old vendetta he had against my family. We'd managed to put it behind us, but we definitely didn't interact much. He looked tired, dark smudges under his eyes, his hair grayer than a few months ago, his chin covered in stubble. As much as I'd been angry over what Daniel had done to me, I'd forgiven him. He'd lost his wife because of my family, blamed them, and had carried that revenge for years. Still, he'd managed to be an amazing mayor to this town, and completely turned Whispering Willows around. So I decided he deserved a second chance. He'd taken it and was thriving, and that made me happy. Plus, my little hometown benefited from his leadership.

Someone from beside me threw a plastic cup at the mayor, and he flinched when it hit him. Preston tensed beside me. We'd never actually talked about my relationship with Daniel, not in much detail, and I wondered if it bothered him. I glanced over at him. Maybe that's why he'd been acting so weird lately? Last night was definitely odd. I mean, I knew he wanted the perfect kiss, but taking me down into those tunnels? What had he been thinking? I shook my head and focused my attention on the mayor.

"What's the plan?" a leprechaun yelled from where he sat in a booth. "We can't just sit here and expect the Demon Slayer to handle it. There's a whole other portal growing in our town."

"Beneath our Academy!" someone else cried.

"We'll have to assign extra patrol shifts for the packs," Myrtle said from where she stood by the door, her blue tracksuit as shimmery as ever today. "I'll take first shift."

Daniel held out his hands. "Let's just calm down, everyone. We can't be assigning shifts or making plans before we actually know what is happening."

"What's happening is the demons are trying to take over our town again!" a fairy yelled in her high-pitched voice, which of course, caused everyone to start talking at once.

Daniel's shoulders slumped, and I could see how this was weighing on him, but worse, I could see how it was tearing our town apart, everyone disagreeing, talking over each other, no one listening.

Gene just rolled his eyes from the corner, Helen looking the tensest I'd ever seen her. Before I could change my mind, I stood and let out a loud whistle.

Everyone stopped at that, staring at me. Wow, I didn't actually expect that to work like it did in the movies. Now I had to say something. Something intelligent, preferably.

I cleared my throat. "Listen. We have some of the most capable people in this town. We have a badass Demon Slayer." I gestured to Helen. "We have strong packs, who fight the demons with a ferocity I've never seen." I gestured to Myrtle and the other werewolves. "We even have the Demon King's former employees here with us." I motioned to Martin and a few other imps.

Martin's brows rose. "Who, me?" he squeaked out, running a hand over his green skin. "Oh no. No, no, no. I am not getting involved. I worked for the Demon King for a century, and no way am I going to talk to that psycho any time soon."

I glared at him. He wasn't exactly helping my case right now.

"The point is," I gritted out, "we have to work together if we want to figure this out."

"You also have the Council on your side." My head snapped toward the voice and there my dad stood by the door, his big figure filling up the frame. "I'll have to take this back to the Council, see what they think about all this."

No one in the supernatural world would want to hear about a new portal opening up. That could mean other portals opening in other places. A demon threat to one town was a demon threat to all towns.

A few goblins grumbled, and I thought I heard one of them say the Council was useless.

Myrtle just scoffed. "The Council's never been there for us before, so why would they show up now? If we want to deal with the portal, we're going to have to do it ourselves."

I bit my lip and looked at my dad, who didn't seem to take any offense to that. "The Council has been negligent in the past, focusing on the wrong things, but we're trying to be better, be the leaders we need to be for the supernatural community. We won't make Whispering Willows face this alone. In fact, I'm going to take a look at the portal later this afternoon, report my findings back to the Council."

"So what, the Council gets to decide what's best for us?" a vampire shouted. "I don't think so. We should get to vote on what we want to do."

Everyone started yelling again, and I dragged a hand down my face. This was going about as bad as it could.

"Are we at war?" another voice asked, but I couldn't see the face.

Daniel shook his head. "Now let's not get ahead of ourselves. No one said anything about a war." His face paled, and I knew the mention of "war" scared him senseless. He was a good mayor, no doubt, but having to lead an entire town into war against an army of demons? That would be a bit much for anyone.

My dad stepped further into the diner, a few fairies fluttering past his face and toward the counter, where they landed, bits of dust sprinkling from their wings.

"The Council will not decide anything without consulting with Whispering Willows. We are entering a new era where the Council wants to work together with supernatural towns. We don't want to dictate your futures. We want to work with you to mold them. And what Mayor Greenburg has done with Whispering Willows over these last few years is nothing short of amazing."

Chatter slowly died down as my dad spoke, everyone's gaze turning to him, some supernaturals' mouths hanging open.

"The Council has been paying attention to what you've done with this town, how you all have worked to build a community you can be proud of. One that thrives."

My father was usually such a soft-spoken man, and I remembered how when we first met it was hard to get more than a few words out of him. So seeing him like this, addressing this room full of people, angry and scared people, at that, was nothing short of amazing. He had such a command over the room, a confidence in his words that I hadn't yet seen. I'd have to tell him later how good he was at his job. He seemed self-deprecating the times that I'd talked to him, so sure that he didn't have any skills, that it was my mom who had helped him become who he was, but I could see a fire in him that was all his own. He didn't give himself enough credit.

Now my dad was walking throughout the diner, the residents hanging on his every word.

"I promise you that any Council intervention will not be without first consulting with you. We will only strive to work together in this venture."

Silence filled the room, mouths open, no one expecting a speech like that, especially from a Council member. The Council tended to be mysterious, this vague body of law that laid down rules and sent out edicts but didn't deign to grace us with their presence. It must've been a shock to everyone to not only have a Council member in their midst, but for that Council member to be so reassuring, so calm and steady. A pride swelled within me, and Preston must've felt the change in my demeanor because he reached down and squeezed my hand.

My dad's gaze swept around the room. "Now, before I contact the Council to alert them of this situation I will need to go and scout out this new portal so I can give the most up-to-date situation. I'd like someone to accompany me who is familiar with Hell, with portals, with how demons work."

My gaze flicked to Helen, our own Demon Slayer. She'd be a good candidate for that.

Helen must've been on the same wavelength, because she stepped forward, but my dad held up his hand. "No, we need the Demon Slayer to be on patrol, on the watch for any demons that might spring out of the portal in the square." His eyes flicked away from her. "Anyone else who might be a good candidate?"

"Martin," I said, the name slipping out before I could even think about it.

The imp's green skin paled, and he pushed a hand over his thick black hair, silvered at the temples. "Mmm . . . No." He crossed one leg over the other, placing his hands in his lap. "I'm good. Thank you, though."

I pinned him with a look. "You're the most qualified. You worked for the Demon King for years."

"Yes, Clara, and I'd like to not have to see him again, since our last meeting didn't go over so well and he threatened to chop a certain appendage from my body should he ever see me again. A very important appendage. One I use quite often—"

"Okay, we get it," Myrtle said.

I knew the Demon King didn't want to let Martin go, but the imp had somehow bartered for his freedom years ago. He'd avoided the portal to Hell and any run-ins with demons since, maybe because it was too much of a reminder of the past.

"It'll just be a short trip," my dad said, stepping toward Martin. "I promise."

Martin heaved a sigh. "Well, I only have three rooms to clean, a frittata to make, and bread to proof. But sure, why not add a trip to the portal to Hell to my agenda? Honestly."

"Martin," I said, a warning in my voice.

Others murmured, and someone nudged him from behind, as if to say "go on."

Daniel nodded from next to my dad. "Yes, Martin, you can go with the councilman. Give him any details for information that may help him. Leave nothing out."

"Oh for god sakes." The imp shook a finger at me. "It's not enough you drag me out to sea in my boat for all your little escapades, now you volunteer me for this."

"I really am sorry, Martin, but you're the most familiar with the Demon King, with how portals work. You can help save this entire town."

That seemed to mollify the imp a bit, and he sniffed. "Well, when you put it that way."

Daniel clapped his hands, making me jump. "Great. Then it's settled. The councilman and the imp will go to the portal, and we'll continue to monitor the situation as we come up with a plan on how to deal with an extra portal. We've solved a lot of issues today. Great work everyone!"

With that, the townspeople began to rustle, standing and gathering their things, exiting the diner. The meeting was adjourned, but a pit had formed in my stomach at the thought of my dad going to the portal, and I couldn't shake the feeling that things were far from solved.

# Chapter Twenty-Six

Preston and I parted ways. He'd gotten a substitute for his classroom so he could come to the meeting with me, but now he had to go back to school. My nerves were too frazzled for me to grant any wishes today, so I went back home to relax. I sat on the couch, my knee bouncing. I tried to read a book, to lay down and close my eyes, to turn on the TV. Finally my phone lit up with a text.

> **ISAAC**
> On a scale from one to ten, how ready for the runway do I look?

A photo followed of Isaac draped in a faux cheetah print cape, wearing an all-black ensemble.

> **CLARA**
> You're choosing to ask me about this?

> **ISAAC**
> I texted five other people before you, and no one else answered.

I couldn't imagine why Isaac needed to look like he was ready for the runway while he was visiting his mother, but I also wasn't sure I wanted to know the answer.

**CLARA**

> Uh . . . eight?

**ISAAC**

> EIGHT??? That's it? Oh my god. If you're giving me an eight, my outfit must be awful.

**CLARA**

> I thought an eight was good!

**ISAAC**

> . . .

What did dots mean? God, I needed Remy here to interpret these things. Before Isaac could spiral, I shot off another text.

**CLARA**

> Listen, I have a lot on my mind so I'm really not the best person to ask right now.

**ISAAC**

> A lot on your mind? What happened?

I could just imagine his dramatic gasp.

> Did something happen to my room? Did the paint samples not arrive that I ordered?

I rolled my eyes.

**CLARA**

> Your room is fine.

ISAAC

> Oh, thank god. Well, use that journal you found. Write down your thoughts and feelings or whatever it is you do. Because I need you at the top of your game to rate my outfit. And you better come back to this text chat with a clear mind and a ten rating.

I set down my phone, sitting up straighter. I'd forgotten all about the journal, but he was right. It had made me feel better the last time I wrote in it, and, well, I had found myself in yet another stressful situation. The journal could help. I put my phone down and marched up the stairs to my bedroom with a determination settling in my bones.

I sat with the journal in my lap, staring at the last entry I'd made what felt like forever ago when my dad had first arrived in Whispering Willows and I'd felt so confused about his presence. Now I felt excited, ready to get to know him and have an actual parent here for me when I'd been lacking one for so long. But this second portal . . . what did it mean for me and for us as a community? It felt like the threats were never-ending.

The shiny cover of the journal glinted, and I trailed my finger along the cover, still wondering why my mother decided to buy this journal but never write in it. Why she'd even kept it for herself. I wished so badly she'd written something inside, left me with something else of her rather than the scraps I'd gotten. I reached for a pen to start scribbling in the journal, my thoughts racing as I let out my fears, my hopes, all the things that plagued my mind. The more I filled the pages with my thoughts, the lighter the load felt on my shoulders. I'd have to thank Isaac for reminding me of this outlet—and text him that his outfit was definitely a ten and I'd clearly been out of my mind for rating it an eight. I reached for my phone and the journal fell to the floor, flipping over on its backside, the sunlight catching it once again.

I cocked my head and squinted. Wait a minute, there was something on the backside of the journal. I reached down and picked it up, studying the back cover. A symbol was engraved, old and worn with time so that I could barely see it. I ran my fingers over it, tracing the symbol. It was a star, our family crest. This journal must've been personal, then. It wasn't just a random booklet she picked up or that someone bought for her. It had to have been special to have this engraving. I couldn't believe I'd missed it before, but then again, time had clearly erased most of it, so it had been easy to miss. I opened up the back, curious if maybe there was an inscription or something I might've missed.

When I flipped open the cover, my mouth dropped at what I saw. Oh my god. I'd had this whole thing backwards and upside down. I wasn't writing in the front of the journal, I'd been writing in the back. The pages were blank, so there was no way to know back from front, but now, reading this little note written on the inside of the cover, I realized I was looking at the front. My gaze locked in on the message written as I tried to decipher who wrote it and what this was all about. What was I missing, here?

*May this journal be with you in the most difficult of times. May it provide you a path forward. Help you in times when you don't have a voice to guide you. May it be there for you when I can't be. I'm sorry. I'm so sorry about how things ended between us. It wasn't what I wanted. It wasn't what I would've chosen for us, but I know now that it's over. I've chosen my path and you yours. Please forgive me for everything that happened. Know that I only want the best for you moving forward, that I was only trying to be the best that I could be for you.*

My heart dropped as I continued reading, and my stomach twisted tighter and tighter.

*Just know that I won't forget our time together, and I only wish you the best as we go our separate ways. I know right now the wounds are too fresh, but I do hope that we can eventually be friends. Please accept this as my gift to you in spirit of that sentiment. I hope this can be a peace offering, that you can look at this and think of all the good times we had. We had so, so many good times.*

I already knew who wrote this, already knew who gave my mom this journal, and now I understood why she'd never written in it. There at the bottom, the signature was clear, not marred by time or elements. No confusion in the swirl and loops of the letters. This was a breakup letter, and it sounded like my mother hadn't been the one who initiated the breakup.

This journal had been from my father.

# Chapter Twenty-Seven

BEFORE

Isabella lay wrapped in Jeremiah's arms. It rained outside his mountain cabin, rain pattering down like drumbeats on the roof. Isabella loved coming here to his little home in the woods.

He snuggled behind her, and she could feel his yawn against the back of her neck.

"Mmm," he said sleepily. "Good morning."

Isabella smiled as his hand skimmed down her stomach, resting on her belly. She pressed her own hand against his, reveling in the fact that she had a little life inside of her, one they'd made together.

Jeremiah didn't know yet. Isabella had just found out yesterday, and she knew it was still early, very early. She wanted to wait to tell him until she was further along. But also, she wanted to make the announcement special, and though she loved their morning cuddles, this wasn't exactly what she'd had in mind.

He pressed his hard body into her, and she groaned as a wave of nausea hit her. She'd have to tell him soon. She wouldn't be able to keep this a secret for long, not with the morning sickness already hitting her, and not just in the morning, as it turned out. She turned around to face him and he pressed a kiss to her forehead.

"You okay?" he asked. "You look a little pale."

"I'm fine, really."

"It's your father, isn't it?"

Isabella stilled in Jeremiah's arms. Did he know . . . No, he couldn't know what she'd done. No one could know. Jeremiah wouldn't approve of such a thing. He saw the world so black and white, whereas Isabella saw shades of gray. What she'd done to her father was necessary to protect her mother, to protect herself. She pressed her hand against her stomach once more. To protect this new little life. But Jeremiah wouldn't see that. He'd only see the dark magic Isabella had used, the way she'd gotten that dark magic, how she'd sent her father on a little trip through the portal to Hell and let the Demon King do what he wished with him.

"What do you mean?" Isabella asked, trying to keep her voice steady.

"He's been missing for a month now," he said.

Relief flooded Isabella.

"Right. Of course." She bit the inside of her cheek. "Can I tell you a secret?"

Jeremiah's eyebrows furrowed. "You can tell me anything."

"I'm glad he's gone," she said quickly, like ripping of a Band-Aid. She might not be able to tell Jeremiah everything, but she could at least admit this and hoped he'd understand.

His face softened. "That's okay. He wasn't a good father, wasn't a good man. He didn't deserve you or your mother." He sucked in a breath. "How is she doing with all this?"

"She's okay."

In truth, her mother had been a wreck since Isabella had sent her father away. Isabella thought she would be overjoyed that her father, her mother's tormentor, was gone, but instead, her mother spent all her time sitting by the window, staring out. Like any day she expected him to walk through the front door. Isabella didn't know how to tell her mother that he was gone for good.

"Well, in time, it will get better." Jeremiah's voice drew her from her thoughts. "And you're running The Wish List now. You've got your own place. You're out from underneath your father's thumb. I'm proud of you. So proud of you."

He took her hand in his, rubbing his thumb over her engagement ring, then bringing her hand up to his mouth to press a kiss to it.

"So when do you think you'll move here?"

That took Isabella back, and she reared her head away. "Move here?"

"Well, yeah. Once we get married, I figured we'd finally move in together."

"No, I understand that part," she said. "But why wouldn't you move in with me?"

He laughed like she'd made a joke. "You live in a small apartment. I own this entire cabin, and we have land here, space for our kids to roam around."

It warmed her heart when he mentioned kids. They'd spoken many times over the course of their relationship about wanting them but never talked about when they'd want children or how many. Still, it rankled that he just assumed she'd give up her apartment, the life she'd fought hard for.

"Well, I don't know if I want to move out here. That's a long commute to The Wish List."

"Not if you're on your broom," he said. "You don't even drive, Isabella. You ride it everywhere."

She huffed. "Well, I'm not sure that I can live out here."

"Why?" he asked, genuine confusion on his face.

That was the thing. She couldn't tell him why. After she'd sent her dad to Hell, Isabella found herself looking for ways to get that power back, that rush she'd felt when wielding dark magic. It had made her feel powerful in a way she never had before. She'd found an object, a necklace, that allowed her to collect the pieces of souls given in exchange for a wish. All she had to do was wear the necklace containing the souls, and she could perform any kind of magic she wanted. No more quills, spell books, cauldrons. Of course, she still used all of those things as a front, so no one would suspect anything else was going on. She used Whispering Willows as a base to meet these supernaturals she was granting wishes to, then taking their souls for her own use. Up here, in the mountains, she was too far from civilization. It would be harder to take the souls since that was all after hours work.

"Let's talk about it another time," she said to him.

And even though he agreed, she could feel the sense of dissatisfaction, of hurt. A little crack had formed in their relationship, one that would ultimately spread until the entire thing came crashing down.

# Chapter Twenty-Eight

My entire body shook as I tore from the house and hopped into my car, journal in hand as I drove toward the school. I'd always thought my mother was the one who'd broken my dad's heart, that she was the one who ripped it out of his chest and stomped all over it. But no. It had been him. That much was clear from that little inscription he'd penned. My mother must've loved him more deeply than I ever thought to keep that journal all this time. But she never wrote in it. Once again I was left with more questions than answers.

Except this time I had access to a direct source. I drove blindly before realizing I didn't even know where I was going. Where was my dad right now?

The fog cleared from my mind, and I realized I knew: the portal. I swerved the car around and headed toward the school, parking it in the circle drive, not bothering to even go to the parking lot. I turned on my blinkers and hopped out, journal clutched tight in my hand as I stomped toward the school.

Anger built, stacking like heavy stones in my stomach, over the whole thing, even if I knew it was irrational. He'd been the one who broke it off with her, and he never thought to tell me? He dated her, agreed to marry her, and then crushed her heart. He was probably the reason she never wanted to be in another relationship, the reason she couldn't even tell me she loved me. Though I felt it. I always felt her love. Still, it would've been nice to hear it every once in a while.

I thought I heard a voice call my name, but I didn't register it. I didn't register anything as I strode into the school and marched to the secret passageway. I opened the portrait, not caring that I wasn't supposed to know it existed, and turned on my phone flashlight, which guided my way as I carefully walked down the stairs, mind racing.

It wasn't fair to be angry at my dad. I mean, people broke up all the time. I knew that. And he surely had his reasons for ending their relationship. I took a few calming breaths. I knew I tended to jump to conclusions, jump to anger. I remembered how I'd attempted to bind Isaac and his golden lamp back to the basement, so blinded with anger when I'd discovered Isaac's deception. Then, in my fury, instead of trapping Isaac in the basement, I'd somehow gotten myself trapped in the lamp. It hadn't been my best moment, and I didn't want to repeat those same mistakes. I needed to give my father the benefit of the doubt.

Darkness consumed me, except for the glare of my flashlight, which illuminated spots around the seedy underground. Rough stone and faded brick surrounded me, and my flashlight caught on a few stray bones that made me wince. Human or animal—I didn't want to know.

Soon, the glow of the portal came into view, and there stood my dad with Martin, both of them frowning down at the portal.

Martin shuddered, his pointy ears standing straight up, as tense as the rest of his rigid body.

"No, no, no," Martin was saying. "Dear old Demon King will not take kindly to any kind of negotiation. If he's sending up more demons, then that means he's planning something. And if I know my old boss, it's not good."

"Do you think you would be willing to help with negotiations?"

Martin's eyes bugged out of his head. "Help with . . ." He put a hand to his chest. "Are you listening to a word I've said? No, absolutely not. You and the Council are on your own."

I took a deep breath and steeled myself, clicking off my flashlight and stuffing my phone in my pocket. I took a step closer to the portal and some rock crunched underfoot.

Both my dad's and Martin's eyes snapped to me.

"Clara?" my dad asked, thick eyebrows bunching. His gaze traveled over my shoulder. "Remy?"

I whipped around, and my daughter stood behind me, a guilty look crossing over her features.

"What are you doing here?" I asked.

"I called your name and you didn't answer!" She shrugged. "So I followed you."

"You need to get back to class, Remington." I pinned her with my most menacing Mom Look.

"Relax, it's lunch right now. And I'm not hungry. I'd rather see the portal."

"Why would you follow me all the way down here and not say anything?" I rubbed my temples.

"Because you would've told me to turn around and go back?"

"Not a good enough reason. We are going to have a talk later, young lady. Right now, you just stay there until I'm finished, and then I am walking you back upstairs."

I whirled around, and my dad's flashlight caught on the journal clutched in my hand.

Even in the dark red glow of the portal, I could see his features slacken. "Where did you get that?"

So it was true. He recognized it, which meant he gave this to my mother. Those words in the back of the journal were his. Not some other Jeremiah who might have signed that inscription. Which, thank god. Two Jeremiahs might have been a little too much for even me to handle.

I held up the journal. "I found this in my mother's attic."

"She kept it all those years?" he asked, and I could see the way that thought pained him. He swallowed and it looked like he had a rock stuck in his throat.

"What happened between you two?" I asked, heart beating fast. "I know it's painful to talk about, but it's time."

"Really?" Martin asked. "Now? When we're standing at the portal to Hell that we just discovered. That's the right time to have this discussion?"

I ignored the imp, holding my dad's gaze. I knew he didn't want to talk about it, but we couldn't avoid this anymore. It was only fair he told me what happened between him and my mother, all of it instead of just bits and pieces of their history, which I still had to work to put together like a puzzle.

"So you read my note, then?" my dad asked, and I felt Remy step up beside me.

Both of us inched closer to my dad and Martin as the imp huffed and crossed his arms.

"Yes," I said. "You ended it with her. Why?"

He swallowed, looking away like he was ashamed. "Because I was an idiot."

My heart clenched at his words.

"What's going on, Mom?" Remy looked from the journal to me. "Is that Grandma's?"

I nodded. "I found it a while cleaning out the attic with Emerson, and I just discovered an inscription in it today, one that he wrote." I couldn't help the accusing tone in my voice, and I reminded myself to give him a chance to explain. My mother was a lot of things, did a lot of bad things, but I couldn't help the protectiveness I felt rising up at the thought that he could've done something to hurt her so badly, even if it wasn't intentional.

"What does it mean that you were an idiot?" I asked, my tone pleading. For once, I wanted more than a few words from him in answer to a question. I knew this couldn't be easy, but it was time.

"Again, maybe we can choose a different place to have this conversation?" Martin asked, eyes darting to the portal, which belched out a large red bubble that popped in the air.

My dad shook his head. "I'm sorry," he whispered. "I—it's the biggest regret of my life, what I did."

"What did you do?" My voice shook.

"I chose power and prestige over your mother."

"What does that mean?" Remy asked, eyes wide.

His shoulders sagged. "Your mother was never a fan of the Council, and she made that clear throughout our relationship. She didn't like the way they would lay down law among the supernaturals without consulting anyone, without actually talking to the community at large. She thought the Council did more harm than good." He hesitated. "I wanted to impress her, so I got an appointment with the Council myself, went to them and presented her ideas. I added on some of my own, solutions to the problems that Isabella had talked about. I thought I was doing some good."

A few red embers rose in the air, and the heat from the portal brushed my face.

Martin tapped his foot impatiently. "Can we get the Spark Notes version of this story?"

My dad shifted. "A few weeks later, an invitation came from the Council—I was being invited to join their board."

My mouth dropped open.

"I went to your mom, excited over the whole thing. I told her what I'd done, what had happened, and I thought she'd be proud. I thought she'd be ecstatic that I could get a Council position and make some positive change in our world. I know I was. For the first time in my life, I felt a purpose, a drive that I'd never had before."

My throat grew thick at his words. If I knew my mother, that's not at all how she'd react. She would've felt hurt, betrayed over the entire thing.

"She didn't react the way I'd hoped," he said softly, his voice laced with hurt. "She said a lot of mean things, things about my character, about the kind of person I must be to even entertain a Council job. She told me if I took that job, we were over, that I wasn't the kind of man she wanted by her side."

That sounded like my mother. As awful as it was, I could understand why she felt betrayed, but even as he spoke, I knew it was just a bluff. She kept that journal, which meant she would've fought for the relationship, if she thought there was something to fight for.

"Her words hurt me," my dad said. "They hurt my pride. I thought she'd be so proud of me, and here she was, listing out every insecurity I had about myself. She said I wasn't meant to be a leader, that I was taking her ideas and passing them off as my own. I tried to tell her how I'd come up with solutions myself, ones that I truly thought could make a difference, but she wouldn't listen. So I did something I'm not proud of."

Remy stilled next to me. Even Martin stood frozen like a statue, hanging onto every word that came out of my father's mouth.

"I told her that she was jealous, that she spent her days complaining about the problems of the world instead of actually trying to make change."

I winced, dreading what came next: the inevitable end of my parents' relationship.

"Then I told her that I was taking the position. That if she thought so little of me, then we shouldn't be together. I told her it was over, and that I never wanted to see her again."

Tears welled in his eyes. "I still remember it all so well. The smell of fresh rain as it pounded outside my mountain cabin. Watching Isabella storm toward her car and not look back. How close I was to wrenching that door open and chasing after her. But I didn't. I didn't fight for us. And I regretted it every day since. I stayed on the Council for five years. I tried to put my solutions into play, but I got outvoted constantly. No one wanted to make any kind of change. But I realized I didn't have to be on the Council to make a difference. I went back home to live a quiet life among my pack, rose in the ranks as a pack leader, where I instilled policies I was proud of. I was happy. But something was always missing. I wanted to reach out to your mother, but the truth was her words burrowed so deeply inside of me, and I started to believe what she said. I also started to believe what I'd said, that we didn't belong together. I didn't think any kind of apologies could fix us. So I never tried."

My heart sank. He'd been so close to us. A mere hour's drive away. And all because of a stupid fight, because of how stubborn he and my mother were, he'd never found out about me.

"So how did you come back to the Council?" Remy asked.

He shrugged. "They approached me again a few years ago. When your mother was at her worst." He made eye contact with me. "They told me they needed my help talking sense into her."

I could barely breathe, hearing him talk about my mother in what would've been her final days.

"I agreed and came with them when they wanted to capture her. Of course by then I'd heard all about your mother's dealings. The horrible things she'd been doing as a Witch Granter. So I agreed, hoping I could see her and, I don't know, keep her safe." His voice broke. "I knew the Council was planning on doing whatever necessary to incapacitate her, but I'd hoped I could help de-escalate the situation." Tears welled in my eyes and dropped down my cheeks as my dad shook his head sadly. "I failed her again."

"What happened?" I asked, my voice nothing more than a whisper.

"The Council knew the area she was in, so they sent me to talk to her. It was the first time I'd seen her in forty years, but she somehow looked as beautiful as the day I first met her. She locked eyes with me and had just stopped, staring at me with an open mouth." His head hung. "That's when the Council attacked. They'd lied to me. They didn't want me to help bring her in safely. They used me to bait her."

Tears poured down my cheeks now. My mother had done unspeakable things, but she hadn't deserved that kind of ambush.

My dad's shoulders shook as his own face was wet with tears. "I tried to save her, to stop the bleeding, but I couldn't. That's when she told me about you." He locked eyes with me. "That you were my daughter, a secret she'd kept from everyone."

I swallowed.

"She told me to find you, to take care of you, to be the parent she never was."

Remy's arms came around my waist, and Martin wiped away a few tears, sniffling.

"But even then I was a coward. I didn't know how to face you, not when it was my fault . . ." He stopped, unable to finish his sentence. "It took me a few years to finally work up the courage to come find you, but I couldn't. Not until recently."

Because I'd been in hiding. He was able to find me once I returned to Whispering Willows.

"And I wanted to tell you the truth, but the more time I spent with you, the more afraid I became." His voice was almost a whisper now. "I fell in love with you and Remy and this town almost immediately, and I was so sure if I told you what really happened you'd never forgive me, that I wouldn't deserve that forgiveness."

I couldn't speak, my throat so thick with tears and heartache that no words would come out. My heart wrenched in two at the visual of my mother, in my dad's arms, dying, and her last wish had been for me, for him to find me and take care of me. Something broke inside of me at the same time as a gaping wound healed, and sobs shook my shoulders.

"I'm so sorry," my dad said. He reached out but then bit his lip and let his arm fall. "I don't deserve you. I know that. But I wanted to try. I wanted to be there for you, and it's okay if you don't want that anymore. I wouldn't blame you."

Remy hugged me harder, and her wet cheeks pressed against me. I knew my mother loved me, of course. I knew it was my choice to remove her from my life, to go on the run and hide from her all those years. But to hear that after twenty years apart, she still just wanted to make sure I was safe and protected . . . it meant the world to me. Those words healed something inside of me, a wound I hadn't even realized needed healing.

I lifted my gaze to my father, wanting to speak but unable to form words.

"This is a lot to take in," I said, and he nodded.

"I know. I know that. I wish I could do more right now, but all I could do was tell you the truth."

I swallowed, not sure what I was feeling. It wasn't anger, exactly. Maybe disappointment? No, no that wasn't it either.

The portal burbled, more red bubbles of heat rising in the air and popping, burning red ash raining down.

"We should go," I finally said. "It's probably not safe to be down here any longer."

My father's shoulders sagged, and I knew he wanted me to say more, but right now, I didn't know what I could say in response to all that. I needed time to think, to work through everything he'd revealed. His and my mother's relationship had gone so, so wrong. And it was hard not to wonder if she'd have turned out differently if they'd stayed together. What my life would've been like with two loving parents?

"Uh, Clara?" Martin said. "Step away from the portal."

"What?" I asked, and then looked down.

The portal was widening, almost to our feet. Remy and I jumped back, and so did my father and Martin.

I grabbed Remy's hand, ready to run, but it was too late. The portal widened again, and my mouth opened in a scream as it pulled us all forward and sucked us right into its dark red depths.

# Chapter Twenty-Nine

I was falling. Again. This time blazing red surrounded me, flames licking and leaping toward me as my body careened through the air. Remy's hand slipped from mine, and I couldn't see where she'd gone.

"Remy!" I screamed, but it was no use. I couldn't hear anything but the savage wind rushing through my ears.

After what felt like forever, my feet landed firmly on the ground, and I swayed a bit, my vision unfocused as I tried to orient myself to my surroundings. Red. Orange. Black. Flames and lava and a hazy gray sky above.

I looked down at the rocky uneven ground where I stood. It was like I'd fallen inside a volcano. Maybe I had. This was Hell?

"Well, you've really done it now." Martin stomped up to me.

"What are you doing here?" I looked around, eyes wild. "Where's Remy?"

"I'm here, Mom." She walked from the opposite direction where Martin came. I ran to her and hugged her tight, running my hands over head, her face, her shoulders, as if to check her for any wounds.

She swatted at me. "Mom! I'm fine, really."

"And my dad?"

"Doesn't look like he fell." Martin rolled his eyes. "Of course the councilman isn't here. You know they track Council members? He could absolutely get us out of this mess."

"He still might," I said, though I had no idea if he'd be able to. I mean, how did you get someone out of Hell? I gulped.

A river of molten lava flowed past us, and the rocky ground wound through it and toward tall dark peaks in the distance. My eyebrows furrowed.

"What are we supposed to do?" I turned to Martin. "You're the expert."

"Oh no." Martin crossed his arms. "I am not getting involved." He sat down on the ground, cross-legged, avoiding any eye contact with me.

I looked at Remy, who shrugged, then I turned back to Martin as he sat there, ignoring me completely. He shifted a bit, wincing, then he groaned and stood, throwing his arms in the air. "Dammit, this is too uncomfortable! Fine. Fine. The only way we're getting out of here is by visiting my old boss."

"The Demon King?" I asked.

"Yes, the Demon King!" Martin snapped. "And let me tell you, the guy's no picnic. In fact, he doesn't even enjoy picnics. Who doesn't enjoy a picnic? Someone demented, that's who."

"So how do we find this Demon King?" I asked, and Martin gestured toward the tall gray mountains in the distance.

"His lair is that way, so we better get walking. And whatever you do, don't look him in the eye."

Martin stomped ahead of us, grumbling to himself.

"What happens if we look him in the eye?" I asked as we followed the imp. The very angry imp.

"He turns you to stone?" Remy asked.

"No, I'm pretty sure that's a gorgon."

Remy gasped. "Do those exist too?"

"Just walk," I said.

Martin huffed. "You know, you better hope nothing jumps out of that river. Can't tell you how many times one of the Demon King's creatures used to pop up and try to eat me. One time I got swallowed whole."

"Like Pinocchio!" Remy said, and Martin turned and pinned her with a look.

"No, not like Pinocchio." He scrunched his brow. "Who's Pinocchio?"

I shook my head. "Okay so what about the flesh-eating creatures? I feel like this is important information."

Martin flung his hand out. "They'll just jump right out of the River of Death and snatch you up in their mouths."

"The River of Death?" Remy asked. "That sounds ominous. Um, why's it called that?"

My foot kicked up a rock that skittered across the gray, uneven ground and fell into the River of Death, immediately evaporating as soon as it hit the lava.

"Because if you fall in, you die," Martin said like it was the most obvious thing in the world.

I grabbed Remy and drew her closer to me. Well, this was just great.

"Where is everyone?" Remy looked around. "Don't all the Demon King's minions live here?"

"Not in this area. No one comes here unless they have to. Actually." Martin pointed up ahead to a blackened tree, its leaves brittle and hanging off the branches precariously. "That's a popular make-out spot because of how secluded it is." His eyes twinkled. "Brought many a lady here back in the day."

"Charming," I said.

The rocky path ahead of us wound away from the River of Death and toward barren land, the ground gray and lifeless, the only plants either cacti or trees that looked dark as death. Which made sense, I supposed, given we were in the land of death.

I had no idea how we were going to convince this Demon King to let us go, especially not with Martin in tow.

From everything the imp had said, the Demon King would not be happy to see him.

We walked further along the rocky path, now smoothing out to less rocky and more sandy, the grains dark and inky. I swiped an arm across my brow, slick with sweat. It turned out Hell was hot. Who knew?

I turned to Martin. "Can you tell us anything about the Demon King? Any weaknesses he has? Ways to earn his favor, maybe?"

"Weaknesses? He doesn't have any weaknesses. Well, except for the high cholesterol and blood pressure. I told him he needed to get both under control, but would he listen? No, not to the imp. And you can't earn his favor. He doesn't give favors. You either do what he tells you, or he kills you."

I heard Remy audibly gulp next to me, and I slung an arm around her shoulder. "It's going to be okay," I whispered to her, trying to sound more assured than I felt.

This sounded bad. Really bad. But there was no way I'd let Remy get stuck down here. I didn't care how foreboding this Demon King was, he couldn't scare me. Not when I had a daughter to protect. I'd find a way to save us.

Remy worried at her bottom lip.

I nudged. "Hey, how was the Samhain Ball? We haven't had a chance to talk about it."

She needed a distraction, and so did I.

Her eyes brightened. "It was the best night. I had so much fun with my friends."

"Good, hon. That's really good." I paused. "Though I couldn't help but notice you were without a date."

"Mom." There was a warning to Remy's voice.

"What? You said you were going to explain everything later." I gestured around us to the barren land. The sky above rumbled, dark, plump clouds forming. "What better time than now?"

"I agree," Martin said, eyes wide and innocent.

Remy shot him a look. "Fine. If you must know right this second, which I really don't think you must, I decided that I wanted to go to the Samhain Ball with my friends and focus on me, not some guy who's been hot and cold all year. One day he likes me, one day he doesn't. I don't want the games, Mom. I want what you and Preston have."

That took me aback. "Me and Preston?"

"Yeah. Mr. H has been telling me so many stories about you two, your love story, how he loved you almost the minute he first saw you. I want that."

I gave Martin a Help Me look, and he shrugged as we continued walking the sandy path, the heat emanating from the River of Death now cooling off marginally.

"Remy, you can't know if you're going to find your great love story without even giving anyone a chance. I mean, you have to trust your gut. And if your gut told you that this vampire of yours was just playing games, then yes, you made the right choice. But if you pushed him away all because you want some lightning-strike love, well, that's just not realistic."

"Why? It was for you and Preston."

Martin barked out a laugh, and Remy whipped toward him. "And for you and Isaac!"

That sobered Martin's expression.

"Isaac and I are definitely the number one couple in Whispering Willows," Martin agreed.

"What does that mean?" I asked. "Number one in what category?"

"All of them," Martin said.

I just rolled my eyes as Remy smirked.

"But I would never have found that love with Isaac without making all the mistakes I made over the years. And there were a lot of mistakes," Martin said. "So many. One-night stands. Ghosting. Once, I broke up with a fairy by turning her into the Demon King for breaking his laws."

"You what?" I asked.

"I'm not proud, Clara," Martin said. "Well, I was a little proud at the time, but I'm not proud now." He shook his head. "The point is, all those mistakes made me realize not only what I want in a partner but what I need." He roped an arm around Remy. "You gotta make the mistakes to get the reward."

Remy donned a thoughtful expression. "I guess I never thought of it that way. But still, the vampire wasn't right. No matter what. I don't know. I feel like I'm meant for something greater. It's just a feeling, you know? Something passionate and exciting and epic." Her voice grew excited.

I patted her shoulder. "Okay, calm down, there, Casanova. Just keep trusting your gut. It hasn't steered you wrong so far."

We approached the base of the towering mountain. Lightning struck above, zigzagging blue lines through the darkened sky. Oh, hell no. I was not about to climb this thing.

Martin gestured to a set of steep stairs cut into the mountain. I sighed heavily. Looked like I didn't have a choice.

"This is going to take days," I whined.

"The Demon King doesn't live at the top. Relax." Martin shooed us toward the steps. "Let's get this over with."

We climbed higher and higher, my legs aching with each step I took. I had to stop a few times to catch my breath, and each time I did, I made the mistake of looking down, my stomach filling with rocks at the steep drop down below. Gargoyles flew around us, paying no mind to the three supernaturals climbing the mountain. Other winged creatures I couldn't identify zipped through the air, releasing awful screeches.

From up here, I could see for miles. Towers rose in the distance, and a large black pit sat in the ground, demons jumping out of it.

"Is that where they're spawned?" I asked, and Martin nodded, face grim. Each demon that rose from the pit was uglier than the last.

My feet stumbled over a step, and after that, I focused my attention on climbing, my lungs squeezing tighter with each breath. Finally we came to a stop on a flat part of the mountain that led into a cave. The stairs continued up the side, but Martin stepped off and onto the large mesa.

On the one hand, I didn't want Remy going anywhere near the Demon King. But on the other, no way was I leaving her alone out here. I grasped her hand and gave her as assured a look as I could while we approached the cave.

Two demons stood guard outside, their large black eyes fixed on us. Wings sprouted from their backs, misshapen and filled with holes. One of the demons stuck out its forked tongue and hissed at us. I winced.

They both locked eyes on Martin and stepped aside. I was surprised the sway the imp still had. Martin nodded to each of them, his shoulders tense in a way I hadn't seen before. If Martin was tense, that was definitely not a good sign.

We stepped inside the cave, candles in sconces along the wall. The warm glow lit up the cozy round space. Holes filled with bubbling lava covered the ground, and in the center of the cave sat a large red throne, skulls building up its base and bones making up the back and the armrests.

I gulped, not wanting to know whose bones.

Martin's mouth dropped open. "You," he said, pointing at the Demon King, who sprawled out across the chair.

My head snapped to the imp. "What? What's wrong?"

"That's not the Demon King," Martin sputtered. "It's his son."

# Chapter Thirty

My mouth dropped open. The Demon King, or his son, anyway, was very . . . un-demon like. In fact, objectively speaking, he was, well, gorgeous. I mean, way too young for me, and really not my type, but damn.

He stroked his strong jaw, which was cut like a freaking stone. He might actually have been made of stone. I didn't know for sure. I looked at Remy for confirmation that I wasn't the only one surprised, but her gaze was locked on him like she was in a trance. I'd never seen her so taken aback, and I nudged her. She shook her head, her curls skimming her shoulders, and then she glanced at me, letting out a nervous laugh.

"Remington," I said, a warning to my voice. "You're staring."

"Pretty sure you were staring too," she shot back, under her breath.

"Balazar, where is your father?" Martin asked, hands on his hips. "Long story short, we fell into the portal, got stuck in Hell, blah, blah, blah, we need to get sent back."

Martin pointed to a small tunnel behind Balazar, swirling and red. That must've been our way out. Except the Demon King sat right in front of it.

Balazar's gaze swept over us, briefly pausing on Remy, and I pulled her into me protectively. No, sir. I did not care that my daughter was eighteen and capable of making her own decisions. Whatever heated looks lingered between them—I wasn't having it. Gorgeous or no, this Balazar was the Demon King's son, which made him evil, terrible.

At the mention of his father, Balazar's eyes flashed, and I swore I saw something like sadness reflect in his yellow irises. Red light flickered against his creamy pale skin, and rings glittered on his fingers. "My father is dead," he said, his voice low and melodic.

"I'm sorry," Remy said to him, and his eyes snapped to her.

Martin stepped forward. "How did he die?"

Balazar sighed heavily. "Turns out even the Demon King can get heart failure."

"Well, that makes sense given the high blood pressure and cholesterol," Martin mumbled, and I elbowed him.

"Listen," I said, "I'm very sorry for your loss, but we need to get back up to earth. Can you help us?"

"No," Balazar said simply, then paused. "Well, I can, but I don't want to." His gaze once again strayed to Remy in a way that made my throat close up. "Maybe I want to keep you all here, for myself."

"Absolutely not," I said.

"Wait a minute." Martin pointed at Balazar. "Is your father's death the reason why all the demons are invading Whispering Willows? Why there's a second portal?"

Balazar studied the shiny black rings on his fingers like he was bored. "I don't know what you're talking about."

"Your father isn't here to control them. We made a pact with him when the Demon Slayer arrived in Whispering Willows over twenty years ago."

Helen. They'd made the pact when she and Gene had gone into Hell to barter with the Demon King. Every time Helen killed a demon, it physically hurt the Demon King, and so they made a peace treaty that he'd stop trying to wage war on Whispering Willows. Of course the occasional demon still broke through the portal, but for the most part he'd kept them in control over the years. But now, with him gone . . .

Balazar still sat sprawled over the throne, his jaw locked. "If you came here to imply that I don't know how to do my job, then I'd suggest you watch the next words that come out of your mouth. They might be your last." He flicked his wrist and the guards standing outside the cave had crept in, their wings fanning behind them.

"Maybe try a different tactic," I whispered to Martin.

"Oh I'm sorry I'm not the Demon King whisperer." He glared at me.

"Is war really what you want right now?" I asked.

"War is what my father wanted," he said, which wasn't really an answer to my question. "He hated that peace treaty, hated that he'd been forced to sign it, to sign away what he thought was his power." Balazar's lips thinned. "And now that he's gone, I'm the only thing left to uphold his legacy."

Suddenly, it was clear exactly how I could get us back up to earth. Balazar's dad had died, leaving him with all this power that he wasn't ready to wield. He was following in his father's footsteps, and it was clear he wanted to be just like him. I could use that against him. It wasn't right what I was about to do, but I had to do it. I had to get Remy to safety and that meant doing whatever needed to be done, even if it was poking at the Demon King's obvious wounds.

I stepped closer.

Balazar held out his hand. "Don't."

I raised mine up. "Your father didn't think much of you, did he?"

Balazar frowned. "What are you talking about?"

"He never believed you could be the king he was."

Just a guess, but one based on the way Balazar spoke about his dad.

"You don't know what you're talking about," he said, his eyes flashing.

I'd struck a nerve.

"Mom," Remy hissed from behind me.

"Your father was disappointed in you, but why? What was it about you that was such a let down?"

"Shut up," Balazar said.

"I agree with the Demon King." Martin mouthed *knock it off*, but I kept going.

"I mean, here you are, barely able to control your demons, and now you're telling me you don't even have the power to get us back up to earth."

Balazar shook his head. "It's not going to work, whatever you're doing. You can't goad me into returning you. You fell into the portal, you can figure out how to get back."

"That's fine," I said.

"No it's not!" Martin cried. "It's definitely not fine."

I didn't take my eyes off Balazar. "You know, your father would never have let this happen. Not on his watch. Sure, he might've wanted demons to attack Whispering Willows, but not because he couldn't control them. That would've killed him, knowing demons were running wild without his permission."

Balazar's jaw ticked, and I could tell I was slowly chipping away at his self-control.

"He'd be horrified at what you've become, barely able to control your demons, letting humans just waltz into your territory."

I'd heard the Demon King hated having humans in his lands, couldn't stand the sight of us. He'd always been so afraid we'd come to Hell and wage war on him, that we'd sneak down into Hell and learn all his secrets. Little did he know, humans wanted nothing to do with this place.

"Shut up!" Balazar roared, standing and rushing forward, his chest heaving.

Remy and Martin took a few steps back, but I stood my ground.

Oh, I hoped this worked. Hoped I wasn't a complete idiot for this. But I needed to push him over the edge.

"Until you learn to control those demons, you'll never be able to stand in your father's shoes. They'll never see you as their king. And you'll be nothing more than that little boy your father always thought couldn't live up to him."

Remy stared at me, horrified, and Martin's mouth dropped open.

Balazar's fists curled tight, and I could see his nails digging into his skin. "You're going to pay for that," he said, close enough now that I could reach out and touch him.

"No," I said, my hand shooting out as I grabbed him and threw him toward one of the bubbling lava holes. "You are. Now!" I shouted to Remy and Martin. "Run!"

They took off toward the portal floating behind his throne, and I ran after them as Balazar screamed on the ground, the bubbling lava burning his skin. He'd be fine.

The demons behind us screeched and I could hear the flapping of their tattered wings. Martin pushed Remy through the portal, and then jumped in after her. I stretched out my hand, so close to escape, when I felt the demon's jaws snapping at my heels.

"Get her," Balazar roared.

I shot a look behind me and jammed my foot into the demon's nose, then with one final push of strength, I lunged through the portal and back home.

# Chapter Thirty-One

The portal propelled my body and spit me out onto the cobblestone ground of the old square. I groaned as I hit the hard ground, and rolled onto my back, my vision going sideways. Remy lay beside me, and Martin lay closer to the overturned tables and chairs that surrounded the little square.

"Remy!" I cried, pushing myself up and launching toward her, ignoring my creaking joints and bones that protested with the movement.

She sat up, rubbing her head, eyes groggy. "Mom?"

I pulled her into my arms and pressed kisses into her head. "Oh, Remy. Are you okay?" I kissed her again. "Are you hurt anywhere?"

She pushed me gently. "I'm fine, Mom. Balazar? Not so much. Did you have to be so hard on him?"

My mouth dropped open as Martin stood and came closer.

"Hard on the Demon King?" I looked between her and Martin. "She's joking, right?"

"You were kind of mean." The imp lifted a shoulder in agreement.

"Because he was going to keep us trapped in Hell for all of eternity. I had to do something to save us."

Remy studied her nails. "I think he might've been hurting. I mean his dad just died and he's the ruler of Hell and dealing with demons who won't listen to him, so maybe you could've found a different approach? One that didn't completely piss him off?"

"She has a point," Martin said.

"I can't believe you two." I stood and brushed off my dusty knees. "I saved us, and you're complaining about how I might've hurt the Demon King's feelings."

Remy now picked at a nail. "I guess I just felt a little bad for him is all."

I squinted at her, noticing the pink that flushed her cheeks. "Please tell me that's all."

Martin's gaze bounced between us. "What does that mean?"

I pointed at Remy. "You thought he was cute."

Remy crossed her arms and rolled her eyes. "Of course I did. Did you see him? He might as well have been a statue carved from stone. He was . . . gorgeous." Her voice came out breathy in a way I didn't like, and suddenly I remembered her words about lightning striking, about wanting to feel an all-consuming passion. I did not like where this was going.

"Yes, Remy, he was attractive, but he's also the king of demons and lives in Hell."

She threw out her arms. "I know that."

"Okay," I said slowly. "Just making sure we're clear that there cannot be a relationship between you two."

"Mom, you are losing your mind. First of all, he's the Demon King. Second of all, I spent like five minutes with the guy. Third of all, he's the Demon King. Even if he is the most beautiful thing I think I've ever seen in my life. And he's my age. And both of us have experienced our dads dying. Anyway." Remy gave me a look that told me she wanted to drop this entire thing, and I intended to once I knew that she understood the Demon King was off-limits.

"I trust you," I said. "You know I do, but the Demon King, no matter how good-looking he may be, is evil, Remy. Just like his father. That kind of thing, it doesn't skip a generation."

She cocked an eyebrow. "Really? Because it did with you and Grandma."

I thought I heard Martin snort, but when I looked over at him, his lips were pressed together as he rocked on his heels, a twinkle in his eye like he was enjoying this far too much.

"That's not the same thing at all."

"What is going on here?" Helen and Gene burst into the little square from a nearby alleyway. Helen ran to me and Remy and pulled us both in for a hug. "Please tell me it's not true. You didn't actually fall into the portal, did you?"

I bit my lip, and Helen gasped.

Gene swore. "Seriously? You three? In hell? How did the demons not rip you to shreds right away?"

Martin's hand flew to his chest. "Excuse me. I worked for the Demon King for years, and I did just fine."

"Yeah, and you don't think you've gone a little soft running a B&B the last forty years?" Gene said.

Martin glared at him. "Oh, you're one to talk, *Gene*."

"It's the Serpent to you," Gene growled, flashing his fangs, then he glared at me. "It's all your fault, you know, going around town, calling me Gene, revealing my given name to everyone."

Helen hid a smile behind her hand.

"Can we focus on the problem at hand?" I asked.

The portal behind us let out a loud shriek and a rain of hot lava flew over the cobblestones as we all jumped out of the way. Embers burned on the ground, flaring a bright red before turning to black ash.

"So what happened?" Gene asked, running a hand over his bleach-blonde hair, gelled and slicked back, not a hair out of place. I swear, he could stand in the middle of a tornado and it wouldn't sway his hair one bit.

We recounted our tale, and Helen's eyes grew wider as Martin, Remy, and I delved further into our story.

"The Demon King died?" Gene asked when we finished. "Of heart failure, of all things?"

I shrugged.

"He ate a lot of donuts," Martin said, and I just rolled my eyes.

"I don't think donuts are a cause of heart failure, Martin."

Helen started to pace. "No wonder demons are popping up everywhere. So the new king doesn't have control?"

"Well he might now," Remy mumbled. "After my mom pushed all his buttons."

"To save us," I said, still annoyed that she clearly didn't appreciate what I'd done for us. Part of me worried it was because in the short time we'd spent in the Demon King's lair, Remy had developed a crush.

"Hey, I'm proud of you," Helen said, looking at me. Then she turned to Remy. "The Demon King, whether or not he's young or just lost his father, isn't someone you want to mess with. Your mom did what was necessary to save you all."

"Thank you," I said. Finally someone appreciated what I'd done.

"So what do we do now?" I asked. "We have a Demon King who can't control his subjects."

"Well, maybe your little scheme did more than get us home." Martin tapped his chin. "Maybe you snapped him out of whatever funk he was in after his father's death, and now he'll be on a mission to prove his worth, to prove he can maintain control over the demons just like his father did."

Gene cocked his head. "That's not a bad thought. I say for now we wait. And watch. If we see any signs that things are escalating, we'll have to visit and see the new Demon King ourselves." He winked at Helen. "I wouldn't mind making another trip. Our last one was pretty fun." He waggled his eyebrows and Helen shot him a sly smile.

The last time they'd made a trip to Hell, about seventeen years ago, was when they'd finally admitted their feelings for one another and officially became a couple.

I bit the inside of my cheek. "Well, maybe my father will have some insight."

Oh my god. My dad. With everything that had happened, I'd completely forgotten how we ended our conversation. His confession. Everything that had happened between him and my mom. The journal.

I shook my head, his revelation flooding back to me all at once.

"You okay?" Helen asked, nudging me. "You look a little pale."

Remy put an arm around my waist and hugged me tight, and she must've realized exactly what was going through my mind. "She found out that her dad is the one who broke her mom's heart and that he chose a position in the Council over Grandma."

"What?" Helen's eyes bugged out. "Seriously? I did not see that coming. Totally thought your mom was the one who screwed that up."

"I think we all assumed Isabella was the one who ruined that relationship," Martin added.

"Well, she didn't," I said, my voice curt. "It's a lot to digest, but I need to find my dad so we can talk it through. I feel like we didn't end things on the best note, and I want him to know that I'm not mad, just surprised by everything."

"Well that's going to be hard," Gene said.

"Why?" I asked, stomach dropping.

"He's gone," Helen said. "He was supposed to meet with us and the mayor after he went to go check the portal, but he never showed to our meeting. We stopped by your house and no one answered. We've called him and it's gone straight to voicemail. No one can find him."

"Oh my god," I said. "He left?" My tongue felt thick and heavy, my head cold. No. I couldn't lose another parent. Not when I'd just found him. But I knew it was true. That's what had happened with my mom. He got in a fight with her and then they literally never spoke again. Panic rose in me, fast and hard. "This is all my fault. He thinks I'm mad at him, that I want nothing to do with him."

"You don't know that," Remy said. "That doesn't seem like something he'd do."

"He did it with my mom," I said. "He disappeared on her, for years."

Remy opened her mouth to respond but closed it again, probably realizing she didn't have an argument for that.

"Well great." Martin planted his hands on his hips. "There goes any Council help we hoped to receive."

But I wasn't thinking about the Council or the aid they could give us. I was just thinking about my dad. About the fact that there was still so much to learn about him. About how scared he'd been to tell me the truth about what happened between him and my mom, so afraid I'd shut him out of my life. But no. I wouldn't. I didn't want to. He deserved more than that. I deserved more than that. I had to fix this.

"How do you get to Council headquarters?" I asked the group. "If there's any way I could contact him it would be through the Council."

Everyone shot uneasy glances at each other.

"No one knows," Gene said. "The Council has always been secretive about their location. That's why when you're summoned, you just up and disappear, then reappear in their building."

I groaned. "There has to be a way." I thought about my last visit to see the Council, thought about any details I could grasp onto that might help me. But there was nothing. No landmarks, no distinguishing features. All I had was the warning they gave me: that they'd be watching, and if I . . . I snapped my fingers.

"I know how I can find my dad."

"How?" Helen asked.

They weren't going to like this, but I'd already made up my mind. I knew what I needed to do, and hopefully, it would fix everything.

# Chapter Thirty-Two

"Mom, have you completely lost it?"

Remy followed me into The Wish List, and I headed straight for the shelves lining the walls of the shop, gleaming crystals sitting there just waiting to be filled with a wish.

"She's right," Helen said from behind me as I plucked a crystal off the shelf.

"Does anyone actually think she's going to listen?" Gene asked, leaning against the doorway of the backroom.

I muttered to myself, wondering where exactly I'd left my wand. Aha. It lay on a shelf by the cauldron, just waiting to be used on a wish.

I scurried over to it and snatched it up, feeling the smoothness of it against my skin. A sense of calm washed over me, the way it always did when my wand was in hand. Martin paced, Helen worried at her lip, Gene just looked irritated, and Remy's eyes had gone wide.

"This is insane. You know that, right?" She looked at Helen. "She knows that, right?"

Helen just shrugged. "She's got the determined look on her face, the one that she makes when she's not going to let something go."

Myrtle burst through the door. "What in the feck is going on?" She held up her phone. "I'm getting text after text, here, about you losing your mind." She looked at me when she said that last part, eyes wild, twigs in hair. She must've been in the middle of a hunt or a run, in her wolf form.

Her glittery green tracksuit sparkled bright, and she scrunched her nose, which caused her glittery green glasses to tilt. She adjusted them and harrumphed.

"I swear, every day I'm getting some new text about you and your antics." She pointed at me. "Can we give it a rest already? I just want one day of peace."

My phone dinged with a text from Isaac.

> ISAAC
>
> You must really be off your rocker if Remy is resorting to texting me to talk you off the ledge.
>
> I'll admit, I don't know much about granting wishes since you haven't had a chance to teach me yet, but this sounds like a terrible idea, even to me.
>
> And that's saying something.
>
> Anyway, if you go and mess up this wish and somehow off yourself, I call dibs on your room.
>
> I need somewhere to store my shoe collection.

I just rolled my eyes and put my phone on the counter, staring at the crystal ball and my wand.

"Listen to me," I said to everyone, who was currently staring at me, varying looks of horror pasted on their faces. "I am not putting myself in danger. I promise."

"You just got yourself trapped in a lamp like a month ago doing this exact same type of thing," Remy countered. "Well, not the exact same thing, because then you were casting a stupid spell instead of this time, when you're going to grant a stupid wish."

"But it's not the same." I slowly walked to Remy and cupped her face with my hands. "I was deranged then. So blinded by anger and this lust for revenge that I couldn't think straight. That was a stupid choice, but I promise this isn't. My mind has never been clearer," I told her. "Listen, over twenty years ago I walked out on my mom. And it was necessary, because she was making dangerous choices and she wanted me to follow down that same path as her. Since my dad has been back, I've been so focused on using him to learn about my mom, I didn't spend enough time trying to just get to know him. We just finally got to a good place, a place where he started to open up to me."

She opened her mouth to argue, but I cut her off.

"And now he thinks I'm mad at him. He's run off because he thinks he's not good enough to be my dad. Just like he thought he wasn't good enough to be with my mom. But he is. He's enough. And I have to prove that to him, Remy. Don't you see? My mom never fought for him, she didn't fight for their relationship. So I have to. He deserves that much."

I let my hands fall from her face, and Remy just stepped back and nodded. "Okay, yeah. I get it."

"What?" Martin screeched. "Is anyone else still very confused?"

Everyone in the room raised their hands.

Myrtle peered at me through her glasses, the wrinkles on her ancient face more pronounced than ever as she frowned. "What, exactly, are you about to do, Clara?"

"She's going to make a wish," Helen said.

"For who?" Myrtle asked.

"Herself," Gene answered gruffly.

Myrtle's eyes widened behind her glasses. "But that's not allowed! The Council forbid any Witch Granters from making wishes for themselves over thirty years ago!" Her Irish accent thickened, a sure sign she was stressed, which was saying something, because the werewolf rarely worried about anything.

I bustled behind the counter and glanced at the empty crystal ball one more time. Soon enough it would be filled with my wish.

"If anyone can do this, it's Mom," Remy said simply, the worry gone from her voice. She trusted me, and that meant the world.

I was glad I'd at least reassured her.

"But you're on probation already!" Myrtle said. "If you go and do this, you're gonna get your powers revoked!"

"Christ," Martin muttered, still pacing. "I don't know where we went wrong with her. I know Isabella was absent all the time, and we did the best we could to raise her, but this . . ." He gestured at me like I was a lost cause. "Hopefully, we can still save Remy."

I glared at him.

The door to the shop burst open again, and Preston stood there. My heart stopped in my chest at seeing him, the sun behind him lighting him up with a glow, dimples pecking his cheeks, those hazel eyes boring into me.

"Finally," Gene said. "Will you talk some sense into your girlfriend?"

"I support whatever she's about to do," Preston said firmly, and I smiled at him.

"Everyone's lost it!" Martin threw up his hands. "Completely lost it!"

I picked up my wand, now holding the crystal in one hand, my wand in the other. "Or we're thinking clearly for the first time in a long time."

Martin shook his head, his thick hair shifting with the movement. "No, no you've definitely lost it."

"What is this even going to accomplish?" Helen asked, stepping toward me.

"It's simple." I straightened and my gaze swept around the room. "I'm going to wish that I am wherever my dad is. I can see him, explain everything. I'll get him back. And I'll deal with the Council later."

"Why not just cast a normal spell?" Myrtle asked.

"I don't know how to cast a spell like that, one that'll take me to where he is right now." I shook my head. "It could possibly take weeks to find the right ingredients, to write a spell like that. I don't have that time. I need to find him and explain everything before it's too late."

I didn't know why I felt a sense of urgency, but I just did.

"But your powers . . ." Helen trailed off. "Your ability to grant wishes!"

I waved her words away. "They're not going to ban me forever. Isaac will be back soon and I can train him, and Remy is going to graduate in less than six months, and she can run the shop if I'm still not allowed to grant wishes by then. Either way, it's worth it."

Remy's eyes shined with pride.

"I'm really not worried," I said. "Plus, I do know someone on the Council, and I think he might put in a good word for me."

Preston strode to me and put an arm around my shoulder, bringing me in for a tight hug. "I believe in you. You've got this."

"Thank you," I whispered into his chest. "For always being in my corner."

He let me go, and I took the little crystal ball in my hands and brought it to my lips, then whispered my wish to it. The ball ignited in color, swirls of magic whipping around inside, purple and pink and blue. The ball glowed brighter and brighter, everyone shielding their eyes against the color.

Then the light zapped back into the ball, the color gone. I closed my eyes and steeled myself to go find my father. My feet lifted from the floor and my body whirled, spinning faster and faster at a dizzying speed. Then everything went dark.

# Chapter Thirty-Three

"Well, she's really done it now," a voice said from somewhere in the distance.

"I can't believe this is your daughter," another voice said. "Are you proud of this? Blatantly breaking the law with no regard to her powers?"

"Just like her mother," someone else added.

Fog filled my head, and it pounded fiercely. Is this what it felt like to get a wish granted? Did everyone feel this effect, or was this the price I was paying? No, the price would probably be something greater. I didn't know what yet. I slowly sat up, all my joints aching, and I blinked several times when I finally opened my eyes.

The Council sat before me. I was back at their headquarters? But why? I was supposed to go where my dad was. Had the Council already found out about my illegal dealings and brought me here immediately? My stomach twisted, and for the first time, I thought maybe I'd made a grave, grave error. Then my vision cleared, focused, and . . . there sat my dad, frowning down at me.

"Clara?" he asked, eyebrows bunching.

I shot to my feet, wincing at the pain that jolted through my knees. "I'm so sorry," I rushed out before he could speak, everyone else's faces falling away. "I'm sorry that I brought that journal and that I ambushed you like that. I was so shocked to find it that I wasn't thinking clearly until it was too late. And then we fell into Hell—"

"Hell?" one of the Council members repeated, a woman with dark skin and a thick accent that made me think she was possibly Israeli.

"What is going on here?" another Council member asked, looking between me and my father.

I ignored them, keeping my gaze locked on my dad.

"The truth is a small part of me did want to jump to conclusions at first. I saw that journal entry from you, and I thought you'd lied to me, betrayed me, just like she did."

A tear slipped down my cheek.

"But you're not like my mother. I know that. And I also know that it's okay that she was evil and did bad things. I mean, it's not okay." At that, I glanced at the other Council members, all of them frowning at my words. "I obviously don't condone anything my mother did, but what I mean is that my mom was a complicated person. She had so many different facets to her, and just because I saw one side doesn't mean I didn't know her."

"Oh, Clara," my dad said. "Is that what you think? That somehow I saw some real version of her that you didn't?"

I gave a helpless shrug. "I did, for a while. I worried that I never really knew her. But that's not true. She showed you a side of herself that I never saw, sure, but that's because you were her fiancé. I saw a lot in my mom that you probably never did."

He nodded, a small smile on his lips.

"I mean, yes, my mother was gone a lot, and yes, she cared about power and magic and me following in her footsteps. But she also packed my lunch when she was home. She took me on adventures with her every chance she got. She was the mom who insisted on taking my pictures before a school dance, on being there for every big event, even if it wasn't big. Like my sixth grade science fair or the spelling bee I had in high school, where I got last place, by the way. She loved movie nights and always insisted we had popcorn with marshmallows and chocolate chips. I think this whole time I was so worried that my mom wasn't her real self with me, but she had just grown and evolved from who she was with you. At the end of the day, she was my mom in all her complicated glory. That's it. That's all I needed, and that's what she was."

"Yeah, honey," my dad said. "That's exactly what she was."

"And now I need my dad. I know I'm a forty-year-old woman, but I want you in my life. And I'm so sorry if you thought I was mad at you. I didn't mean to make you run away or feel like you did something wrong, and I definitely didn't mean to make you confess the most painful part of your life to me like that. I know you would've told me eventually."

"No, Clara—"

But I cut him off.

"No, really this is my fault. I shouldn't have been so impulsive and impatient. I could've gone about that in a much better way, and you deserve an apology. I get why you ran. I wish you hadn't. I wish you'd stayed and given me a chance to explain myself, explain that I wasn't angry with you, but I'm ready to move past all of this and start fresh if you are."

My dad stood, the other Council members all staring, their gazes pinging between the two of us. "I didn't run away."

My eyebrows furrowed. "What do you mean?"

He gestured toward me. "You fell into Hell. I came to the Council headquarters to alert them and assemble a team so we could immediately come and do a rescue mission."

"Oh." Well now I felt pretty stupid. "That actually makes a lot of sense."

He stepped down from the high dais, walking toward me until he came to a stop right in front of me. "Thank you for coming, but just like you know I'm not your mom, I also realize that about you. I never thought you'd leave me or be so angry you'd just abandon our relationship. I just wanted to find a way to save you and Remy. To bring you both back so we could keep getting to know each other." He heaved a big sigh. "I actually just put in my resignation."

"Y-you did?" Hope fluttered in my chest.

He smiled big. "I did. Turns out I'm moving to Whispering Willows. Going to retire and get to know my daughter and granddaughter."

I sniffled. "That sounds really nice."

"Oh, for god sakes," a Council member said from behind my dad. Regus, I think his name was. "You know, as sweet as this little reunion is, there are still going to be consequences in place for you breaking the law so blatantly and irresponsibly."

"But she did do it to come see her dad," a shaggy-looking werewolf said from two seats over, still in his wolf form. "That was kind of sweet."

I expected a punishment from this, though part of me hoped my dad might be able to use his sway to lessen the blow.

My dad turned. "Regus, come on. She used her powers to find me. No, it wasn't okay, but her wish wasn't something reckless or dangerous, like you're implying."

"The law is the law," Regus said, though other Council members looked unsure, murmuring to each other and frowning.

The whisper chain started at the end, one Council member saying something into the ear of the next Council member, and it spread down the line until it got to Regus. The line between his brows deepened the longer the vampire next to him whispered until it was practically a crater in the middle of his forehead.

"You've got to be kidding me," Regus said. His gaze snapped to me, eyes darkening. "Certain Council members feel your punishment deserves to be lightened."

My dad's shoulders sagged in relief.

"Lightened from what?" I asked, grateful.

"Instead of being banned from wish granting for life, you'll be on a six-month probation."

"Deal!" I said.

It wasn't ideal, but Remy could grant wishes under my supervision —if that's what she wanted to do. And Isaac would be back soon and was eager to learn more about wish granting. Plus he said he needed to find a job to support his "lavish" lifestyle, so it wasn't exactly going to be a hard sell trying to get him to work at The Wish List.

My father still frowned, turning to me. "I can't believe you risked all of that for me."

I shrugged. "I had a feeling it would all work out, and you're important to me. To Remy. I want you to know that."

He just shook his head. "I do. No more stunts like this trying to prove it to me."

Regus sighed. "Can we get this little family reunion over with now? As touching as it is, we do have other cases to see."

Before anyone could respond, one of the Council members went rigid, her entire body tensing and a white film forming over her eyes.

"Oh great." Regus rubbed his jaw. "Mariella is having another vision."

My dad leaned over. "She's been having a lot of uncontrolled visions lately, interrupting summonings, and it's got Regus in a very bad mood."

I could see that. The councilman crossed his arms and huffed like a petulant child throwing a fit. Two lights shot out of Mariella's eyes, twining together and forming a picture that all of us could see. I squinted at the vision, wondering what it was of. Seers could have visions of the past, the future, even the present. The stronger a seer, the more they could control these visions. Still, no matter their strength, visions could come at any time and if the seer was taken by surprise or the vision was particularly forceful, it could be on display for everyone. Like this one.

I took a step closer as I studied the vision, recognizing The Wish List. Main Street. Helen, Gene, Martin, Myrtle, and Bones, all standing in a line that crossed the street. What were they doing in the middle of the street? Was this a vision of the past or the present? But no. It had to be the present. Helen was wearing the same outfit, her black leathers with those dangly red earrings, and Myrtle was in her green tracksuit. This vision was of today. What could possibly be important enough that—

Then I saw it, and my heart stopped beating. Lines and lines of demons marching in a formation. Like an army. And there at the front was the Demon King. The one I'd just escaped from. Oh my god. He was leading an all-out attack on Whispering Willows.

I spun to face the Council. "We have to do something! Whispering Willows is under attack!"

"Of course we'll help in any way we can," my father assured me.

Regus looked to the vampire sitting next to him. "Call in the packs and put out word to the half-giants. Also start contacting all the Demon Slayers and arrange transportation to get them to Whispering Willows now."

I might not have had the best experience with Regus so far, but I appreciated how he was taking command.

I turned to my dad, gripping his arms. "We have to get back. Remy is there! Alone!"

He nodded. "Then let's go."

# Chapter Thirty-Four

BEFORE

"You have to push!" the nurse yelled again as Isabella lay in her hospital bed, grunting and heaving and wishing more than anything that she wasn't so alone in this moment, with only a handful of nurses and a doctor she didn't know yelling at her to force this tiny baby out of her body.

She fell back into the hospital bed, exhausted.

"Come on, girl," the red-headed nurse said, hair frizzy and wild. "You can do this."

"I can't," Isabella said weakly, probably for the first time in her life feeling like giving up on something.

If only she could use her powers here. The necklace of dark souls sat nestled between her breasts, exposed for everyone to see, but no one paid any attention to it, their eyes focused on Isabella. Besides, she might use this power for a lot of things, but she'd never use it to bring her child into the world.

The doctor's brows furrowed. "If you don't push, we're going to have to cut it out of your stomach."

Isabella swallowed a few times. What would her mother say if she were here? What would Jeremiah say?

But no, Isabella's mother had died a few months ago. It was sudden, unexpected, and it broke something inside of Isabella. And Jeremiah... well, he was a councilman now. Big and mighty and choosing a job over Isabella. He didn't deserve her or her son. Isabella just knew it was a boy, and he'd probably look exactly like his father. But she couldn't let the councilman know about their son. Then he'd be in their lives forever, and with Isabella's new side hobby of collecting souls to perform magic, well, she couldn't have the Council breathing down her neck. Plus, Jeremiah had made it clear the last time she saw him that he wanted nothing to do with her. She doubted he'd want anything to do with his son either. It was easier this way.

"We're going to lose the baby," she thought someone said.

She was truly alone.

"C'mon," the red-haired nurse said. "I know this is scary and hard, but you've got someone depending on you."

She sat up straighter. No, no, she wasn't alone. She had her son.

Pain radiated up her legs and down her spine, bursting in huge waves that ebbed and flowed. She gritted her teeth, took a huge breath, and blew out as she pushed with everything she had.

Sweat rolled down the sides of her face, and she bore down, down, down until, just like that she felt a release. Then a cry.

Everyone was talking all at once, and one of the nurses shoved a wriggling little baby into her arms. Isabella could barely believe this was real.

"Congratulations," the doctor said, taking his scrub cap off to reveal thick blonde hair. "You've got yourself a beautiful little girl."

Isabella's eyes widened. But... she'd been so sure...

Still, she looked down at the little baby and knew this was exactly right. Just as it was meant to be.

Everything around her faded away, no one else mattering but Isabella and her sweet little girl. She wasn't alone. She would never be alone again.

Her heart swelled in her chest, feeling like it might burst, and she brought a hand to her cheek, realizing it was wet with tears. Tears of joy. This little girl was so perfect. How could something be so perfect?

Isabella vowed right then and there she'd protect her for always. She pinched her necklace between her thumb and forefinger. She'd always keep her safe, at all costs. She'd keep her happy. She'd make sure her daughter had everything she could ever want or need. She'd give her everything Isabella didn't get during her childhood.

Just then, her sweet little girl peeked open her bright blue eyes, which would surely change with time, to look at Isabella. The world stopped as they locked eyes.

"Hi, little one," Isabella said, her voice shaking. "I'm your mom. It's nice to meet you. We're going to have a lot of fun together. Do you know that?"

The baby let out a wail that made Isabella laugh.

"You're just full of surprises. You were supposed to be a boy, you know. And you weren't supposed to come for two more weeks. But I can already tell you have a mind of your own. Your path is going to be so different from mine, but that's okay. It'll be yours to take."

The baby yelled again, and Isabella realized she might be hungry. Instinctually, she started nursing her, the baby eating hungrily, her cries quieting.

"You're already a natural," the red-headed nurse said, snapping Isabella from the little bubble that had formed over her and her daughter.

"I don't know about that," Isabella said. "I'm not sure I have any idea what I'm doing."

"That's the secret," the nurse said, leaning in. "No one really does. You just do the best that you can."

Isabella nodded, grateful for her kindness.

"Have you picked out a name?" the nurse asked.

Isabella thought of Jeremiah, of a time when they'd just been laying on the couch, throwing out potential baby names for fun. Jeremiah had said he loved the name Clara, after his grandmother, a very kind werewolf Isabella had met a few times. She certainly didn't have anyone she wanted to name her daughter after on her side of the family. She could give Jeremiah this. He'd never meet their daughter. But he could name her.

"Clara," she said softly. "That's her name."

# Chapter Thirty-Five

We dropped out of the portal into utter chaos. Demon bodies surrounded us, the residents of Whispering Willows fighting them off. Helen stood a few feet away, slashing her glowing golden sword and dismembering demon after demon.

I ran to Helen. "Where's Remy?" I shouted over the noise of the battle.

"She's at the school. Don't worry, all the kids are there, and it's protected by wards. They can't be harmed."

Relief flooded me. That was all that mattered.

Helen looked behind me, then drove her sword straight over my shoulder.

I winced and glanced behind me at the demon. The dead demon, with a long, pointy piece of metal sticking through his skull. I gave Helen a pointed look and she rolled her eyes. "You're welcome."

Bones picked up a demon and ripped it in half, while werewolves fought against the creatures, snapping their jaws. I didn't see my dad anymore, and I wondered if he'd already shifted and was fighting. I looked above to see witches flying on their brooms, using attack spells that we kept in reservoirs, there when we'd need them. They dipped their wands into liquid-filled jars they held, then pointed their wands and laser-like lights shot out, zapping the demons, who fell when the spells hit them. I didn't have my broom, and there would be no time to go home and get it. If I wanted to help, I'd have to stay down here and fight.

A demon barreled my way, and I yelped, not sure what to do without a weapon. The demon's black eyes locked on me, and it licked its mouth with a forked tongue that made me shudder.

When it got close enough I brought my knee up to my abdomen and then stomped down as hard as I could. The demon yowled in pain, and I elbowed it in the stomach. It doubled over, the spikes on its back protruding out. My hand shot out as I jabbed it in the nose, and it howled in response. Sweat formed at the base of my neck, on my upper lip. I could only do so much, here. Without an actual weapon I wasn't sure how to kill this thing, and eventually it was going to regain its strength and come after me.

Supernaturals and demons packed Main Street, and a window shattered in the distance as a supernatural threw a demon straight into the glass.

Demons crawled up the lampposts, then jumped down into the masses, on top of unsuspecting supernaturals. This was a mess. Far in the distance, I spotted the Demon King, sitting atop one of those winged creatures, studying the war that was raging down below. This was my fault. I'd goaded him, told him he wasn't as good as his father, that his father would be disappointed in him. Remy had been right. I'd been so desperate to get him angry enough to distract him so we could escape that I wasn't thinking about the consequences of my words.

The demon I jabbed straightened, popping his neck as he moved his head from side to side. His lips widened into what I thought was supposed to be a smile. My gut twisted. I was out of tricks, and the creature knew it.

Still, I wouldn't give up fighting. I didn't get this far in life to just cower to some bully. I lifted my foot, ready to kick him in the gut, when he caught it and twisted. Sharp pain shot through my ankle and radiated up my leg.

"Ow, ow, ow," I cried, tugging my leg back and falling onto my butt.

The demon loomed over me, its black eyes growing wider and

wider, its sharp teeth gleaming under the sun. Fear twisted my body like a knot, paralyzing me.

A knife plunged straight through the demon's back, poking out of its chest. It looked down, then back up as blood spilled from the wound. The demon dropped to its knees, then collapsed on the ground, revealing the person who'd saved me.

"Preston," I said, relief flooding my body.

Preston pulled me up and into his chest, and I heaved out a sob as he petted my hair. "It's okay. I'm here now," he whispered into my ear.

He pulled a knife from his pocket and handed it to me.

"Thank you," I said. "I can't believe we're under attack like this."

We took a moment to survey the carnage around us. Demon bodies piled on the ground while supernaturals continued to fight. Steel against steel rang out in the distance, and the resonating bang of a gun vibrated the ground. Above us, witches continued to throw down their attack spells.

I turned back to Preston, wanting to savor this moment for just a little longer before reality sank in and I'd have to fight. "I love you," I said.

He stared at me for a moment, his face unreadable. Then he slowly bent down.

"What are you doing?" I looked down at his leg. "Are you hurt? Is your leg okay? Do I need to find a doctor?"

His knee hit the ground, and he reached into his pocket with a shaking hand, pulling out a black velvet box.

My hand flew up to my mouth as a demon flew over my head and hit the ground next to Preston with a crack. "Oh my god," I said. "Oh my god. Are you—No, no you're not—Are you, though, because it looks like—"

"Clara, shut up," Preston said, a smile quirking his lips.

A demon ran at me from my right side, and I lifted my knife and stabbed it right in the throat. I pulled the knife out and returned my attention to Preston, still kneeling in front of me.

"I'm sick of waiting for the right moment," he said. "Do you know how many perfect dates I've planned now to try and propose to you? The picnic, the yacht, the town square, Samhain Ball—"

"Wait what?" I stared at him in shock. "You were planning to propose in all of those places—Oh, demon!" I pointed over Preston's shoulder, and he stood, whirling around and slicing his knife across the demon's neck. It fell to the ground, and Preston turned again, returning to his kneeled position.

"The Samhain Ball?" I asked my mind reeling. "Is that why everyone was there?"

He nodded. "I thought maybe you'd like having your closest family and friends there. Plus it was my fourth attempt at a proposal, so I had a lot of time to adjust."

"Your fourth attempt." I swayed, my head feeling woozy. "You've wanted to marry me all this time?"

He shot me a wicked grin. "I've wanted to marry you damn near since the day we first met." He stood, still holding the box, the beautiful emerald ring sparkling. "I told you on our picnic date, there is no path, no life, for me without you."

Tears welled in my eyes. "Oh, Preston." My gaze snapped to a demon lifting its clawed hand and swiping at us. "Oh, Preston!"

We both ducked, and a fireball flew over us and incinerated the demon to nothing but ash. I looked to my left and saw Martin with his hand outstretched, smoke rising from it into the air. "You're welcome," he said before forming another fireball in his hand and launching it.

I shook my head and looked back at Preston, who now had a full-on grin. "I feel the same way. I hope you know that. And I'm sorry all our dates got ruined. I just thought you were trying to kiss me. I had no idea you wanted to propose."

"Well, the kiss and the proposal were kind of supposed to go hand in hand."

My chest fluttered. "Does that mean I'm finally going to get my kiss?"

He held up the black box. "Well, you haven't said yes yet."

"You haven't asked," I reminded him.

"Clara Westfold, will you please marry me?"

"Yes," I breathed, and he took the ring out of the box and slid it onto my finger. "It's perfect." I hugged him. "This is perfect."

"It's the opposite, actually."

"I think that's the point." I laughed through the tears.

"You know"—he stuffed the black box into his pocket—"I think maybe the kiss should wait. I mean I don't want to kiss you here on this grimy—"

I wound my arms around his neck and reached up, pressing my lips to his. He froze for a minute under the contact, then his lips moved against mine.

Fireworks lit in my belly, warmth spreading through my body. He pulled me closer with his strong arms, and for just a moment, the entire world melted away around us. Just his lips and mine: touching, tasting. It was familiar, yet like nothing I'd experienced. And I didn't want it to ever stop.

"Really? You two are choosing now to have a make-out session? Have a little class, Clara Westfold and Preston Hammond."

And moment over. Preston and I split apart to see Martin, holding a fireball and rolling his eyes.

"There is a time and place, you know," Martin said.

"Oh, shut up." I grinned at Preston and looked at my finger, the ring fitting perfectly.

"Watch out," Martin yelled, and Preston and I both whirled, now back-to-back, fighting our own demons. I used the pressure of Preston's back to give me leverage to kick out, and I sent my demon flying. Meanwhile, Martin threw another fireball, annihilating the demon fighting Preston.

We whirled, facing each other again. "Is your dad here?" Preston asked. "Did you talk to him?"

I nodded. "We worked everything out." Then I pointed over his shoulder. "Behind you!"

Preston whipped his knife up over his shoulder without even looking, and it embedded itself directly through the demon's eyes. The demon fell to the ground.

"So was it worth the risk?" he asked, and I nodded.

Bones stomped past us, demons clutched in both his hands. They shrieked as he squeezed them tight.

"I've spent so long living in my mother's shadow, afraid of becoming like her, afraid that her evilness was in my blood. I think even though I resolved a lot of that trauma after we first arrived in Whispering Willows, I still held onto some of it, and that's why I wanted to hear more stories about her, to get to know her. So I could see that there was good in her, that that good passed onto me."

Preston's eyes crinkled as a demon flew over our heads and tumbled into three other demons, sending them all sprawling onto the ground like bowling pins. "Clara, you are good. You are your mother's daughter in some ways, the most important ways."

"I know that now." I looked around at the mass chaos surrounding us as demons and supernaturals continued to fight. "But I'm afraid I made a whole mess of things." I stared up at the Demon King, at his face as he watched the battle below.

He didn't look gleeful or happy—he looked scared, and suddenly it reminded me of Remy, of how she'd looked as we fell into the portal to Hell. He had to be about Remy's age. He was just a kid, thrust into this role much too early in life. And on top of that, he was living in his father's shadow.

I thought about his words, how he'd said his father just wanted war, hated being locked into a peace treaty with mortals. He hadn't said that was what he wanted.

My eyes widened, and I looked at Preston. "I need to get up there," I said, pointing to the sky where the Demon King rode on the back of his creature.

"But you don't have your broom? And"—he shook his head—"why do you need to be in the sky?" He gave me a look. "Don't tell me you're going to try and fight the Demon King."

"No, I don't need to fight him," I said. "I need to talk to him. I think I can fix this, end this entire war without anymore bloodshed. I just need a broom."

Preston stared at me for a minute before nodding his head and grabbing my hand. "Then let's go get you one."

# Chapter Thirty-Six

The broom shook underneath me, twisting from side to side as I clutched on for dear life. Every witch had a broom, and when it was your own broom, it bonded to you, keeping you safe and steady. But using another witch's broom? Well, that was unpredictable at best and downright dangerous at worst. We'd pawned it off some witch who'd been standing in an alleyway, clutching her broom and hiding from the fighting.

I looked at the raging war below me as Preston stared up, his eyes widened in fear. He said he'd trusted me, but as a witch, he knew as well I did how brooms could be. Still, this was the only way I had to get to the Demon King and talk some sense into him, which was exactly what I intended to do. We could keep fighting, and we'd most likely drive the demons back, but at what cost? And what would the Demon King do in retaliation?

If my suspicions were right, then maybe I could connect with Balazar and get him to stop this entire war.

My broom twisted again, this time spinning me upside down. I cried out and clutched it even tighter, the ground seeming much farther away than it had just seconds ago. The broom righted itself, and I smacked it.

"Will you please stay upright?" I asked it, which was pointless because even if it was spelled, it was still just a broom. It's not like it could talk back.

Balazar sat on his winged creature up ahead, only about twenty feet away. His gaze snapped to me, his yellow eyes alighting with a fire.

"You," he snarled as I approached. "What, did you come to fight me? Because I don't think you'd win."

I shook my head as my broom vibrated, and I did my best to hold on for dear life. "I have a feeling I'd lose that fight, too."

That seemed to mollify him, and the sneer on his face turned to mere annoyance. "Then what do you want? Don't tell me you're here to beg me to stop. You were right. My father would be disappointed in who I've become. How weak I am. He hated that peace treaty with the mortals, hated how he was basically forced to bow to you all." Balazar shook his head. "He'd want this. And he'd be proud that I'm doing what he didn't."

"Is that what really matters?" I asked.

Balazar narrowed his eyes at me. "What are you talking about?"

I gestured to the fighting down below. "It sounded like you and your dad didn't exactly agree on everything when he was alive."

Balazar shrugged. "It doesn't matter now."

"So why are you still trying to please him?"

He swallowed, and I could tell I hit a nerve. So I was right. This was a thorn stuck in Balazar's side. One I thought maybe I could remove. Before Balazar could answer, I continued on.

"Had you ever heard of my mother? Isabella Westfold?"

Balazar's eyes widened at that. "Isabella? The evil Witch Granter?"

I winced at his use of evil, even if it was true.

"She was your mother?"

I nodded. "The thing is, I see myself in you."

He scoffed. "Please, spare me the sordid details of your pathetic little life. You're nothing like me."

"No, really. I do. Because, like you, I had a parent who didn't make the best choices, and I lost her far too early. She didn't die when I was nineteen, but I made the hard choice to run away from her, from the life she wanted for me."

Balazar's creature continued to flap its wings, air rushing out at me each time the wings lifted up and down.

"What life?" he asked.

I waved my hand at the question. "She had started abusing her power, granting wishes she shouldn't have granted, collecting supernaturals' souls for her own evil purposes. I never did figure out exactly what she wanted or why she did what she did. But it doesn't matter. The point is I spent a long, long time running. I left my life of magic behind, left my heritage, I married a mortal who had no idea magic existed, I hid magic from my daughter."

"Remy," Balazar said, and I didn't like the way he said her name, like something he admired, treasured even. What was it with those two?

I continued on, ignoring his interruption. "Do you know why I did all that?"

He shook his head.

"Because I was afraid I would be exactly like her. But more recently, I've figured out that's not all I was afraid of. I was afraid she would see me as a failure because I didn't follow in her footsteps. Recently, I've been so desperate to prove she was good, because I wanted to know that she had some goodness in her, yes, but also because if there were parts of her that were good, then that would mean maybe she would be proud of this life I'm living." Tears welled in my eyes. It was the first time I'd admitted that out loud. "I'm forty years old and still so desperate for my mother's approval that I almost lost sight of other relationships that I could nurture."

I thought of my dad, how little effort I'd made to get to know him, all so I could learn more about my mom, about the good parts of her life.

Now Balazar's eyes filled with tears, and he hung his head.

"You don't have to prove anything to him, Balazar," I said gently. "You're enough. Just you. Don't make the same mistake I did. Don't waste twenty years of your life afraid that you'll end up like him, afraid you won't. Just afraid. He's gone, and the truth is, even if it didn't seem like it, he loved you."

"How do you know?" Balazar asked, now lifting his head to look at me.

"Because I'm a mother, and I know that no matter what my daughter does or who she becomes, I'll always love her. I may not always like her choices, but that's okay."

Balazar's chest rose and fell with each breath he took. His eyes flicked down to the battle below. Yells and cries rose up, filling the air. Metal clanged against metal. Gunshots rang out. It was a mess.

"I don't want this," Balazar said softly. "Did you know I once showed my father a proposal I'd written up? It outlined a new Hell, one where instead of spawning demons and treating them like nothing but soldiers, we taught them actual skills, created communities, ruled over them fairly and justly, traded with humans and supernaturals on Earth."

That sounded truly lovely.

Balazar swallowed thickly, his Adam's apple bobbing. "My father went ballistic, said that's not what we do. He crumpled it up, threw it away, and we never spoke of it again. But after he died, I found it in his office, still in his desk drawer."

"He knew it was a good idea, a better one than he'd ever thought up. But his pride got in the way."

"I still want that," Balazar said. "I think I could achieve it."

"I think so too."

"You're just saying that."

I urged my broom closer, close enough that I could reach out a hand and lay it over Balazar's arm. "No, I'm not. Demons are evolving. They've learned to speak, whereas twenty years ago they couldn't do anything more than grunt. If they can learn to speak, then that means they can learn other skills too. Under the right leadership."

I squeezed his arm and let go.

Balazar stared down below. "The Council will never forgive me for this."

"They will and they can. There will be sanctions because of this. There will have to be, but that doesn't mean you can't learn from this and grow."

Balazar stared, his eyes growing misty before he gave a firm nod. "Okay. Okay. I'll call them off."

"Is it that easy?" I gestured to the demons below.

"I can control them with a snap of my finger. It's the power I inherited after my father died. The power every Demon King has. I don't like to use it because it takes away all their bodily autonomy, puts them in a trance, like zombies. They don't ever speak out against it, but I think every time my father used it, they lost respect for him. But now, this is what's necessary to end this, and I'll just have to work extra hard to earn back their respect."

I leaned forward. "We will help you," I said. "The Council, me, the Demon Slayer."

Balazar winced. "Maybe not her. The demons have a very strong reaction to her."

"That's fair," I said. "But we'll do whatever you need to help make this dream a reality. We could have two worlds that co-exist in peace, and you could rule over a realm you're proud of."

He swallowed a few times. "I'd . . . like that."

With that, he snapped his fingers, and the demons straightened. Just like he said, it looked like they'd fallen into a trance. Supernaturals quickly realized what was happening and stopped fighting. They cocked their heads, some scratching in confusion, others staring. Swords dropped, guns stopped firing.

Helen's golden sword dimmed and started fading away, no longer needed.

"I'll close the portals immediately, and I'm sure the Council will come calling for a meeting soon." He sat straighter, rolling his shoulders back. "I'm willing to accept whatever punishment they deem fit to give."

I reached over again and squeezed his shoulder. "I believe in you, Balazar. I know you'll make better choices than I did. You're doing the right thing."

He took a deep breath and tugged on the reins attached around his winged creature's shoulders. The creature turned, flying off through the sky, and the demons all marched after him, leaving the wreckage of Main Street behind.

It started as a clap, then broke out into applause, and then, before I knew it, everyone down below was cheering as the demons disappeared toward the portal. The war was over.

But I had a feeling for Balazar, the problems had just begun.

## Chapter Thirty-Seven

"Ugh, I think I just broke a nail," Isaac whined from the other end of the couch we were both carrying into my dad's new apartment.

He'd returned from his months-long trip to visit his adopted mother, Greta. They'd made up after Isaac found out that Greta had kidnapped him and taken him from his birth family, my grandparents. The story was a bit more convoluted than that, and in the end, it hadn't really been Greta's fault. She'd been manipulated by my grandfather, who hated magic. Either way, now Isaac knew we existed and he was in our lives. I'd finally told my father about Isaac, and surprisingly, they actually got along great. My father was teaching Isaac how to fish, and Isaac was teaching him what a French tuck was. It was an interesting relationship, to say the least.

"Isaac!" I hissed. "Do not drop the couch!" My arms felt like jelly and shook with the effort of holding the red loveseat.

Isaac frowned down at his hand. "Yep, split it right in half. Ugh. Great. I knew I shouldn't have let you talk me into this. Do you know how much nail glue I'm going to need to fix this?"

"Just keep moving so we can put this down!" I said through heavy breaths.

Isaac rolled his eyes and walked backwards into the house and we maneuvered the couch against the little living room wall. This whole place felt so sterile, white walls, beige carpet, gray counters. Remy stood in the kitchen, unpacking plates, cups, bowls.

"I don't really know where Grandpa wants all this stuff," she said.

She'd been trying out the name lately, moving from calling him Jeremiah to something more familiar. I think they both loved it.

"I'm sure whatever system of organization you pick will be fine," I assured her.

Isaac collapsed onto the couch we'd just moved, laying down and resting his arm over his eyes. "Well, I think that's enough for the day."

"Isaac, we've moved one piece of furniture." I frowned at him.

"What do you think?" My dad stood in the doorway, rolling in a suitcase.

"It's perfect," I said, looking around at the small space. It was open concept, the living room and kitchen bleeding into each other, with a bedroom, an office, and it backed right up into the mountains so my dad could shift and run whenever he wanted. He was already talking about joining the local pack, and I knew he was as excited about this move as I was.

Isaac frowned at the space around him, and he opened his mouth to speak, but I elbowed him, giving him a look that said *be nice*. Knowing Isaac, he was about to give his full opinion on the sparse little home, which would probably include that it felt like the type of place a serial killer might live.

Which was true.

But like I said, my dad could add his own touches to the little house.

"It's . . . great." Isaac grimaced.

"Who's ready to celebrate?" Martin stood in the doorway, holding a bottle of champagne.

"Martin, get out . . . of the way."

Martin looked behind him at Preston and Bones, who carried an armoire that looked like it weighed about five hundred pounds. "Ooh, someone's testy." He flounced over to the kitchen. "Remy, have you unpacked any champagne glasses?"

"Uh, there's solo cups?"

"That'll do."

Remy handed over a plastic package of red cups.

At that, Isaac uncovered his eyes and shot up. "Oh, thank god. There's alcohol."

Preston stepped into the house, his muscles gleaming with sweat and bulging as he clutched onto the underside of the armoire. Bones had to duck to enter, and he fared much better with his end of the heavy piece of furniture. In fact, it looked like he was carrying a rag doll instead of something akin to a small boulder.

"Bedroom's right back there." I pointed down the hallway, and Bones and Preston moved in that direction. I stared after them, admiring my fiancé in all his glory.

"Quit with the googly eyes," Isaac said. "I still cannot believe Preston proposed to you in the middle of a demon battle."

"It was romantic!" I said.

Isaac looked at Martin. "Please don't ever do that to me."

"Oh, god, I would never." Martin poured the champagne into the red solo cups.

Remy came to stand at my side. "Well, I think it's romantic."

"So do I," another voice said from the doorway. Helen and Gene stood there, hand in hand, as they entered the house.

"We're here to help," Helen said, her eyes growing desperate. "Please let us help."

Red frosted the tips of her spiked blonde hair. That was new. I raised my eyebrows at Gene as Helen practically dove for a box and started unpacking it. He just shrugged and shook his head.

She'd been going a bit stir crazy lately. After my little chat with the Demon King, there hadn't been a single demon sighting in Whispering Willows. The Demon King was doing what he promised, and I only hoped the Council wouldn't be too hard on him.

Helen grabbed a stack of plates and placed them in a cabinet, then turned, gaze settling on the champagne bottle. "Oh, thank god there's alcohol."

Martin handed her a cup and she cheers'ed him, then started gulping it down.

"Take it easy, there, Demon Slayer."

She raised a finger. "To be a Demon Slayer, you have to actually slay demons."

"There will be more demons to slay, eventually. And, you know, you could expand. It doesn't just have to be demons. You could work with the local sheriff's office and help catch the bad guys. I'm sure they'd love your skills."

Gene came up behind her, setting two hands on her shoulders and rubbing them. Helen closed her eyes, like the movement was slowly easing the tension from her body. "Or she could relax," Gene said. "She's been fighting demons for twenty years. A break wouldn't be a bad thing."

"I'd love a break," Isaac said, and I gave him a pointed stare.

"A break from what?"

"Believe it or not, I live a hard life, Clara."

Bones and Preston reappeared from the bedroom, now armoire-less, Preston with red cheeks and a sweaty forehead. Bones looking like, well, like he normally did with his black bowl cut and pale skin stretched over his large features.

"Where's my dad?" I asked. I just realized he'd disappeared from the room with his suitcase, and I had no idea where he'd gone.

Everyone else looked up, as if realizing the same thing. Preston walked over and slipped an arm around my waist, then leaned in for a kiss. "I think he's out back."

"Thanks, hon." I shot him an appreciative glance, then turned to everyone else. "Please do not wreck my dad's new house."

"Why are you looking at me?" Isaac asked, putting a hand to his chest.

"I'm looking at all of you. You tend to do more harm than good when it comes to unpacking."

Martin took a sip of his champagne. "She's talking about when we helped her move into her house." He shook his head. "Ungrateful, that's what that is."

"You broke an entire box of plates." I glared at Gene and Myrtle. "And you two got in a fight that ended with a hole in my living room wall."

Everyone looked down sheepishly.

"Like I said. Behave while I'm gone."

I turned and made my way through the hallway and toward the office, where patio doors led to the backyard. Sure enough, there stood my dad, admiring the view of the green mountains rising up before us.

"What are you doing out here?" I joined him at his side.

"You know, once upon a time, your mother said she wanted a house with a view. I'd asked her what kind of view she wanted, and she said the mountains."

"The mountains reminded her of you," I said, hooking my arm with his and giving his shoulder a squeeze.

"You think?" He shook his head. "She's the first one I thought of when I saw this house."

I took a moment to appreciate the view, standing in silence with my dad and listening to the chitter of birds, the flit of wings, the buzz of bees. His backyard had no fence, no barrier, and wildflowers surrounded us. It was beautiful.

"After all this time," I said, "you still think of her fondly? Even after what happened between you two?"

He chuckled. "No. Not until I met you. I spent so many years bitter and angry over how we'd ended, how she'd changed, how I'd finally reconnected with her, but it was too late. Then I met you, and you wanted to know all the good parts about our relationship, about your mom. And it made me realize I had nothing to be bitter about, that I'd loved and been loved wholly and completely. A love that many don't even get to experience in their lifetime. It was hard, not getting to see you grow up, not even knowing you existed, but then, I get you now. I get to see the amazing woman you've become, and I get to see my granddaughter grow up. That's not nothing."

"It's not nothing," I agreed.

"You're the one who helped me let all that anger go so that I could finally see clearly for the first time." He spread out his arms. "And what a view I have."

He nudged me. "By the way, the Council officially dropped all charges against you."

My mouth dropped open. "Are you serious?"

He nodded. "You should've seen Regus. His face turned so red I thought he might have an aneurysm. But other than his vote, it was unanimous. After what you did at that demon battle, the way you saved everyone, no one thought you deserved to have your powers revoked. Congratulations. The Wish List is back in business."

Relief swept over me. It would've been okay, not granting wishes for six months, but knowing I got to keep doing what I love with no interruptions was the best news I could've asked for. Plus, that meant I didn't have to train Isaac so hard, a task that might've driven me mad since my uncle was not the best student.

"I don't suspect you had a hand in that?" I eyed him.

A smile crept over his face. "I might've been the one who suggested it as my last act before retirement."

A flock of birds burst from the trees and rose into the air like smoke from a chimney. They cawed as they flew off into the distance.

"So what are you going to do now?" I asked him. "Other than spend time with me and Remy?"

He rocked on his heels. "I'd like to join the local pack. Maybe volunteer somewhere. Maybe take some trips. You know, there's a lot more places I could show you where your mother and I frequented."

"You know, I want to meet your family too."

"Well you're in luck, then. I just got an invitation to a family reunion happening next summer."

I laughed. "We'll be there."

We both fell into silence again, soaking in the sunshine and nature surrounding us. A crash from inside broke the silence. I grimaced. It could only last for so long.

"And that's our cue," I said. "I knew I couldn't trust them alone. Sorry." I made an *oops* face, feeling a little guilty that my dad had to deal with this crazy town.

He slung an arm around my shoulder as we walked back to the house, and I heard the distinct sounds of Myrtle cussing at Gene in Gaelic.

"I wouldn't have it any other way," my dad said.

And as entered the house and approached the chaos, I realized that neither would I.

# Chapter Thirty-Eight

**BEFORE**

Isabella had so many regrets. Over the years, she'd done so much wrong, the first of which had been using dark magic to send her father to Hell. The second had been continuing to use dark magic to get what she wanted, to secretly start working against the Council, to try and amass power so that she could take over as the ruling body in the supernatural world. But the one regret she'd never ever had was her daughter.

She watched as Clara burned down The Wish List, with the new Demon Slayer by her side. It would rebuild itself, of course. The family protection spell Isabella's great-aunt Eloise had put over it ensured that. Isabella had finally revealed the truth about herself to her daughter. She had to after she'd learned the Demon Slayer had discovered her dark dealings. She knew the slayer would tell her daughter everything. So she did it first, even though it would break Clara's heart, would be the final stake in their relationship. It was the hardest thing she'd ever done, because she knew her daughter would never follow her into darkness. She'd cut Isabella out of her life, and Isabella would let her.

Now Clara was burning down their shop, trying to stop Isabella in her quest for power, but that wouldn't stop her, as much as she wished something could.

The Demon Slayer put an arm around Clara, drawing her in for a hug, and something painful twitched in Isabella's heart.

She'd done unspeakable things over the years, targeting the weak, those who could easily become addicted to wishes, then took pieces of their soul until they were nothing but husks of their formers selves, eventually becoming demons—which is what happened when you gave away too much of your soul. She'd send the demons to the Demon King, who in turn, helped Isabella's cause against the Council.

It was too late for her own soul. She'd chosen her path, become addicted to the thrill of collecting souls, and she knew she wouldn't be able to stop. Didn't want to stop.

But Clara. Clara was so good.

Isabella followed her daughter home from their burning shop, watching in the shadows as the Demon Slayer helped Clara pack everything she could into a little suitcase. Isabella wanted to hate the Demon Slayer, but Clara would need her in the following years, would need a mother figure.

Their exchange earlier that day echoed in Isabella's mind, after Isabella had told Clara the truth.

*"You're doing what?"* Clara had asked. *"I don't understand. I don't— you've been collecting souls? That's why you're gone all the time? Why you're always away on trips? Because you're trying to take down the Council? What in the hell, Mom?"*

Isabella had made a weak attempt to get Clara to join her efforts, but she knew her daughter never would. She'd carve her own path in life, just like she'd been doing since the day she was born. And it made Isabella both proud and broke her heart into pieces she wasn't sure she'd ever be able to put back together.

*"I can't believe you, Mom,"* Clara had said while they stood in the living room of their home just hours earlier. *"I—I, um, well give me some time to think about it? What you're offering? Me joining you and fighting against the Council."*

The words had been so weak, so forced, Isabella knew her daughter was lying, likely trying to buy herself time so she could get away. Isabella shook her head now, watching as Clara scurried to the car she'd bought her two years earlier, surprising her for her birthday. Unlike her mother, Clara liked to travel by more conventional modes.

Isabella wanted her daughter to stay in Whispering Willows, but she worried her growing list of enemies would come find her, use Clara to draw out Isabella. The truth was that Clara was safer staying away, starting a new life somewhere else. Isabella had known this for some time, but she'd been too cowardly to do anything about it, knowing once she revealed the truth Clara would want nothing to do with her. And she was right. The Demon Slayer had discovered her secret and forced her hand, but the truth was that it was time. Isabella needed to let Clara go, because that's how she would be safest.

She'd let her daughter believe she needed to run, to stay away from Isabella, but really, she wanted Clara safe from her enemies, and this was the best way to ensure that. She'd leave her daughter alone.

Her heart shattered as Clara got into her little car and started it up.

She only hoped that one day Clara could return to Whispering Willows, that she could return to her life of magic. Isabella had done so many bad things. But this was the one good thing she could do for her daughter. She could let her go. It was the biggest act of love Isabella could think of, because she loved Clara more than anything in this world, and she'd do anything for her. She thought back to that night she'd stormed away from Jeremiah's cabin, vowing she'd never love again. How wrong she'd been.

Clara's car drove away, and Isabella emerged from the shadows, making the Demon Slayer jump.

"You," the blonde woman breathed, donning a fighting stance.

"Relax." Isabella held up her hand. "I'm not here to fight you, Slayer."

"It's Helen," she said.

"Helen," Isabella amended. "I need you to do something for me and to never speak of this to Clara. Ever."

Confusion clouded Helen's eyes. "I don't understand. Clara said you tried to recruit her, that you were going to force her to join you."

"I just want to keep my daughter safe," Isabella said. "She would never join me. Because she's everything I'm not. She's so much better than me."

Helen paused. "What . . . I don't understand."

"I have enemies," Isabella said. "A lot of enemies, and I'm only going to become more well-known. People will use Clara against me. I need her to run far away, to hide herself, and start a new life far away from here."

Helen shook her head. "Why don't you just tell her the truth? She believes you're trying to force her down your path, that you want to make her evil."

The word *evil* stabbed Isabella in the gut, even if it was accurate. "Do you know what Clara would do if I told her the truth? That I was scared for her life? That I wanted to protect her?"

Helen's shoulders sagged. "She'd probably try to save you, to go with you in hopes that she could help you become good again. She'd see you trying to save her as some sign that there's good left inside you. She'd refuse to leave . . . So you pretended you want her to join you in hopes of making her believe you were a lost cause."

Isabella gave a sad smile. "Glad you're catching on. Will you watch over her for me? She's going to need you, even if she's far away."

Helen swallowed, then nodded. "I can do that. I want to do that."

"And you promise to always keep this conversation between us? To never reveal the truth to her?"

Helen didn't look so sure.

"You have to bind the promise," Isabella said.

"What does that mean?" Helen asked, and Isabella took her hand and pressed her necklace of souls to it. The dark magic encompassed the Demon Slayer's hand like a binding, dark smoke swirling and tightening around it.

Helen gasped. "What did you just do?"

"I bound the secret to you."

Isabella's necklace was now drained, dark smoke filling the bottom half of it, the top empty of souls. She'd need to replenish it soon.

"You can now never tell Clara the truth of this meeting, no matter what."

Helen frowned. "I don't like that."

"You can still guide her, be there for her. From afar."

Helen closed her eyes. "You're breaking her heart, you know."

"I know, but it's the only way I can keep her safe. I have to live with the consequences of my actions."

"And what are the consequences, exactly?" Helen asked.

Isabella felt tears prick her eyes. "I'm losing my heart. My soul. My everything."

"Was it worth it?" Helen asked.

"Of course not," Isabella snapped. "If I knew what this would cost me . . . but it's too late now. I've chosen my path and there's no going back."

Helen gave an unsure nod. "Then we're done here."

"We're done," Isabella said. "Good luck, Demon Slayer. You're going to need it in this town."

With that Isabella snapped her fingers and her broom appeared. She climbed on and flew up into the sky, finally allowed the tears to come. She cried for herself, she cried because everything was about to change, but mostly she cried for Clara. She only hoped her daughter would find her way. She hoped her daughter would have an amazing life. She hoped one day her daughter would know how much she loved her. She hoped her daughter would find love that filled her with joy, just like Isabella had. But, unlike Isabella, she hoped her daughter would hold onto that love, to choose love over hate.

# Epilogue

I twirled in front of the floor-length mirror, my light pink dress flowing to the ground. It cinched at my waist, accentuating my curves, and plunged down my neckline, exposing just the right amount of cleavage that I knew would make Preston's mouth water. The top and the bodice were made of a delicate lace, and the back dipped down, exposing most of my skin. It was perfect.

Sunlight streamed into the room through the big windows. A white couch sat against the wall with two white chairs and a white coffee table. The entire room was so bright and airy.

I'd decided I didn't want white for my wedding day to Preston. I'd been there, done that. Besides, my wedding to Greg had been traditional, catering to his beliefs and religion. I'd just been so grateful he wanted to marry me, to give me his name and safety net that came with it, I'd been willing to do whatever he wanted.

But today I was marrying this man as my authentic self, ready to start our new lives together.

"Oh, Mom."

I turned and Remy's eyes filled with tears. She was my maid of honor, naturally, wearing a navy blue dress that hung just below her knees. Helen, Emerson, and Myrtle stood next to her, wearing matching dresses, everyone sniffling and wiping at their eyes. It was the first time

I'd ever seen Myrtle in anything other than a tracksuit, and it was hard not to stare. I'd told her she could wear a navy tracksuit, and that would be just fine with me, but she insisted that if she were going to be part of the wedding party, she would match with everyone.

"Don't ruin my makeup." I flapped my hands, gesturing for them to stop with their sniveling.

"You look amazing." Remy's voice shook.

"Thank you, honey."

"The girl is right," Myrtle said. "I'm not usually one for all the pomp and fanfare. I eloped myself, but you look beautiful."

"Wait, you were married?" I asked.

Helen, Emerson, and Remy all did a double take. Myrtle just shrugged. "I've been alive for three hundred fecking years. Of course I've been married."

She left it at that, and I didn't have the bandwidth to dive into that particular story, though one day I would insist she tell it.

Emerson stepped forward, holding a necklace with a shining blue gem. She clasped it around my neck. "Something blue," she whispered, then moved back, patting at her blonde hair, piled on her head in a bun.

Helen stepped up next, taking a bracelet that matched the necklace off her wrist and slipping it onto mine. "Something borrowed," she said, voice wobbly. She kissed me on the cheek.

She had come to my first wedding with Greg, had actually asked me not to go through with it. She knew it wasn't a marriage of love but one of convenience, but it was what I needed at the time, and ultimately, Helen supported me like she always had.

Helen moved away, and Remy came to a stand in her place. She lifted up a matching set of earrings. "Something new." She smiled big. "Emerson helped me pick them out."

She put them on my ears, and I had to work very hard not to burst into tears at this entire exchange.

"You guys are the best," I said, voice wobbling.

"Oh, who's making who cry now?" Helen dabbed at her eyes.

"Okay, do another twirl!" Emerson motioned with her finger, and I obliged, turning round and round to everyone's cheers.

Myrtle and Helen went to sit on the couch against the wall, and Helen leaned over to grab wine out of the ice bucket that sat in the center of the coffee table. Myrtle grabbed a glass and Helen poured each of them some wine.

"I can't believe you were able to plan this wedding so fast."

It was true that Preston and I had decided we didn't want to wait. After all, we'd already been waiting for twenty years. Life was short, and we wanted to be married as soon as possible.

So I'd gathered all the resources I had. It turned out I knew a few people who were good at getting stuff done. Martin had offered up his beautiful gardens for the ceremony and reception. Plus he offered us two rooms, one for the groom and groomsmen and one for the bridal party so we could get ready and spend the day here at his B&B. Emerson had offered to decorate. Helen took care of the invitations. And Bones was busy in the kitchen, cooking up delicious appetizers and desserts for the reception. With all that help, it only took us a month to put everything together and settle on a date. One amazing month of being Preston's fiancee, and now I would get a lifetime of being his wife. Life couldn't be any better.

"Oh!" Remy put a hand to her head. "Where's your bouquet?"

"Don't worry." Emerson put an arm around her. "I've got it covered." She winked. "Well, actually, Martin has it covered. He does have an entire garden full of flowers, so he offered to make up your bouquet."

"Are you going to throw it?" Remy's eyes twinkled, and I rolled my own.

"That's such a silly tradition."

"But it'll be so much fun. Whoever catches it will get married next!"

Myrtle put up her hands. "Don't look at me. Not interested in going that route again."

Helen shook her head. "I already have one husband. Two might send me over the edge."

I laughed. Helen was head over heels in love with her husband, even after fifteen years of marriage. She wouldn't want anyone else, even if she liked to joke about how much Gene drove her insane.

I pinned my gaze on Emerson, who just looked away. She'd been very quiet about her relationship, or lack of one, with a certain werewolf, and I was eager for some details. I'd wrangle them out of her later.

"Well, it can't be me. I have no interest in getting married any time soon," Remy said.

My eyes practically bulged out of my head. "Of course you don't! You're eighteen and still in high school. You're not getting married until you're at least thirty. Maybe even forty."

Remy just crossed her arms and rolled her eyes. "Calm down, Mom. It's not like there's even anyone in my life I could see marrying."

Pink tinged her cheeks, and I narrowed my eyes suspiciously. We'd been visiting Balazar quite a lot recently, trying to give him the support he needed as he worked to completely overhaul his realm and the demon population. I'd let Remy come with me quite a few times at her insistence and didn't miss the way she and Balazar seemed to hit it off. I liked Balazar, especially now that I'd gotten to know him more, but there was no way my daughter was going to date the Demon King. At least, I'd strongly discourage it. She was eighteen and didn't have to listen to me, and I would never force my opinions on her. But she had to know that was a relationship that would be doomed from the start.

Emerson just shook her head at me, and for what felt like the millionth time today, I dropped yet another conversation I was planning on having at some point. I knew Remy confided in Emerson, both of them bonding, and there were things Remy told Emerson she didn't tell me. Maybe her feelings for the Demon King were one of them.

But Emerson was right. It was my wedding day, and that meant today I should focus on me and Preston—and not things that might result in me going into cardiac arrest. You know, like my daughter's relationship with the actual king of Hell.

A knock sounded on the door, and it peeked open. My dad's green eyes appeared in the crack of the door. "Can I come in? Is everyone decent?"

"Yes, come in!" I called, and the door swung open, my dad's big frame filling it.

Helen stood and shooed everyone out. "Let's give them a moment."

I mouthed "thank you" to her as everyone filed out and she shut the door behind her.

My dad stepped closer, wiping at tears forming in his eyes.

"Oh, not you too," I teased as he stepped closer.

"I'm sorry, I'm sorry." He pulled a handkerchief from his pocket and patted his cheeks. "You're just so beautiful. If you'd asked me a year ago if I thought I'd be attending my daughter's wedding, I'd have told you that was crazy."

I raised a finger. "Not just attending, walking her down the aisle."

Of course I'd asked my father to do me the honor. I didn't have that at my first wedding, and even if the tradition was a bit archaic and silly, I couldn't think of a better way to involve my father. Besides, we agreed he wasn't giving me away. He was walking me into my future. I loved the sentiment and decided we could make the walk down the aisle have whatever meaning we wanted it to.

He scratched his head, shuffling from foot to foot. "I, uh, I wanted to give you something. I know you already have your something old, something blue, and something new, but I thought maybe you could use two something olds?"

He reached into his pants pocket and pulled out a delicate silk handkerchief. It was pink, almost the same color as my dress. Intricate flowers were sewn into it, roses. It was beautiful.

My breath caught in my throat. "Is that . . . ?"

He nodded. "Your mother's. She'd bought it one day when we'd been at some little town market. She thought it was so beautiful, too beautiful to use, she'd said. She told me that it was the type of thing she could imagine passing down to her kids one day, if she ever had them. She left it at my house, didn't take it with her after we broke up, and I couldn't ever bear to get rid of it."

I reached out and touched a finger to the smooth silk, cool against my skin. "Wow. I love it."

He looked away as I took it from his outstretched hand. "Anyway, I know it might be silly, and maybe today wasn't the day to give it to you."

"It's perfect." I reached out and tucked it into his front pocket. "But I don't have anywhere to put it, so how about you wear it for me? Plus, then we can match."

"That's a great idea."

"I wish she was here," I said.

"I know," he said.

"But I'm so, so glad you are."

He stuck out his elbow and I looped my arm through it. "You know

I wouldn't miss this day for anything. So are you ready?"

"I don't think I've ever been more ready for anything in my life," I said.

He smiled at me as we walked out in the hallway and down the stairs. We got to the bottom, and through the big glass patio doors, I could see the garden, see everyone sitting in rows and rows. My breath caught in my throat, and my heart thrummed at the sight.

There at the end of the aisle stood Preston, with Martin behind him ready to officiate. He'd gotten his license just for our wedding. Because of course he did.

"Then let's get you married," my dad said, and we walked through the doors and out onto the aisle just as the music started playing. We walked down the aisle, everyone nodding at me, giving bright smiles. We walked arm in arm. We walked toward my future. And I couldn't wait to get there.

THE END

Thank you for reading my book! This is the end of Clara's journey, but if you want just a little more of Clara and Preston's love story, **Click here (or use the QR code below)** to get access to their bonus story.

Haven't had a chance to read the first book in the series? **Read Be Careful What You Witch For now.**

Even though Clara's journey is over, Emerson has quite a story of her own. Keep reading for a sneak peek of **Death Witch**, a retelling about a witch named Emerson, who has a lot to learn, and the ghosts of the past, present, and future are ready to teach her the errors of her ways.

# Death Witch: A Sneak Peek

A bass boomed to the sound of some overplayed pop song, vibrating the aluminum chairs where I sat and watched as Haley Babcock leaned against the railing in the lower level of the packed stadium. The crowd roared as the offense took the field, some team that I probably should've known but didn't. Instead of keeping her gaze on the football game, she was basically eye-tapping my boyfriend, who stood right next to her. Gary Kim. Tall, dark, handsome, and a coworker at Witch Inc., the company that employed all of us. The reason why we were here today. On assignment. Haley's assignment, specifically, but I was incognito. Gary was here for backup, in case anything went wrong with the spell. Haley finally tore her gaze away from Gary, and I rolled my eyes and focused back onto the field, waiting for the magic to happen. Literally.

The quarterback took a few steps backward, football raised in the air as he readied himself to launch it to one of his wide receivers. It was supposed to be a perfect Hail Mary, the ball sailing through the air just like Haley had spelled it to, the receiver catching it and running it back for a touchdown, and then everything that could go wrong for the other team would go wrong. Dropped balls, missed catches, fumbles, and whatever other football-y things there were that could happen. I wasn't sure. I fell asleep halfway through Haley's presentation on the whole thing.

Either way, it didn't matter what was supposed to happen. Little Miss Perfect Haley Babcock, the Haley Babcock who was currently hitting on my boyfriend, the Haley Babcock who hated me for no reason I could understand, wasn't going to like what was coming in three . . . two . . . one. The ball left the quarterback's hand, and a defender batted it from the air, right into the arms of another defender, who ran the football in for a touchdown. The stadium roared. I rubbed my hands, trying to hold in my squeals as I shoved the ball cap further down my head and waited for all hell to break loose.

Below, the coach was going ballistic, and I could see the way he was looking up into the stadium, searching for Haley, wondering what in the hell just happened. After all, his organization paid a lot of money to guarantee a win and a playoff spot, which hadn't happened for their team in over thirty years. The organization was getting desperate. Usually people had to be pretty desperate to hire us, to do enough digging to even find out about our existence. So they paid us a boatload of money, and we created spells that would help them lie, cheat, bamboozle their way into whatever they wanted.

Except Haley's spell had just failed. Or well, I'd sabotaged it. Potato, potahto. Now, there was no way Haley would be getting any kind of promotion—and I'd sail into the senior position with no problems. She might even get fired for this. The thought made me giddy.

Below, Haley had started hyperventilating into a paper bag, eyes wide, breaths coming in short spurts while Gary tried to calm her, patting her back, rubbing it. I wanted to march down there and wrench Haley away from him, but Haley wasn't going to be a problem after this, so I sunk further into my seat and pretended I was just another fan here to watch a game. On the field, the coach was screaming at his team on the sidelines, no doubt in complete panic over what had happened. The tide had turned, the momentum in the other team's favor, and that didn't bode well for the outcome of the game.

"Uh, Emerson, what are you doing up here?"

Fitz stood on the opposite side of the bleachers and did the awkward "excuse me" to everyone in the row as she balanced her way past them to where I was sitting. She plopped into an empty seat next to me. I was up in the nosebleeds, so there were more empty than not-empty seats available.

"Um," I said nervously, fidgeting with my hands. Crap. I hadn't counted on being spotted. "Well . . ." My brain scrambled for an answer to Fitz's question. She hated Haley as much as I did, but as the company psychologist, Fitz would never approve of what I'd just done.

"Oh, Emerson, no," Fitz said in a disappointed tone as she crossed her legs beneath her bottom. I had no idea how she did that in these tiny stadium seats, but the woman was flexible. She did yoga in her office every morning to start the day and tried to convince me to join, but I just did not bend that way, not at the ripe age of almost-forty. It didn't matter that Fitz was forty-five. I contended that at this age, being able to bend over backwards so your body looked like a literal rainbow was not natural. But Fitz tended to defy the norms.

My stomach twisted at Fitz's words. Oh god. She knew. She knew that I'd just sabotaged Haley's spell. I was found out. Done for.

I followed her gaze to Gary as the wind tousled his messy black hair and ruffled the sleeveless shirt that showed off his toned muscles. My chest tightened.

"Seriously, Emerson? You're checking up on Gary?"

Oh. Oh, I could work with this. I looked down, twisted my hands together. "Um . . ." It was all I had to say for Fitz to launch into a lecture.

"You should trust your boyfriend. So what if he was assigned to this case with Haley? That wasn't his choice—you know Brian is the one who chooses the assignments. Really, I thought you were better than this. You shouldn't be in a relationship if you can't even trust your boyfriend." She took a deep breath, her dark skin flawless and glowing in the sunlight, while my pale skin was no doubt blotchy and red by now from the searing sun.

"You're right, Fitz," I said. "I should trust Gary. I just had a bad feeling about this whole thing, and you know, I was right. I saw Haley stroking his arm earlier in the game. Who does that? Who strokes a taken man's arm like that?"

Fitz sighed. "Who cares? Maybe you can't trust Haley, but you can trust Gary. He loves you, Emerson. He'd never do anything to hurt you."

I snorted. That may be true, but Haley would do everything in her power to destroy me. "Well, I do trust Gary. It's her I don't trust. You know she doesn't like me."

Fitz propped her feet up on the chair in front of her while the football game continued to play out on the field below. "You know her and Gary have a long history. They dated for years before you came to our department, caught Gary's eyes. I mean he broke up with Haley and weeks later started dating you."

I glared at Fitz and she held up her hands. "I'm not saying any of that excuses Haley's behavior. It doesn't. I'm just saying, she adored Gary. He was her entire world, and then you sashayed in and Gary fell for you."

I bristled in my seat. "I suppose that makes sense."

I'd worked at Witch Inc. for ten years, but I'd only transferred to this department in the last year. Before I became a Spell Caster, I'd been working behind the scenes, in the department that was responsible for scoping out clients, recruiting, interviewing clients, making them sign spell-binding contracts that would keep our deals completely secret. But I'd dreamed of being a Spell Caster, one of the elite in the company responsible for creating the spells clients so desperately wanted. And a year ago, another witch had a mental breakdown after she cast a spell that helped a certain big-time politician's affair get buried in the news, and he ended up getting elected, beating his wholesome opponent. She left the company, opening up a spot that I interviewed for. I got the job, and that's when I met Haley and Gary and Fitz. It wasn't my fault that Gary broke up with Haley. It's not like he'd cheated on her. I would never condone that. He broke up with her, and then we started talking, and, well, one thing led to another.

Now I had the perfect job, the perfect boyfriend, and soon, I'd get that promotion that would allow me to rise to the top of this company. My life was perfect.

". . . and besides, don't you have some big date tonight?" Fitz was saying.

I realized I'd been zoning her out. "Oh, date, yes!"

Gary told me he wanted take me on some romantic getaway he'd planned for my fortieth birthday, and he said he had a big surprise in store.

Below the game was ending, the teams filing into their tunnels, and

Haley and Gary had disappeared. No doubt Haley had to go face the coach, the team's owner, and explain exactly why her spell had failed.

"Do you think he's going to propose?" Fitz asked.

I stared down at my empty ring finger, wiggling it. A diamond would be a good look on me. So would the name: Mrs. Emerson Kim.

"I think so," I said. "I mean, what else could it be?"

Fitz nodded, her box braids twisted into an updo, piled on her head. "He's definitely proposing. And how do you feel about that?"

I shook my finger at her. "Oh no. Don't you dare try to psychoanalyze me. I'm not one of your patients."

Despite how much she'd tried to get me into a seat in her office, I'd never scheduled an appointment with Fitz. I didn't need it. Her job was to keep the witches in this department mentally fit, able to do a hard job that sometimes was morally and ethically questionable. In other words, she helped people keep from having mental breakdowns due to the stress of the job. I had no moral qualms about what I did. I mean, if I didn't cast these spells, someone else would.

Fitz's phone dinged. "Oh, no. I'm needed." She stood, shaking her head. "Haley is having a breakdown."

"Oh no." I did my best to muster a sympathetic voice. "Better go attend to that."

Fitz gave me a look. "Enjoy your night with Gary, and text me all the details."

I leaned back, crossing my arms and staring at the empty field. Let's face it: forty was going to be my best year yet.

# About the Author

Tee Harlowe writes paranormal and fantasy romance focused on strong and determined women. After years spent traveling, Tee settled down to start writing her own adventures and is now living out her dream. When not writing, Tee can be found wrangling her children, attempting to bake, and losing to her husband at pretty much every game they play.

Printed in Great Britain
by Amazon